HUNTER'S
OATH

BOOK TWO
OF THE CHANGELING BLOOD SERIES

HUNTER'S OATH

BOOK TWO
OF THE CHANGELING BLOOD SERIES

GLYNN STEWART

**FAOLAN'S PEN
PUBLISHING**
faolanspen.com

This edition published in 2018 by:

Faolan's Pen Publishing Inc.

22 King St. S, Suite 300

Waterloo, Ontario

N2J 1N8 Canada

ISBN-13: 978-1-988035-37-6 (print)

A record of this book is available from Library and Archives Canada.

Printed in the United States of America

1 2 3 4 5 6 7 8 9 10

First edition

First printing: May 2018

Illustration © 2018 Shen Fei

Read more books from Glynn Stewart at faolanspen.com

1

THE CALGARY STAMPEDE is supposedly the greatest outdoor show on Earth, or so its advertisements brightly proclaimed all over the city. It had a rodeo, barns to introduce your children to the farm animals they'd never otherwise see in a city, races, games and a carnival.

It might have been fun under other circumstances, but right now all I cared about was that it was cold, it was raining, it was full of people —and that somewhere among the hundreds of horses that show up for a rodeo event like this was a shape-shifting cannibalistic fae.

My name is Jason Kilkenny, and this is how I spend my Saturdays.

By now, everyone was used to the rain that the current summer was determined to drown Calgary in. Despite the storm, the wet streets were still crowded, and I could barely keep my eyes on the man I was supposed to be escorting. It helped, at least a little bit, that Robert Grace had acquired at least some of the instinctive arrogance of the Fae Noble he'd become, and that the crowd parted ways around him without thinking.

With Robert around, at least, I didn't draw too much attention. The slim youth with the long dark hair that covered his ears attracted admiring glances from men and women alike in his cowboy boots and hat and long black raincoat.

Since we were trying to blend in, we were dressed identically. We had almost the exact same hair color and we both wore our hair long to cover visibly pointed ears. Robert and I could have passed for cousins to a stranger, but there was always something extra about Fae Nobles, even one as young and untried as Robert.

An older Fae Noble like Robert's father, my friend Talus, would have been sent after a Pouka alone. Robert got escorts. Two Gentry, the lacking-in-magic but otherwise terrifyingly physically powerful middle tier of fae...and me.

A three-quarters fae changeling who was a sworn Vassal of the Queen of the Fae. Lord Oberis, the master of Calgary's Fae Court, could order the Gentry to be here and guard Robert. Technically, he had no such authority over me.

In practice, my mistress disliked her Vassals aggravating their local Lords, *and* Oberis was teaching me to use the newly-awakening gifts of my unknown father's blood. When he asked a "favor," I didn't argue.

Which left me sighing in the rain as I caught up to Robert through the crowd.

"Do we have any idea where she is?" I asked him.

"I'm thinking the petting horse stables," he told me. "Public with plenty of prey but still easy to hide. We don't know when she got into town; she's probably hungry."

"Too public," I told Robert, considering as we continued to move through the wet crowd. "She'll want more privacy—there's prey in the public stables, but too many other people would see."

"Prey." What a wonderful euphemism for the fact that the fae we were hunting ate people. From what Lord Oberis had told me, terrified people by preference.

Robert stopped, and half-glared at me, ignoring the ripples he sent through the crowd. "What do you suggest, then?" he demanded.

Six months ago, as part of a political mess that had almost torn the city apart and nearly killed me, oh, three or four times, Robert's previously concealed parentage had been revealed. He'd spent six months learning how to be a Fae Noble, but was still even younger than my own twenty-four years old. By the standards of the fae, we were both children. That didn't make him any happier with his babysitter.

"She spends a lot of her time as a horse, right?" I asked in my quiet Southern drawl, glancing around the crowd to be sure no one was paying us too much attention as we stood still and got even wetter. Our renewed halt had caused further ripples that Robert hadn't noticed, but they were fading and everyone else was more focused on getting out of the rain.

My question wasn't just to salve Robert's ego. I was more experienced, slightly, but he'd been raised fae. He knew things about the world we lived in that I didn't yet.

"Pouka are insane," he said bluntly. "They're born looking human, like any other Unseelie fae, but once they can turn they'll spend as much time in that form as their birth form, yeah."

"So, she's a horse, and will be hiding among horses," I concluded. "But she's not going to be one of the 'pretty but not valuable' ones they have out for petting—she'll be one of the racers. No Unseelie is likely to resist the option to show up everyone."

One of the two Gentry who'd slipped in beside us shifted uncomfortably at my words, and I belatedly recalled that the man was Unseelie. Seelie like Robert and myself had their prejudices against the other half of the fae species—but it wasn't like the Unseelie disagreed with the point, however.

"Which means she'll be in the stables for the rodeo horses and the racers," I concluded. "How do we get in there?"

"You've met my father," Robert said dryly as he pulled a cellphone from under his coat. "He has horses in there."

———

A QUICK PHONE CALL LATER, we approached the private stables armed with a name and a new feeling of something resembling dryness as we ducked under the canopy over the door. A cowboy-outfit-clad security guard stopped us outside the door.

"Excuse me, gentlemen, this area isn't part of the public exhibition," he informed us politely. "I'll need to see some ID, please."

"I'm sorry," Robert immediately told the man, equally polite.

What is it with Canadians and always being polite?

"We're from Angolian, Inc. and we're here to check on Strawberry Dancer. We were only issued one access card and I apparently left it in my hotel room. That's back downtown and I'd prefer not to have to leave and come back!

"Can you call in to security and let us through?"

Angolian, Inc. was a shell company with no real employees, fully owned by Talus through about two other shells and a lawyer. However, by the time we got to the stable, our names should have been added to the authorized list under that company.

"Give me a moment," the guard told us and turned away, shielding his radio from us as he called into the security center hidden somewhere in the carnival grounds. A short conversation followed, and then he turned back to us.

"What were your names again?" he asked, but it was mostly a formality. He might have thought we couldn't overhear his radioed conversation, but we weren't human—not by a long shot—and fae ears were far better than human ones.

"Robert Angel, Jason MacTavish and assistants," Robert replied, giving the false names his father's lawyer would have had put on the list, including our two Gentry bodyguards with an airy wave of his hand.

"All right, you're on the list, go in," the guard told us, gesturing us through into the building.

Stepping out of the rain and into dry air, the first thing we noticed was the sudden overwhelming smell. This was a working stable, and there was only so much you could do about the smell of horse manure in one of those.

Out of the view of the crowd and the guard, I took a moment in the near-privacy of the front entrance to the stable to check my weapon. I'd acquired a snub-nosed .38 Special revolver in recent weeks. For today's excitement, I'd loaded with cold iron rounds, the ancient bane of the fae.

Since I could *feel* cold iron in a way even most fae couldn't, carrying it was uncomfortable. I could also tell that the heavy semiautomatics our two Gentry companions carried were similarly loaded.

Seeing as how the Gentry were each capable of tearing large cars or small tanks apart with their bare hands, they probably didn't need them.

Robert hadn't bothered. Unarmed, the Fae Noble was probably the single most dangerous individual in the entire fairground.

"So, how are we going to find the feeder in here?" one of the Gentry asked Robert and me. "Is there any way we can tell her from the regular horses?"

"If she's anything like me, wave the cold-iron-loaded guns around and see which horse spooks," I said dryly. Of course, more likely than not, the Pouka—fae, yes, but also a feeder, one of the supernatural creatures that fed on mortals—was not an iron-seeker.

"I can sense her at close distances," Robert told the Gentry. "Keep an eye out for humans; this building should be occupied."

I was grateful that Robert didn't mention that I would also be able to identify the Pouka, by sight if nothing else. We weren't entirely sure yet of the full extent of the abilities I'd inherited from my apparently Hunter and Vassal-sworn father. Keeping what we did know secret was useful.

I'd already concealed my little revolver inside my coat, and at the reminder, the two Gentry followed suit. As we paused to work out where to go next, I listened carefully.

"It's too quiet," I told the others. While the Gentry were physically superior to me in, well, every way possible, my senses were on par with theirs—and they were nodding in agreement. "I don't hear anything except horses—shouldn't there be people in here?"

"Keep your eyes open," Robert repeatedly, a new edge to his voice, and then led the way in what was, so far as I could tell, a random direction.

We'd made it down one row of stalls, during which even I could tell that the horses were spooked by something, before we all stopped as one. We could all smell it, even through the earthy scents of the stable. Blood. Human blood.

"THAT WAY." Robert pointed, taking off at a flat run. Before he'd taken three steps, I was beside him and the two Gentry were already ahead of us.

We'd only made it a few more steps before a feeling of deep and utter foreboding hit us. Something was wrong; something terrifying was going on. The feeling hit me down to my bones with a chill that whispered in my mind it was time to run, time to leave—time to be anywhere but here.

"That's her," Robert snarled as even his steps faltered under the influence of the Pouka's aura. Her Power could be turned to this purpose, weaving an aura of fear around her so that none would interrupt her feeding.

With a swallow, I pressed onward. Robert and I led the way again, with the two Gentry catching up a moment later, staying even with us. Numbers gave us the extra bit of willpower to overcome the miasma around the stables and approach the heart of the dark aura.

At the end of the row of stable stalls full of horses cowering against the back walls, a single door marked the entrance into what I guessed was an office. Both the scent of blood and the miasma of fear emerged from the door, and Robert led us to it with a sharp gesture.

"Now," he whispered, and the two Gentry kicked the door open. They charged in first and Robert and I followed, guns now fully in the open.

The office behind the door was a small, cluttered room. Filing cabinets, several drawers overflowing with paper, lined the walls. A door on the opposite side of the office showed a storage room through a window. The plain desk in the center of the room had once held a computer, now brushed off the desk and shattered on the floor as the desk had been turned into a table—and the office's presumed owner into a meal.

A small black horse, little larger than a pony really, had its face buried in the woman's guts. The Pouka reared back, whinnying and spraying gore from its fangs as we broke into the room. Three pistols focused on the horse, a frozen tableau of potential violence as Robert entered the room carefully, avoiding the line of fire, and faced the horse.

"Maria Chernenkov," he greeted the horse quietly. "Surrender or be destroyed."

"I am fae," the horse spat at us, a perfectly human and feminine voice that was utterly strange emerging from the Pouka's very inhuman mouth. "I have rights."

"You are a recognized Pouka of the Unseelie Courts," Robert agreed, calmly facing her as if her miasma of fear was nonexistent. "This grants you certain rights and certain assistances in meeting your...dietary requirements.

"You chose, however, to enter this city by stealth and murder one of its mortal inhabitants," he told her. "Surrender and face the Court's justice, or I will deliver the justice required by the Covenants here and now."

Chernenkov's response came in the form of a crippling wave of fear. My bones seemed to melt in my flesh as that fanged horse became more terrifying than anything I'd ever faced. Even a Wizard in full rage paled beside the terror the Pouka's Power drove into my flesh and mind.

I heard the two Gentry groan, their weapons falling to the ground as fear drove them to their knees. There was a thud as Robert backed into one of the filing cabinets—but my attention was focused on the Unseelie fae as her Power drove into my mind.

Unfortunately for her, whatever else my late and unknown father had been, he had been a member of the Wild Hunt, and had passed his gift of stepping Between onto me. The reaction of a Hunter or a Hunter's changeling to fear is to step Between worlds to dodge the blow.

The cold of that place Between realities crashed into me like a bucket of water. The shaded hues of the world I'd left behind still took the form of rooms and stables around me, but the fear was gone. The Pouka's Power didn't cross the wall to affect those Between, which gave me a moment to regain my composure, check the cold iron rounds in the chamber of my Colt Special, and then calmly, slowly step back into the real world.

I'd been gone only a few seconds, long enough for the Pouka to advance on my fallen compatriots while clearly wondering just what had happened to me.

Her answer came in the form of cold iron jacketed rounds at point-blank range. The first slammed into the Pouka's long horse head from less than two feet away, and I kept firing as the revolver dropped back onto her, each round pushing her farther back until she stumbled over the desk where she'd been feeding.

The hammer finally clicked home on an empty chamber. Six cold iron rounds would kill any fae, so I was starting to turn to check on Robert when the harsh, high, laughter echoed through the room. I returned my gaze to the Pouka to watch the fae, suddenly in the form of a human woman clad in a black, formfitting bodysuit, stand back up, her cackling laughter filling the tiny office.

"You'll need to do better, my little friend," she told me. "I have walked the path of shadows and darkness, child, beyond where mere cold iron can bring me down. You will die, and I feast upon your flesh and Power."

"Jason," Robert's voice murmured, barely audible even to my hearing, and I glanced at him. Still clearly struggling to overcome the fear my jaunt Between had cleared from my head, he gestured. A tiny, tiny flicker of Power trembled through the room, and then my two Gentry friend's heavy pistols shot into the air, flying directly at me.

I had just enough warning to drop my own pistol before the guns arrived. I managed to somehow grab a gun in each hand before turning back to face the Pouka with a cold smile.

She'd finished transforming, but even in human form, her mouth was filled with fangs as she snarled at me.

"Right," I said dryly. "Let's try this again."

A human who tries to dual-wield .45 caliber automatics firing full-metal-jacket rounds would find hitting anything impossible. For a changeling like myself, well, it's merely very difficult. Half of the heavy slugs missed, but each slug that hit Chernenkov was like a hammer to her chest. The bullets drove her back through the room, and she crashed backward through the door into the storage room behind her.

With a handful of rounds left in the guns, I charged through after her. She was back on her feet like nothing had happened and met my entry with a clothesline punch straight at my head—*of course* it wasn't going to be easy.

I didn't have time to dodge the strike, so I just emptied the last few rounds into her as it hit me.

I went flying one way and the Pouka went flying the other, both of us crashing into racks on racks of what looked like gas canisters. I guessed one of them had cracked in the impact, as the entire room began to smell very strongly like a swimming pool.

"I don't think that's working," she taunted me. "You should have done more research, little fae. I am *immortal*."

I sighed and tossed the guns aside as I calmly stepped between the fanged horse-woman and the door. I don't know why I even bother with guns sometimes. With an effort of will, I called on my half-will-o'-the-wisp mother's gift and conjured a whip of crackling green witch-fire as I faced the Pouka.

"You only get to be immortal if you live to leave this room," I told her. She snarled at me, and then I wiped the snarl off her face with a slash of the whip.

Unlike the bullets, where the wounds faded almost as quickly as they were inflicted, she felt that one. The faerie flame, a construct of fire and Power, burnt into her skin and she lurched back in pain and shock.

That seemed to work. Unfortunately, since Chernenkov now felt threatened for the first time since we'd shown up to bring her in, it also pissed her off. With a snarl, she partially transformed, suddenly producing six-inch-long razor claws out of her hands as her fangs extended and she charged at me.

I slashed my whip at her feet, not doing a lot of damage but throwing off her balance so that instead of ripping out my throat, her claws merely stabbed through the upper right side of my chest. I felt my lung give way as she ripped her claws out, and gasped for breath as she smiled evilly.

"You still lose," she snarled at me through a mouthful of fangs.

By now the smell of chlorine in the storage room filled the air. A number of the canisters were leaking, and the thought of just why this much chlorine was in a storage room at a giant public event was niggling at the bank of my head.

What was also tingling at the back of my head was that this was a maintenance storage shed, and chlorine reacts explosively with turpentine. Like the several jugs of it on the shelf behind Ms. Chernenkov.

My whip vanished away, and the Pouka closed in to finish me off as I gasped for breath. Finally, somehow, I got a full breath of air into my functioning lung and a half and used it to focus.

I shot my hands out as she stabbed down, and launched a blast of *something* that caught her mid-strike. My right hand hit her with pure force, enough to pick her up and throw her into the rack with the jugs of turpentine—and then flung a blast of green flame from my left, which surrounded her and blasted the turpentine cans open.

The Pouka struggled back to her feet, opening her mouth to say something when the chlorine in the air met the turpentine spilling onto her and the sparks from the bolt of faerie flame that had thrown her across the room.

It was a relatively small explosion, all things considered.

2

I WOKE up from what was a thankfully short bout of unconsciousness to the feel of a burst of healing Power being blasted into me by Robert. The Fae Noble was crouched over me in the wrecked office, a cloth held over his mouth.

"The storage room is filled with chlorine," he told me urgently. "We've called in a hazmat team under a 'terrorist threat,' but the gas is spreading and we have to get out of here now. Can you take us Between?"

I blinked away the fuzz of explosion-induced unconsciousness and glanced around the room. fae were far more tolerant of poisons like chlorine than humans—hence my surviving in the storage room at all —but a high-enough concentration in the air would be fatal to us, too.

For a moment, I felt inside myself, where my Power lived. It had produced some odd effects today, but it seemed to still be fully present, a burning furnace that fueled my gifts.

"Everyone grab my hands," I told Robert and the Gentry, coughing slightly in the increasingly acrid air. A moment later, they had taken hold of my hands and arms. With a deep, half-choking breath, I stepped sideways.

Between has no air. This means that those walking with me breathe what I want to breathe, and that's not the poison-laced crap we'd left behind. For once, the cold crash of Between and the icy nature of breath were a blessing, it's chill air free of the chlorine that was close to killing even us.

Lord Oberis had been teaching me the skills of walking Between in recent months, allowing me to focus on a familiar point and move us toward it. The others walked with me, unable to even breathe if I released them. This was only a safe way to travel for those who had the Gift to walk it on their own. Others could only travel Between with the help of one with that Gift.

The easiest place for me to find was where I'd been taking my lessons. A minute or so after our entrance into Between, I returned us into reality standing in front of the desk of the man who ruled Calgary's fae.

A moment of shocked silence followed our arrival, and then Oberis, a tall Fae Lord with shoulder-length blond hair turned off the paper-thin computer monitor sitting on his black walnut desk and leaned forward, steepling his fingers as he faced us with a concerned look.

"I take it this means your mission had problems."

"She'd brought enough chlorine to gas half the Stampede," Robert explained bluntly. "I called in a hazmat team to contain it, but the canisters were broken in the fight. It was messy. Jason blew the chlorine up, but…"

"But it remains a threat," Oberis agreed calmly. "Give me a minute," he instructed. A portion of his desk slid aside at a touch, and he withdrew a plain black smartphone with no branding I recognized.

"This is Oberis," he said briskly into it as he accessed an icon. "We have an incident at the Stampede," he continued after a pause. "A hazmat team got called in to contain an apparent chlorine bomb; make sure any remnants of ours are out of the way and that the team is successful." He paused again, listening. "Good luck," he told whoever was on the phone, and then returned it to its alcove on his desk.

"There are some useful leftovers from the Enforcers," he told the two younger fae in his office. "MacDonald may have dissolved his own minions, but the structures and allies they integrated into mortal authorities remain. They'll make sure Ms. Chernenkov's remains don't attract attention."

"There won't be much in terms of remains," Robert replied. "Jason blew her up."

"Nothing else seemed to be working," I admitted sheepishly. "She took a bunch of cold iron rounds and didn't even seemed fazed. Fire and Power seemed to work, but..."

"Fuck me," Oberis whispered. "Cold iron didn't bother her? At all?"

"Just the impact throwing her back, from what I could tell," I told him. "I may as well have been carrying regular bullets."

A much more comfortable experience for me in general.

"Does that mean something to you, my lord?" Robert asked.

"Yes," the ruler of Calgary's fae said grimly. "It means young Kilkenny has made himself a mortal enemy, and one who will not be brought low by many means."

"She's *dead*," I objected.

"No, she's not," Oberis told me flatly. "If cold iron didn't not kill Chernenkov, even your Power-infused flame will not have sufficed. She is not what we thought she was."

He turned to the Gentry with us and considered them for several moments.

"Karl, Jacques. Can you leave us, please?"

The two men, still dripping onto Oberis's moss-carpeted floor, bowed and obeyed. That left Robert and me alone with the city's most powerful fae.

He rose and turned his back to us.

"Tell me everything," he ordered grimly. "Leave out *nothing*."

———

I HAD BEEN through the Fae Lord's idea of a debrief before, but that didn't make it any less intense of an experience. Some of it was practice on Oberis's part—he'd been leading fae organizations for something like a century, after all—and some of it was magic.

"Telekinesis, huh?" the Lord finally said with an intrigued glance at me. "I was wondering if that was going to come out sooner or later."

"My lord?" I asked. "You were *expecting* this?"

"The evidence suggests that your father was not merely a Hunter but a Noble of the Fae Courts," Oberis reminded me. "He would have not merely possessed the gifts of a Hunter but also the gifts of Force and Glamor.

"You may not inherit all his powers, but I still expected to see more," the Lord told me. "We will increase your training, though you may wish to inform your mistress yourself."

That, I was sure, would please Mabona to no end. A more powerful minion was a more useful minion. On the other hand, for reasons no one was yet willing to explain to me, Mabona *hated* being reminded of my father.

"That comes with the job," I admitted. "But…what was Chernenkov if she wasn't a Pouka?"

"Oh, Ms. Chernenkov is a Pouka," Oberis told me. "But like most of the inhumans that cross the line between breeds of supernatural, the Pouka are extraordinarily hard to kill."

I nodded some understanding. The same cold iron round that would be fatal to Oberis would be excruciatingly painful for me, my quarter-human blood enough to shield me against our bane. My girlfriend, on the other hand, was a wildcat shifter. A cold iron round wouldn't even slow her down, whereas a silver round I could ignore would drop her in her tracks.

Pouka were fae, not shifters, but they had links to that breed as well. And then, on top of that, they were feeders. It was a twisted mix of Power, one that gave them gifts most of us couldn't anticipate…

"But immortality?" I said aloud.

"From what you describe, were Chernenkov a shifter, she would be what they call an Alpha," he said grimly. "Because she is one of ours, we call her type a Noble. She would be a Pouka Noble…and she is not supposed to be."

"We were briefed on her," I noted. "I remember being warned she'd take a lot of killing, but we pumped her full of cold iron and then incinerated her in Power-infused flame. You're telling me she still lives?"

"Yes," Oberis confirmed with a sigh. "A Pouka Noble, along with being simply stronger in every sense than their lesser sisters, has a third form—their shadow. And their true essence *is* their shadow. You can burn their flesh and shatter their bones, but their shadow is invulnerable to such things and will regenerate the body."

That sounded…painful. Regeneration from severe injuries sucked. I could heal from almost any injury, though it took time. Regenerating from being burnt to a literal crisp in a chlorine-turpentine explosion?

"So, she's alive," Robert noted. "Which means we still need to hunt her down."

"Unfortunately, yes," Oberis agreed. "I will speak to Kenneth, see if he can locate her, and touch base with some old friends to see if they can advise how to fight her."

I shook my head.

"I'm going to guess that the process we just put her through hurt, at least?" I asked.

"Oh, yes," the Fae Lord told me. "It will have hurt a *lot*, and it will take her days to reassemble herself. She's going to remember you, Jason. Finding her would be wise, but at this point, she's going to come for us. Specifically, she's going to come for *you*."

I sighed. I definitely needed to talk to Mabona.

"And here I was just getting used to not having anyone hunting me."

"You are a Vassal of the Queen of the Fae," Oberis pointed out. "I would never expect that to be a long-lasting sensation on your part."

———

I'D BEEN in Calgary at this point for a little over six months. I'd spent about two-thirds of that time working for a courier company, before Mabona had finally convinced me that mundane employment was a waste of my time, given what she was prepared to pay me.

Not that I was doing much with the money either way. I didn't have a car and I lived in the same apartment in the basement level of a small complex on a hill above the downtown.

The apartment was empty when I got home. Like me, my girlfriend Mary Tenerim no longer worked for a mundane employer. My employment with the Queen of the Fae was only semi-voluntary, however, where her job as one of the coordinators of shifter affairs in the city was her choice.

Grandfather—few of us who'd met him bothered to refer to the old cougar shifter Alpha as Enli Tsuu T'ina—hadn't wanted the job of running the shifter clans, but the same mess that had nearly killed both Mary and me had left him with no choice.

He'd pulled together a staff from all of the shifter clans, who now took on the task of keeping that notoriously troublesome species in something resembling peaceful order. Mary was one of his most-trusted aides, a position of honor and trust—with commensurate compensation and time demands.

We could afford so much more than this little apartment, but the demands our work placed on us sucked up our time…and it wasn't in the nature of the supernatural to live in flashy homes or, well, to take out mortgages.

It wasn't like our jobs had salaries we could prove to a bank, after all.

Being alone in the apartment was useful for now, however, even if the place felt quiet. I poked at the wards a friend had laid on the space for privacy, my Power sufficient to at least test that they were working even if I couldn't create the magical silencing and protection effects myself.

I turned on the computer and linked into the Fae-Net, a private portion of the darknet no mortal would ever find. Even from there, however, there were private networks and secured sections even most fae wouldn't find.

I logged in to one of those places and entered a request. My mistress didn't do anything so normal as using scheduling software, but she did have a portal that would send a notification to a smart-phone that I needed to speak with her.

There was no easy way to predict how long it would take her to get back to me. So far as I understood, Mabona normally operated on Irish time, and she did, despite her phenomenal level of Power, still need to sleep.

I wasn't entirely surprised, though, for the videoconferencing software on my computer to almost instantly announce an incoming call. I wasn't sure just how much of what happened to me the Queen was aware of, but she registered at least *something* from all of her Vassals.

"Kilkenny," she greeted me brusquely as her dark-haired image filled my computer screen. "How, exactly, did you manage to blow yourself up this time?"

I snorted. Apparently, she knew at least that much.

"In my defense, I was blowing up a rogue Pouka as well," I told her. "Except, apparently, we're dealing with a Pouka Noble."

The Queen glared at me, then sighed and nodded.

"Who?" she asked. "There are supposed to be seventeen of those, *total*, and I know where they all are."

"Maria Chernenkov, the Pouka we were hunting here, is apparently your eighteenth," I told her.

Mabona grunted.

"That would make her significantly more dangerous than we expected when you agreed to Lord Oberis's request," she noted. "You are intact?"

"I am. Apparently, she's likely to have survived being blown up too."

"Sadly, yes," she confirmed. "I will see additional equipment delivered to your apartment, assuming you haven't moved out of the hole in the ground yet."

"You keep me busy," I demurred. My Queen objected to my living conditions more than I did.

"You need to nail her shadow to the ground with cold iron," Mabona told me bluntly. "This is exactly as easy as I suspect it sounds if you've fought her. Once isn't enough, either."

I sighed.

"Three times?"

"Three times," she confirmed. "Three cold iron spikes through her shadow... and even then, you will still have to fight and kill her. If she is a Pouka Noble that the Fae Council does not know of, her life is forfeit."

"She snuck into the city and murdered at least three people we know of," I reminded my mistress. "By Lord Oberis's command, her life is already forfeit."

"That is only going to get more complicated," Mabona told me. "With Kenneth MacDonald having dissolved his Enforcers and stepped back from running the city…"

"So far, everyone is playing nice," I reminded her. "So far, so good."

"Such never lasts," she warned. "I felt a spike of Power when you fought the Pouka. Something new, my Vassal?"

"The gift of Force, My Lady," I told her. "I unleashed a level of telekinetic power I have never wielded before."

Given that until today I'd envied the Fae Nobles their telekinetic powers and completely lacked them myself, *any* level of the gift of Force was new for me.

"This is useful," my Queen told me. "And dangerous. Lord Oberis will not have time to teach you what you need to know, especially if you are to fight a Pouka Noble and win. I will see that a trainer comes to you."

"Lord Oberis suggested he would be able to do it," I noted. I wasn't going to argue with her—but I also wasn't going to turn down Oberis's offer.

"He is about to become much busier," Mabona said grimly. "The High Court of the Fae has received a petition to open an Unseelie Court in Calgary."

That gave me pause and I swallowed as I looked at my boss on the computer screen.

"I thought the Council supported Lord Oberis?" I asked carefully.

"*I* support Lord Oberis," Mabona corrected sharply. "The Fae Council as a whole is…not entirely enthused with the concept of joint courts. I think some of my fellows suspect that if we let too many of them form, the Seelie and Unseelie might start getting along on a grander scale, and who knows where that would end?"

She snorted.

"Even of the nine of us, most class themselves as one or another,"

Mabona concluded. "It's a bloody stupid division in my mind that's caused more blood and heartache than it was ever worth, but it is what it is. And the High Court must not merely be neutral; we must *appear* neutral."

"Of course, my lady," I agreed. I wasn't sure I understood—but what changeling was going to argue with the High Court?

"Which means the petition passed," she told me. "Lord Oberis will be informed by dawn and Lord Andrell will be arriving in Calgary at eight PM in two days on the flight from Dublin. I'll make sure you have the flight number."

I hated what that implied and sighed.

"I'm guessing you want me to meet him?" I asked.

"We must appear neutral," she repeated. "You are my voice and sword in the region, which means it falls to you to introduce Lord Andrell to Lord Oberis's court...and it falls to you to be neutral between them.

"That is why I will send you a trainer to teach you to use your gifts." She shook her head. "You can no longer be Oberis's pupil if you are to act as a neutral mediator between him and Andrell."

"I am yours to command," I said. There was more than a touch of sarcastic grouchiness to my voice, but it was true. Quite literally, Mabona owned my blood. Defying her was unwise for anyone. For me, it was almost impossible.

"Andrell is young for a Fae Lord," she warned me. "He is an Unseelie who grew to adulthood in the fires of the First World War. Step carefully, my Vassal. You are protected by your oaths...but you are not entirely immune to his displeasure."

My own displeasure was probably visible, but she let that slide. Mabona was surprisingly willing to ignore what she called my trouble-some nature.

"I can be nice," I said.

She chuckled.

"Nice is unnecessary. Be inoffensive, my Vassal. If nothing else, we are well served if he sees you as no threat."

"That won't be hard," I pointed out. "I am a mere changeling, after all."

"Perhaps," she agreed. "Promise me one thing, Jason?"

"I am yours to command," I repeated.

"Don't make the Unseelie Lord take a cab. Find yourself a nice damn car before the flight arrives. Have Eric arrange it."

Eric von Radach was Keeper of the Manor in Calgary, sworn to serve the fae race as a neutral in all affairs of the supernatural. His own oath was to the Queen, however, and the gnome was a friend as well.

I'd driven a courier truck for my first job here, until my Queen's demands had grown too time-consuming. Since then, I hadn't had a vehicle. The city had decent transit and, well, I could walk Between when I was in a hurry.

That, however, would be showing off when dealing with an Unseelie Lord.

Equally, driving the Unseelie Lord around in the type of car I'd prefer to own would be an insult. My Queen's objection to my living and transportation arrangements had nothing to do with wanting me to be comfortable—and everything to do with appearances.

"As you command, My Queen."

3

WITH EVERYTHING MARY had going on, it was late by the time my girl-friend got home, and all she did was collapse into bed. Come morning, however, the fact that I was living with one of Grandfather's adminis-trators had its political advantages.

That wasn't why either of us were there, but it was part of why our respective leadership allowed, even encouraged, the relationship. Our races weren't cross-fertile with each other, though there was an open question of whether a regular changeling's human half would be enough to allow for children.

My subtlety at buttering up the first long-term girlfriend I'd had in years, however, left quite a bit to be desired, so when Mary wandered out of the bedroom to find me making breakfast, she dropped into a chair at the table and leveled a sharp green glare on me.

"What's up?" she asked. There was a warmth to her tone that few others heard from her, but there was more business to her than would normally be the case while she was sitting in our kitchen in a skimpy bathrobe and her long red hair.

"Pancakes?" I suggested hopefully, sliding the indicated product onto plates for us both.

"I can see that," she agreed. "And it's appreciated, especially since you've learned to use real maple syrup, but it's *Sunday*, Jason. Which means you aren't normally even awake before me, let alone making breakfast."

I sighed.

"I couldn't sleep well," I admitted. "She dropped a bombshell on me last night."

There was no question who "She" was. My love knew who I worked for and what I did.

"And I'm guessing I'm being bribed to carry some kind of message to Grandfather?" Mary asked as she took the plate and inhaled deeply. She might hate the "table syrup" I'd grown up with, but she had no complaints about the pancakes my mother had taught me to make.

"I'd hate to be so crass about it," I replied, pouring and hand-delivering coffee mixed to exactly her tastes. "But he needs to know what's about to get dropped on our poor city."

She took the coffee and shook her head at me as she inhaled.

"You know you don't actually need to butter me up for that?" she told me.

"It makes as good a reason as any," I said with a smile. "Plus, you need the fortification."

The humor faded from us both at that and she took a long swallow of the steaming hot coffee. Shifter regeneration meant that little things like "let the coffee cool" weren't really necessary.

"What happened?" she asked.

"An Unseelie Lord petitioned for, and was granted, the right to assemble a second Fae Court in Calgary," I said flatly. "Per our traditions and laws, he is still bound by the same Covenants Lord Oberis agreed to, but many other agreements will not apply to him.

"Even if he was coming in with the best of intentions—and he is *Unseelie*—this Lord Andrell would be a disrupting influence at a time when our supernatural community is still disrupted."

We'd saved—okay, *I'd* saved—the city's Wizard from being betrayed and murdered by his augmented human Enforcers. Kenneth MacDonald was a Power in his own right, but betrayal always struck where you weren't looking.

But his Enforcers had been the binding force holding Calgary's supernaturals together and something resembling in line. Through them, MacDonald had controlled the supply of heartstone, a by-product of the oil sands production north of the city that was a critically valuable commodity to all supernaturals.

Now…the Covenants that bound Wizard and fae and shifters to work together were strained, and only the personal friendships and personal *trust* across those lines had kept things together. A new normal was starting to take shape, but it hadn't yet.

Andrell was going to throw all of that into the blender again.

"What a fucking shit show," my lovely and intelligent girlfriend spat. "Is your High Court insane?"

"No, they just have different priorities," I admitted. "To them, keeping the peace between the two halves of the fae is far more important than worrying about order in any single city. A city with Calgary's importance, regardless of the actual number of fae here, should have two Courts.

"So, when petitioned, they can't deny it without appearing biased in favor of Lord Oberis, a Seelie."

Mary didn't look like she bought my explanation, but she ate more pancakes instead of arguing.

"I'll let Grandfather know," she told me. "All of that, including the political BS. *Quietly.*"

"Thank you. For my sins and official neutrality, *I* get to be Andrell's welcoming committee, which means I need to go car shopping."

She winced.

"For something 'worthy' of chauffeuring a Fae Lord around, I presume?" she asked. "How are you going to afford that?"

Theoretically, I had an employment contract from an Irish toy manufacturer that paid me a generous salary to act as a local "customer relationship manager." I could use that to finance a car, but the more expensive the car, the more attention I would draw—and the last thing I wanted to discover is whether or not there were limits to the ninety-percent-false credit history I had in Canada.

"I'll talk to Eric. It is a work expense, after all," I told her. "If She insists that I acquire a fancy expensive car, then She can bloody well pay for it."

Mary chuckled and reached over to take my hand.

"Be careful, my love," she told me. "I grew up here, where there's only ever been one Court. But I don't get the impression being caught between two Courts is going to be good for you."

I squeezed her hand as I shook my head.

"It probably won't be. But I swore an oath and I agree with at least *most* of what She asks of me. I'll be fine."

If Mary Tenerim looked doubtful of that, well, no one had ever accused her of being stupid.

———

ERIC VON RADACH had a thousand roles in the fae community as the Keeper, the acknowledged neutral, the man whose job it was to greet strangers to the city and offer them succor.

In the mundane world, however, he was the owner of an older motel and a gleefully gaudy bar between the university campus and the c-train line. If that motel and bar were something else to the city's supernatural community, the type of people who drank at that kind of bar or stayed at that kind of motel weren't the type to notice.

At lunchtime on a Sunday, the bar was open but utterly dead. There was a single dark-haired young man pushing a broom around and keeping an eye on the door. His long hair suggested he was one of us, and my own odd ability to pick out the supernaturals around me told me he was a changeling.

"Can I help you?" he asked.

"I'm Jason," I introduced myself. "Is Eric in?"

Eric was a gnome and blatantly short to human eyes. He spent most of his time behind the bar where it wasn't quite as obvious, but he was nowhere to be seen this morning.

"He said you might be stopping by," the youth said, bowing slightly. "I'm not sure of the address, My Lord Vassal?"

I laughed.

"You're just off succor and working for Eric to stay afloat, I'm guessing?" I asked gently. He nodded. "I may be a Vassal, but I'm just a changeling. 'Jason' works fine."

"A Hunter's changeling," a familiar gruff voice pointed out. "That means more than you might think. Zach here is still finding his own feet in who and what he is. I may send him to you with questions."

I turned toward the voice and bowed to Eric. Both of us were sworn to the Queen of the Fae, standing outside the normal lines of Court and fealty. Which of the pair of us had authority over the other was…an interesting question, given that the Keeper served a hierarchy sworn to the Queen and I served Her directly.

In practice, Eric von Radach was ninety or so years older than me, so I went with seniority.

"I can probably help," I agreed, offering my hand to the youth. He was, oh, maybe two years younger than my own twenty-four. Based off my own experiences, that meant he'd only had access to whatever gifts he'd inherited for a couple of years at most. "It's a hell of an adjustment."

"It is," Zach admitted.

"Zach should have come to our attention earlier," Eric noted. "He grew up in Saskatchewan's foster system, though, and our reach in the Prairies isn't what it should be."

"Damn lucky my ears didn't start pointing until *after* I'd realized I was getting weird," Zach agreed. "Do you need me, boss?"

"Nah, Jason and I have business to discuss. Can you keep an eye on the bar? We're probably going to have to hit the road pretty quickly."

"Tarva should be here in a few hours," the changeling youth said cheerfully. "So long as George in the kitchen stays awake, I can sling beer and sandwiches till then."

"Good lad." Eric turned to me. "Come on, Jason. I'm guessing there's a reason I was told to expect you?"

"No one briefed you?" I asked quietly.

One old eyebrow went up.

"Step into my parlor, Mr. Kilkenny," he replied.

By the time I was done filling him in, Eric just looked tired. We were in his underground apartment beneath the bar, drinking coffee he'd made himself. The overstuffed chairs down there were almost certainly older than I was—they were quite possibly older than the bar itself—but they were definitely comfortable.

"I was notified about Andrell not long after She updated you," he admitted. Like when I spoke about our mistress, the capital was audible on the pronoun. "All I got with regards to *you* visiting me was to make sure I had funds on hand for an 'authorized business expense of some magnitude.'"

He chuckled.

"I sometimes wonder if the people who send those notes understand what I would regard as 'some magnitude,'" he continued. "Here I was, trying to work out how I was going to move a couple of million from liquid assets into cash on a Sunday."

I winced.

"I need a car, Eric, not an airplane."

"If you needed an airplane, I'd need more notice," he told me. "I can arrange a charter on twenty-four hours' notice, but I can't *buy* a plane in that time frame."

"What about a car?" I asked.

"You want something expensive enough to support the fact that a Fae Lord needs to treat you with respect, without being flashy enough to draw attention from the mundanes."

"Basically," I agreed with a nod. "And I need it ASAP."

"Even in this city, that rules out sports cars and Teslas," he told me. "What's *ASAP*—tomorrow?"

"Lord Andrell arrives at eight PM on Monday, presumably with an escort," I told him. "I don't have details for how many people he's bringing with him, but I presume an Unseelie Fae Lord won't travel alone anymore than Oberis would."

Eric snorted.

"Even less likely. So, you want something that can carry at least four passengers comfortably. You realize that's getting you big SUVs, right?"

"Can't be worse than the courier truck," I pointed out. "I'd still be driving those if you lot left me the time."

"That would be even *worse* for Her image than you not having enough passenger seats for Andrell's bodyguard," Eric said with a chuckle. "You might have managed to get away with a 'day job' while Oberis was the only Lord in the city, but with two Courts that need to see you and me as neutral arbiters?

"No, you're getting a Cadillac, boy. Escalade, eight passengers, big engines, black paint job." He snorted. "I'd recommend *against* black, to be honest, except you need to walk into a dealership, pay cash, and pick the vehicle up with all registration sorted tomorrow morning. So, you're stuck with what they've got…which will be black."

It could be worse, I supposed. Though that left me with the headache of working out where I was going to *park* a massive luxury SUV anywhere near my apartment complex.

"I don't suppose they're bulletproof by default?"

"No, but you're bringing Andrell *here*," Eric reminded me. "He'll come to the Manor, and then we'll take him to see Lord Oberis, then you'll bring him back here. From there, getting around is his own damn problem.

"Leave the car with me after that for a day or two, and your enemies will wish I'd *merely* made it bulletproof."

Eric von Radach, these days, was a neutral arbiter and required to stay out of most conflicts. In his younger days, though, he'd been a gnomish War Smith and forged magical swords and guns for Fae Lords.

Whatever he did to the car, I knew I wasn't going to mind.

4

MANEUVERING the leather-seated and electronics-festooned SUV into Calgary's airport parking was intimidating enough for me—and I'd spent three months driving courier trucks around the city. I couldn't imagine why someone would voluntarily drive a boat like the Escalade.

Its sheer size and mass seemed to get a degree of space and respect even my courier truck hadn't, and with the overpowered engine built into this one, it was actually more maneuverable than any regular car I'd driven.

It was just a monster to try to fit into a regular parking spot in the multi-level garage. Duty, however, called and I took advantage of my literally superhuman senses and reflexes to tuck the wheeled boat into a spot and get into the airport to meet Calgary's newest supernatural power player.

Like the executive sedan drivers around me at the gate, I carried a sign with Andrell's name on it. Unlike them, it was a mere formality. I'd know the Lord on sight. No one else was going to come off the plane radiating Power the way he would.

I hopefully wasn't quite as recognizable to him, but he'd probably be able to guess that the long-haired man in the cheap suit was his fae greeting party. It was even possible that my Queen had made sure he had a picture of his greeting party.

Mistakes would be insults, and insults were a deadly game amongst fae nobility.

In the end, I didn't even need my ability to identify the supernatural to pick him out. Two men and two women, all in matching expensive suits and long hair, emerged from the gate with rolling luggage. All four of them towered over the crowd around them, radiating the kind of calm authority and power than led even mundanes to give them space.

The fifth fae was barely visible through his escort. He didn't come up past the shoulder of any of his friends, probably only came up to my nose or so, but I didn't need the guards to know who he was.

Lord Andrell was short for a Fae Lord, broad-shouldered but still bone-thin. Long red hair covered his ears and was drawn back into a ponytail that highlighted his sharp features, helping him draw intrigued looks from the crowd around him.

He moved with the liquid grace of a tiger, and his green eyes were cold as I met his gaze across the concourse. He was as different from Lord Oberis, the other Fae Lord I'd spent any time around, as I could imagine...but the Power and intensity of his gaze were the same.

Andrell gestured toward me and his mobile square of bodyguards moved in my direction. I folded away my sign and inclined my head toward him.

"Lord Andrell," I greeted him quietly. He'd hear me, as would his guards. Anyone with merely mortal senses, however, would barely notice I was moving my lips. There were courtesies to be observed—but also practical necessities of greeting in an airport surrounded by non-supernaturals.

"You would be Kilkenny, then?" he greeted me in a strong Irish accent. To my surprise, he stepped through his bodyguards and offered me his hand. "I knew your mother, long ago. It's a pleasure."

I shook his hand carefully.

"I'm Kilkenny, yes," I allowed. "I'm your ride to the Manor."

"Of course, of course," he replied. "Do you have space for my friends?"

"Of course, Lord Andrell," I echoed back to him. "If you have all your luggage, you can follow me."

———

THE ESCALADE MIGHT HAVE SEEMED RIDICULOUSLY over the top to me, but my passengers clearly took it as their due, readily loading their suitcases into the back of the SUV. They also took a moment, shielded by Lord Andrell's glamors, to each open their suitcase and remove a magically concealed shoulder holster.

The guns had at least traveled unloaded, and the magazines they loaded them with didn't contain cold iron. I'd have felt more comfortable if my new passengers *weren't* all armed, but I wasn't hypocritical enough to say anything.

It wasn't like I didn't have a cold-iron-loaded revolver in the driver's-side door, after all. Any reasonable Canadian would have been horrified at the amount of hardware suddenly present in my SUV...but even *I* was probably more dangerous than my gun, and I was the least threatening person in the vehicle.

"I do wish I'd known Mellie had a child," Andrell told me softly as we drove through the city. "She had many friends back home, and I don't think any of us knew you existed, Jason. Until Her Majesty told me you'd be greeting me and I looked you up, I didn't realize what had happened to her."

"She made her choices," I replied carefully. My mother had been dead for a long time now—car accidents were no gentler on changelings than they were on regular humans. Before her death, however, she'd never told me anything to suggest that we weren't perfectly normal. For whatever reason, my mother had left fae culture behind when she moved to the United States and raised me as a normal human.

"That she did," Andrell confirmed. "And I'm sure she had her reasons. Your mother was a smart woman. And your reputation, Jason, precedes you."

I snorted.

"I doubt I have much of a reputation," I pointed out. "I think I may be the only changeling whose Fealty is held by a member of the High Court, but beyond that..."

The Unseelie Lord chuckled.

"That was enough, once our Queen told me about you," he said. "The very polite email I got from Kenneth MacDonald was fascinating, though."

I said nothing in response to that. What could I say? I hadn't even been certain that the Wizard had known about Andrell's arrival.

"Magus MacDonald has made it very clear that he regards you as being under his protection and that he will protect the neutrality of Her Majesty's servants in this city," the Lord told me. "Some minor matter about saving his life?"

He waited for me to answer.

"I was one of many," I finally told him. "This last winter was complicated. The city is still unsettled."

If he took that as criticism of his timing on trying to start a new Fae Court there, well, it was indirect enough to be safe.

"I know," he allowed. "Laurie's death was unfortunate. Justified, yes, but it drew the attention of the Unseelie Lord to the concerns of our people in this city, ruled over by a Seelie Lord. That, Jason, is why I am here.

"If the Unseelie in this city want to start a war, they will go through me to do it," he said calmly. "But if the Seelie in this city want to execute my people, they will have to prove the need to *me*. That is the nature of the Courts of our people. How it should be.

"How it will be."

I shivered and turned my focus back to the road. The Unseelie Hag Laurie had tried to kill me, repeatedly, in the service of the conspiracy against the Wizard. Her betrayal had nearly destroyed the Fae Court—and the confession Lord Oberis had forced from her had helped undo the entire conspiracy.

But it was the nature of fae to be clannish. We protected our own first. The Unseelie, it seemed, felt that Lord Oberis had been regarding the Seelie as his own...and the Unseelie as not.

IF MY CAR was what our Unseelie guests had been expecting, the Manor, Eric's bar, was…not.

I'd seen the Manors in about twenty North American cities before I'd reached Calgary, and Eric's bar was pretty low-class even by that standard. The only real requirement was that a Manor had to have the ability to feed people and somewhere to house them—since tradition called for the Keeper to provide three days of succor to strange fae—but I'd seen that fulfilled by anything from a diner and motel to a decent hotel.

The gaudy university bar was definitely closer to the diner-and-motel end of that scale, and from the expression of my *very* Irish guests, they weren't familiar with Manors of that quality.

"This is the Manor?" one of the women asked. "Are you *serious*?"

The tall black-haired woman was glaring at me like a hungry crow.

"Peace, Gráinne," Andrell told her. "You can read the fae-sign as well as I can. Young Kilkenny has done as we asked; lay no insult at the feet of the Queen's Vassal."

Her master's pointed reminder quieted Gráinne, and she and the others exited my SUV at the front door of the bar.

"May we leave our luggage with you for the moment?" Andrell asked me in his lilting accent. "As I understand, Her Majesty asked you to drive us around tonight?"

"That's right," I confirmed. "There's plenty of space for your bags."

I'd only had the car for half a day. There wasn't even a concealed armory or anything built into it yet.

"I don't plan on imposing too harshly, Jason," Andrell promised. "If you'll meet us inside, we have business to discuss with the Keeper —and I think Her Vassal should be present for it."

———

ENTERING the bar a couple of minutes after Andrell and his people was entertaining for me. Probably not so much for the fae-only occupants of the bar, who had the incredible, I was sure, pleasure of trading looks with his bodyguards.

Gráinne was the most noticeable, but all four of the neatly suited

Europeans were looking like they'd stepped into a pigpen several inches deep in muck. The Fae Lord himself, however, was studying the dingy bar with the fascination most people reserved for a *probably* friendly Rottweiler.

"Hi!" Tarva greeted them as I entered, the waitress appearing out of the limited crowd like the sun rising. She was a water nymph, five foot six of hyper-compressed sex appeal. She could turn that down, if she wanted, and it didn't work all that well on fae...but at full power, even Andrell looked somewhat taken aback at the blast of her presence.

"Can I get y'all some drinks?" she asked. "Eric is on his way." She grinned. "I'm guessing you don't need succor, but I think we can spot you some beer."

Andrell chuckled, a liquid sound that was a mild but noticeable threat to my determined heterosexuality, and gestured his people to a table.

"*I* will have a Traditional," he told her, referencing Calgary's local beer. He looked at his crew, then chuckled again. "My people will have Guinness, unless you have anything else from the old country?"

"We've got Smithwick's, most Murphy's, and Beamish," Tarva reeled off instantly. "I've probably got a few varieties of Irish whisky, too."

"Nothing that heavy on the job," Andrell said gently. "Folks?"

His people gave the waitress their orders, and I traded calm nods with Tarva as I took my own seat. Zach materialized a moment later, the young changeling carrying a small tray with coffee.

Eric's bar coffee was usually terrible, but this cup actually smelled fantastic.

"Thanks, Zach," I said, sniffing it. "What did you *do*?"

"Cleaned the pots and started with cold water," he reeled off instantly. "It doesn't take much to make good coffee out of the gear Eric had, just someone who had the time to stop and look at it."

I chuckled my thanks and took a sip. It wasn't quite up to what I'd been drinking the one memorable week I'd stayed in Seattle's independent coffeehouse Manor, but it was a *hell* of a lot better than Eric's place traditionally served.

It was late, though Calgary July meant it was still light outside, and

I was starting to wonder just how long Eric was going to make Andrell wait. Tradition and courtesy said that the Unseelie Lord *had* to meet with the Keeper before anyone else.

Using tradition to make the Lord wait too long, however, would become one of the insults my Queen had ordered me to avoid. I wasn't sure how long would be too long, though…but I would bet dollars to donuts that Eric *did*.

Andrell hadn't even begun to appear twitchy by the time Eric eventually arrived, though several of his guards were less self-composed. The gnome stepped out from behind the bar without hesitation—Tarva had a dozen different ways to make sure there were only fae in the bar when that was needed, after all—and crossed to the Unseelie Lord.

"I am Eric von Radach, Keeper of the Manor in Calgary," Eric introduced himself quietly. "Announce yourself, stranger."

"I am Lord Karl Andrell of the Unseelie," Andrell told him, his voice liquid and calm. "I am charged by Unseelie Lord Jon Andrews of the High Court to establish a new Court in this city, to provide leadership and sanctuary to the Unseelie of these lands."

He paused for a moment to let the mostly Unseelie crowd absorb that. The nature of the crowd was sign enough that Calgary's Unseelie had known he was coming.

"Such was presented to Our High Court and approved," he told us all. "By the Will of the Fae Powers, I am now the Lord of the Unseelie Courts in this city."

Andrell had never actually sat down, even as he drank his beer, and yet he and Eric seemed to be on a level somehow. The gnome came up to his chest, but the Keeper was unintimidated. I didn't know how strong Eric truly was with Power without the chance to forge artifacts —but I also knew that this was his home.

Few were those foolish enough to fight a War Smith on their own ground.

"Do you so recognize me, Keeper Eric von Radach?" Andrell demanded.

"The High Court and Queen we share have made their decision, Lord Andrell," Eric told him. "I see you and I recognize you. I remind you that I stand as Keeper to this city, outside your Courts, and that I have bound the fae of this realm to the agreed-upon Covenants between the races.

"Are you prepared to accept those Covenants, Lord Andrell?"

In theory, Andrell could refuse the Covenants that dictated how the fae would deal with the Wizard and the shifters and the other scattered supernaturals of Calgary. But then, in theory, Eric could actually deny recognition of the Unseelie Court.

In reality, there was no chance I was doing anything except driving Karl Andrell to meet Lord Oberis next.

5

I'D STOPPED at the entrance to the Manor and let the Unseelie go in on their own, but that was the Manor. The Manor was neutral ground, guaranteed as such by the High Court. If someone caused trouble in the Manor, it was part of my job to punish them for it.

So far, that had involved tracking down one drunken banshee and making her pay to replace an entire set of glassware. It had been pretty mundane and tame, but the neutrality of the Manor was sacred.

There was no such neutrality to the Courts themselves. Quite the opposite, in fact, and Lord Andrell arguably took his life into his own hands by entering Lord Oberis's Court. Tradition required it—and equally, tradition required that Andrell be escorted by an accepted neutral.

Today, that was me, which meant that I parked the giant SUV and led the way into the western-themed hotel that held what *had* been merely the Fae Court of Calgary—and was about to become the Seelie Court of Calgary.

Andrell himself walked behind me, but this time, his guards fell in behind us. Leading the way into Oberis's Court with armed Unseelie Nobles was...bad form.

We passed through the normal sections of the hotel, where hay bales and painted cowboys reminded everyone that the Stampede was still ongoing, and into a wing of conference rooms that declared themselves booked by one of Calgary's many and varied oil exploration companies.

It was always a different company...but this wing was always booked. A suited "hotel employee" at the entry desk was actually a Gentry guard, but she waved me through. We were expected, after all.

Charms woven into the walls would discourage any mundane from going much farther than that desk even if it was unguarded, and the actual space back there was larger on the inside. Carpet gave way to carefully grown and magically maintained moss, and we reached a paired set of double doors.

Normally, those doors were kept open when Court was in session. Tonight, however, they were closed. Tradition demanded it.

Robert stood outside the doors stiffly, the young Seelie Noble eyeing his new Unseelie counterparts carefully. With the arrival of Andrell's guards, the number of Fae Nobles in the city had just doubled—and that was assuming Talus was in town.

"Robert," I greeted him with a nod of my head. "I'm here to present Lord Andrell. Are we going to have a problem?"

The words were more formalized than they sounded. We had our assigned roles to play tonight—there had once been a time when this affair would have required more than one part-human Vassal to make sure of the new Lord's safety.

Things were calmer these days. Mostly.

"We were advised of his arrival," Robert said carefully. "There are no hands raised against him tonight; the Court awaits his arrival."

He stepped aside, a small gesture opening the doors with his telekinetic power. My usual thrill of envy at the demonstration of that gift was tempered tonight by the realization that I would soon be meeting a trainer who was supposed to teach me how to wield that power.

It was an odd thought.

Andrell gestured for me to precede him and gave Robert a firm, reassuring nod. He clearly recognized the young Noble's inexperience and was being supportive.

I wasn't entirely enthused with Andrell's presence in the city, but I'll be damned if the man wasn't likeable.

————

CALGARY'S COURT was built on the bones of a normal large business conference center. At one point, it had had mobile walls that could be slid across to divide it into three smaller spaces, but those—like the original carpet—had disappeared after the fae had taken over the space.

Now the walls were covered in murals half-concealed under creeping ivy, and the carpet had been replaced with carefully mani-cured moss. The chairs were about the only thing that resembled the original furniture, and even those had been upgraded to more expen-sive and more comfortable varieties.

A raised dais at one of the hall now held a table with a single chair behind it, the closest Lord Oberis was willing to come to anything resembling a throne. Usually, there would be chairs in front of the table for the people meeting with him, but today there was nothing.

Talus stood to Lord Oberis's right, Robert's equally blond and Noble father looming over the crowd. To the left stood the ash-black form of the nightmare Tamara. Both of Oberis's guardians were friends, though no one would have guessed it from the cold glares they leveled on me.

This was work and duty, though, regardless of what any of us thought of it. I followed the narrow gap at the center of the room, leading my new companions to the front of the hall with a somber step.

There'd been two dozen fae, almost all Unseelie, at the Manor. The rest of Calgary's two hundred–odd fae were gathered here. There was no one in the city of our Courts who would not see Lord Andrell tonight.

There were guests, too. A cluster of wolf shifters were seated in one corner, keeping quietly to themselves. None were Alphas or similarly important members of the Clans—that would be stealing the spotlight—but the shifters were there to bear witness.

Every eye in the room was on me. I *hated* being the center of attention, not least because even now most of the people in the room could break me with one hand.

But this was duty and I would honor my oaths.

I reached the dais and bowed to Lord Oberis.

"My Lord Oberis, Master of the Seelie in this realm, I am here as a neutral arbiter under the will of my Queen and our shared High Court," I told him, the formal words rolling awkwardly off my tongue. "An Unseelie Lord has petitioned the High Court for the right to form a new Court in this realm."

Oberis was silent but gestured for me to continue speaking. The need for me to be neutral was going to be a headache for the friendships I'd forged with Calgary's Court. For that alone, I wished Andrell had gone somewhere else.

"The High Court saw no reason to deny the petition," I told the gathered Court. "Lords and ladies of the Calgary Courts, may I introduce the Lord of our new Unseelie Court, Lord Andrell."

I gestured Andrell forward and stepped to one side. My part in this theater, at least, was done.

Andrell gave Oberis the carefully measured half-bow of equal Lords.

"Lord Oberis and fae of our now-shared city," he greeted them all. "I know this is never an easy transition to make, from one Court to two, and it's hard to swallow for many. To the Unseelie of this realm, I remind you that our shared Lord has commanded this. I will open a new Court in the days to come, and I summon you all to meet me there when the time comes."

He smiled and waved expansively to the room.

"To our Seelie brothers, I beg you to be patient and to give us time. There is no need for conflict," he told us. "This is not a hostile takeover—I don't want to rule this city any more than Lord Oberis does. We are bound by code and oath and Covenant, and we share this city."

He turned back to Oberis, and even *I* could feel the tension in the air between them.

"We *are* brothers, my Lord," he insisted. "The codes and Covenants to lay out peace between Seelie and Unseelie Courts have been written for generations. There is no need for conflict here."

Finally, Lord Oberis rose.

"I agree," he ground out. "I hope we can work together to get through the inevitable teething problems. There are, as always, ongoing issues, Lord Andrell, and I would invite you to meet with me tomorrow to discuss them in a more collegial setting."

From the Seelie Lord's body language, I figured a boxing ring or underground fight club was definitely inside the category of "collegial setting" in his mind.

"For now, know that you are welcome to Calgary and I look forward to us building a new future together, two Courts bound as one race."

"As do I," Andrell promised. "We have much work to do, you and I, Lord Oberis. We shall help our people thrive."

———

THE FORMALITIES CONCLUDED, Andrell returned outside. I gave Oberis and Talus what I hoped were friendly please-don't-blame-me-for-this nods and followed him out.

I found him leaning against the back wall of the hotel studying my car, looking tired.

"Jet lag is a bitch," he told me as I approached. "But even I could pick up that there was more tension than I expected. What happened, Mr. Kilkenny?"

"I don't know what you mean," I admitted.

"I've played bodyguard for this kind of mess before," he said. "And I *know* Oberis. There were a lot more angry people in there than I expected. Which means, I judge, that an Unseelie just managed to cause trouble.

"So, I repeat myself. What happened?"

"Ah." I sighed. "We had a Pouka attempt to gas the Stampede. I don't know why—I'm guessing that dying terrified and screaming makes humans taste better or some shit?—but it happened. And rumor suggests she might have survived us stopping her."

He closed his eyes and exhaled.

"I see," he admitted. "Presumably, that's part of what Lord Oberis wishes to brief me on. That's a headache my new Court doesn't need, but we'll deal with it."

His bodyguards folded in around him and he gave me a tired smile.

"I'm sure it's no surprise I'm not planning on staying at the Manor under succor," he continued. "May we impose, Jason, for one more ride? We're staying at the Palliser downtown. Drop us off there and your duty to our shared Queen is done for tonight. And you'll have my gratitude."

"I can manage that," I replied. It was easy enough, and I had no more interest in aggravating the city's new Unseelie Lord than I did in aggravating our Seelie one.

6

DROPPING the car off at Eric's and bussing home after delivering Andrell left me getting in well after midnight. Mary was already home and asleep, and I carefully closed the door to keep the light out of the bedroom as I booted up my computer.

For once, my email didn't have any metaphorical wriggling snakes lurking in it. Experience suggested that would change by the time lunch had rolled around in Ireland, but for now I only had one email that was expecting me to take any action at all.

That email could easily have been taken for spam, too, if Fae-Net suffered from such a thing. It was titled simply *Begin Your Training* with an address and a time.

The time was early the next morning and the address was relatively nearby. That would be helpful when I needed to meet whoever my Queen had arranged to take over my training—Mabona hadn't given me any more information on that than she had before. Most of my communication with her over the last few days had been around Andrell's arrival.

Clearly, she'd found time to arrange for someone to arrive in Calgary and take over the task of training me in my gifts from Oberis.

Another wedge driven in between myself and the Seelie Court of the city, who had, until today, been my friends.

I sighed and jotted off a quick email to Talus, asking if we could meet up for a meal before he left town. I'd be *damned* if the need to stay neutral meant I had to give up on my friendships in this city. I couldn't train with the Seelie Lord, I could accept that, but I wasn't going to lose all of my friends, either.

I was tired and frustrated enough that even my senses missed Mary coming out of the bedroom until she wrapped her arms around my neck and kissed my hair.

"Rough night, huh?" she asked.

"Politics were bad enough when we had *one* Fae Court," I replied, leaning back against her. "Now…now I don't know if I'm going to find time to *breathe*, let alone sleep. Being the local neutral is sounding like it's going to be a pain in the ass."

"You'll manage," she told me assuredly. "However bad it gets, it can't get as bad as it was when you first got here. Nobody is poking at the soft spots."

I chuckled and turned to face her. For her part, Mary slipped into my lap and cuddled against me. This was the point where I realized she was wearing a flimsy silk robe and not much else.

"In any case, it sounds like you need to actually come to bed and *sleep*, not stress over things," she pointed out with a small wicked grin. "I have some ideas to help with that!"

———

THE ADDRESS I'd been given turned out to be a closed kung fu dojo in a strip mall twenty minutes' walk from my house. That was helpful, seeing as how the Escalade was still with Eric and, well, I was used to getting around on foot.

Stepping Between was something I still reserved for events of greater urgency than "I don't feel like walking today." It wasn't really uncomfortable for me, not like it was for someone with no control over their own trip, but it was still a little nerve-wracking.

Thanks to the wonders of modern smartphones, I arrived precisely three minutes before I was supposed to be there and stood outside the boarded-over windows, studying the space carefully. I'd ridden past it on the bus a few times, and the dojo had only closed a month or so before.

The old signs were still up and there was no sign that anything had changed, but I doubted that someone had sent me that email just to make me look like an idiot. I walked up to the paper-covered door and knocked.

The door swung open instantly, and I found myself face to face with one of the most imposing women I've ever met. She was several inches over six feet, towering over even me, with dark skin that suggested African ancestry somewhere, and blond hair braided into a tightly fitted crowd around her skull.

"Kilkenny," she greeted me in a vaguely Scandinavian accent. "Come in."

She stepped back, allowing me to enter the dojo, and then closed and locked the door behind me.

Someone, presumably my hostess, had cleaned the hardwood floors and cleared out the small office. I was pretty sure I spotted a cot hiding behind the desk in the office, which told me a lot about where my new teacher was sleeping.

"The landlord was desperate," she noted as she led me into the space. "He thinks I'm setting up a new dojo, but I suspect he knows I'm sleeping in here, too."

"Are you setting up a dojo?" I asked carefully.

She shrugged.

"I will think about it. I am supposed to be here for some time, and it may prove to be a useful distraction." She turned to loom over me. "I am Inga Strand, of the Aesir."

I blinked at that. I was vaguely aware that the Aesir were, basically, Nordic fae, but that was all I knew. From the Power Inga radiated, she was a Noble or Greater Fae at least.

"My Lady said she was sending a Hunter," I said carefully. "I'm guessing that is you?"

"'A Hunter,' the boy says." Inga laughed. "Kilkenny, I have trained Hunters and the children of Hunters for two *centuries*. I have ridden with Ankaris, who leads the Hunt today. I rode with Calebrant until his death. I rode with Karos until his death. Before Karos recruited me, I rode with the Valkyries."

The Valkyries.

I was standing in a room with a *Valkyrie*.

The Wild Hunt were basically the special forces of the Fae High Court, the only organized "military" the fae had. They'd once been one of several, but all of them had been absorbed by now.

The Valkyries had been one of the ones they absorbed. Like the Hunters themselves, the Valkyries were a subspecies of fae. Where the Wild Hunt had other fae in their ranks, drawn through Between by the Hunters who led them, the Valkyrie had ridden alone.

They were Hunters, able to step Between, but they were also *legends*.

"I am honored, my lady," I told her.

"Get your jaw off the floor," she instructed bluntly. "From what the Queen has told me, you are one of the strongest Hunter changelings to ever cross my path. The Wild Hunt cannot afford to have you running around half-trained, even if your Fealty to the Queen means we cannot claim you as our own."

She shook her head.

"The Aesir would be Noble if they wielded the glamors that define that caste," she noted. "We have their strength and their gifts of Power otherwise, but we lack the glamors they claim as their own.

"The Valkyries are Aesir who can walk Between. Nothing more. Nothing less. You claim the gifts of Force, and Fire, and Between, but lack the strength of a Noble. If you are to survive at the tasks our Queen has set you, you must learn to use the gift of Force to make up for that lack; do you understand?"

"I think so," I said slowly. I didn't even know what gifts I commanded yet, but her list sounded about right. "I am prepared to learn. I *must* learn. I swore an oath."

"Good. You recognize that much," she agreed, then pulled a silver-hilted sword from nowhere.

"Then we shall begin."

INGA STARTED WITH BASIC EXERCISES, movement and stretches that would have been familiar to any student of martial arts, mundane or supernatural. Without much in terms of training or aptitude, I had the strength and endurance of an Olympic-level athlete, so I was used to this sort of thing being easy.

Except today I was being put through the "basic" exercises by a Valkyrie. If there was a drop of mercy in Inga's training methodology, I wasn't aware of it after the first twenty minutes. Peak human endurance or not, I was dripping with sweat by the time we'd finished her "warm-up".

"All right," she told me, picking up the sword again. It was only slightly reassuring to me that the silver-hilted weapon had a scabbard around its cold-forged iron blade. "Knock the sword from my hand."

I stared at her.

"Are you kidding me?" We'd already established she was faster and stronger than I was—*and* more skilled.

"No. Knock the sword from my hand."

Well, we both knew how this was going to end. I charged at her, trying to fling my entire body weight against her wrist to knock the weapon free.

I didn't even manage to register individual blows. The next thing I actively registered, I was flat on my back on the other side of the room, breathing stiffly past a crushing pain in my chest.

"What part of what I am supposed to be teaching you led you to think I meant with your hands?" she asked acidly. "You have the Gift of Force, child. *Use it.*"

A gift I had used once, while under deadly threat. But that was, as she said, the whole point of this lesson. I slowly levered myself to my feet, letting my body heal the bruises as I regained my breath.

Inga faced me, her eyes grim as she studied me. She held the sword firmly in her hand and I returned her assessment.

This time, I started with fire, hoping to tie Force into the abilities I'd always had. A whip of flame flashed out from my left hand to try and wrap around the sword and yank it away. The Valkyrie grinned widely and dodged sideways, the sword dancing away from my whip.

I tried to adjust, to curl the line of fire out to grab the blade despite her movement...but that was more control than I'd ever attempted before. I lost control and my whip smashed into the wall. For a second, I thought I was going to set the damn building on fire!

Inga had clearly been at least half-expecting the problem, however, as her own Power snuffed out my whip before I did more than scorch the wall.

"Good," she told me, then laughed. "Well, atrocious, actually, but it's a good start. Did you feel the Force in your flame?"

I shook my head.

"That's what I was *aiming* for, but no, I didn't feel it," I admitted.

"That's fine," she said. "*I* did. That's a beginning, anyway. We'll get there."

"How long are you here for?" I asked carefully.

She laughed again.

"As long as you need," she admitted. "I'm *retired*, Jason. For two centuries, I trained Hunters, and for two centuries before that, I rode, as Hunter and Valkyrie alike. Four hundred years is enough to sacrifice to *anything*."

Inga shook her head.

"I'm here as a favor, nothing more. I'm no longer a member of the Hunt and was never a Vassal to anyone."

"I appreciate it," I told her quietly. "I'm surprised the Queen called in a favor from a Valkyrie on my behalf, however."

"I never said I owed the favor to the Queen," she said sharply. "Now, let's try that flame whip again. It's a good starting point, so let's see if we can refine it!"

———

INGA WORKED me over for roughly two hours before I had to call a halt to our training. It was hard for me to say if I'd made any noticeable improvement, though I was certainly glad that I had enough of the rapid healing abilities of the fae to make the bruises and exhaustion tolerable.

Regardless of my need for training, however, I had scheduled meetings and appointments. There was a Pouka Noble loose somewhere in the city, which was at least partially my responsibility, and the thousand other things that the Queen's main representative in Calgary had to handle.

"Acceptable progress," she told me as I checked my phone to make sure I hadn't missed anything critical. "You'll be back here at the same time every day, for two hours, until *I* think you are worthy of being called a Hunter. Understood?"

"You realize I *do* have responsibilities?" I asked dryly. One of my emails wasn't *quite* a bomb. It was more of a ticking time bomb, the kind I couldn't do anything about yet but was going to explode in my face in a day or three.

That was how my job went. I kept an eye on arguments and "discussions" in the fae community and acted as a mediator. I wasn't even the fae equivalent of Interpol. I swear I was the fae equivalent of a nanny.

"Of course," Inga agreed instantly. "But you will be far more able to carry them out once you are ready. Right now, your fealty and oaths make you a target, and you lack the skills to survive what your enemies may throw at you."

She wasn't wrong. I sighed and nodded, then paused at the doorway.

"You said you didn't owe a favor to the Queen," I noted. "Who did you owe it to?"

Inga chuckled.

"I've been asked not to tell you that," she told me. "That silence is a favor to the Queen—but also to you."

"I've heard that before," I replied. It was as ominous from Inga as it was from Mabona. A lot of the more powerful fae around me kept referencing a secret that would be dangerous for me to know.

It was pissing me off, to be honest.

"You will understand," Inga said. "For now, however, I will see you in the morning. Shoo!"

7

WHEN I ARRIVED at the Manor, Tarva quickly directed me out behind the bar, in the not-quite-alley between Eric's bar and motel and the strip mall facing the major street one block over. There, I found the Escalade suspended in the air on a car lift I was relatively sure wasn't normally there.

Eric was just cleaning his hands on a blue strip of disposable shop towel as I approached, and he gave me a firm nod.

"Kilkenny. How's your day going?"

"Training, so far," I told him. "And I have a mediation in about two hours, which I confidently expect to consume the rest of my day."

And, given the way mediating disputes between fae sometimes went, potentially my evening and night, too.

Eric chuckled.

"You have no idea how happy I am to have someone *else* to off-load at least some of those on to," he told me. "Part of why I spent the morning poking at this girl."

The gnome pointed at the Escalade. The car lift descended as he pushed buttons from a distance, allowing the big SUV to slowly drop onto the ground.

"There's only so much I can do without taking her apart," he continued. "A bit of work on the chassis and glass, some standard enchantments and parts in the engine system. I don't recommend trying to drive her through a building—mostly because it would attract too much attention."

There was a faint sense of Power around the Escalade that hadn't been there before.

"That tough, huh?" I asked.

"She'll stand up to small arms fire without a problem," Eric explained. "Most light Power-based attacks will actually strengthen the defenses, though most supernaturals who realize what's going on can overwhelm that.

"Mundane heavy arms or strong Power attacks will give you problems," he continued. "The enchantment will probably stop an armor-piercing grenade or anti-tank rocket, but I wouldn't bet on it stopping two."

He shrugged.

"Otherwise, you don't have to pay for GPS updates, the windshield will protect you from sun glare without impeding your vision, and your gas consumption is a fifth of what it should be. Normal tricks."

"Normal tricks," at least, if you were a gnome War Smith qualified to forge swords that could kill gods.

"I appreciate it," I said. "If She is going to insist I have a vehicle, I may as well have one that will keep me alive."

"You'll probably need it, given your proven abilities at making friends," Eric reminded me. "There, grab that." He pointed at a folded-over leather pouch sitting on top of his toolbox.

As I approached the pouch, I could feel the cold iron radiating from inside it and shivered. I trusted Eric, though, probably more than was reasonable. So, I picked up the pouch and opened it.

Inside nestled six cold iron spikes that resembled giant nails as much as anything else.

"She had me arrange for those," he told me. "That Maria Chernenkov is not going to let the fact that you kicked her ass stand. So, you've got a Pouka Noble coming for you, and they're about as nasty as Unseelie get."

"That will make finding her easy," I admitted, opening the Escalade to drop the leather folder and its cold iron spikes into the central console.

"You want to find her first," Eric said. "If she comes at you, she'll come at you sideways, in the shadows and the dark. You're tough for a changeling, but she's an *Unseelie Noble.* Even ignoring that she's a Pouka, which makes her almost impossible to kill, she's a Noble."

"And the new Unseelie Court isn't going to make this any easier on us, is it?" I asked quietly.

"No," he confirmed. "Thankfully, the order for Chernenkov's termination comes from the full High Court at this point, so Andrell can't screw with it. Doesn't mean he won't try, though."

"Wonderful," I said dryly. "So, what do I do?"

"Keep your ears to the ground and keep those spikes to hand," the Keeper instructed. "You have six. You need three to kill her—nail her shadow to the ground and burn her to ash.

"You've got time. It'll be a day or two still before she can fully rebuild herself—but she is going to be *pissed* once she's done so."

"You'll let me know if you hear anything?" I asked.

"Of course," he confirmed. "With two Courts in town now, the Manor and the Keepers start being their own power center. Not that we're going to be much of one. Tarva's an apprentice Keeper and I'll probably hang on to Zach for a bit, though I should arguably pass him into Andrell's keeping."

"The kid's Unseelie?" I asked. He hadn't felt like it to me, but changelings were hard to read.

"Of the 'a Redcap raped my mom and left her for dead' school," Eric said flatly. "I don't think *he* knows that, but I pulled enough pieces together. If I ever find the kid's dad, he won't live long enough to find out he has a son."

Eric might be small, but I wasn't going to underestimate him. I suspected there were more than a few graves with occupants who'd made that mistake.

"And Andrell's Court?" I asked after a moment.

"Setting up in a warehouse. You and I will have to go visit once he's ready." Eric shook his head. "Don't expect it to be too awful. The Unseelie aren't *that* bad."

"Mostly," I said.

The gnome sighed and nodded his agreement.

———

I GOT AS FAR as starting up the Escalade and starting to plug in the address of my meeting when the car's electronic brain informed me I had a text message. I stared at the note on the screen in confusion for several moments, and then shrugged and pulled out my phone. I wasn't driving anywhere yet, after all.

The text was from Talus.

Meet at my restaurant at 7:30PM. Bring Mary if you can. This MUST be social.

Or, unspoken, it must at least appear to be only social, regardless of what he and I actually discussed. Talus was roughly eighty years old, looked thirty, and was a good friend...and spectacularly rich.

"His" restaurant was a location of a higher-end chain. Technically, he didn't own the restaurant itself—there were no franchises for this one—but he owned the building and sponsored half of the senior staff's immigration visas.

No one was under any illusions who *actually* owned the restaurant, regardless of what the paperwork said.

I sent back a quick text confirming that I would be there. My mediation *might* run too long for that, but his time did give me over four hours to try and talk people down from the ledge.

I considered texting Mary, but given how busy we'd been lately, I was finding myself missing her more and more. So, I called her.

"Hey," she answered almost instantly. "You have good timing. Grandfather just kicked everyone but the Alphas out of the room, so I have a few minutes."

"That's...not a good thing, is it?" I asked carefully.

Mary chuckled.

"It means he's about to rip a strip off a bunch of overgrown furries with ego problems," she concluded. "Michael and the others are freaking out over the new Unseelie Court, where Enli, I think, has a far better idea of just what it means."

"Headaches but not bloodshed," I summarized instantly. "Are you free tonight?"

She hesitated, then sighed in a firm tone.

"Not really, but I'm pretty sure Grandfather will give me the evening off if I point out that it's been about ten days since I wasn't working twelve hours a day. What's up?"

"Talus wants to meet us for dinner," I told her. "Seems like as good a time as any to hit up our rich friend for a good meal."

Mary was silent for a few seconds. She understood what I wasn't saying as well as what I said. I'd acquired a *very* smart girlfriend.

"I'll get the time free," she promised.

I filled her in on the details.

"I'll see you there," I told her. "I love you."

"You too," she replied. "Be careful."

I chuckled.

"I'm dealing with a glorified condo board squabble," I pointed out. "My only *danger* is being bored to death!"

———

SUPERNATURALS of all sorts tended to clump together. There was a lot of fae living with fae, Shifters living with shifters, et cetera, et cetera, but there was also a tendency for the different types of supernatural to congregate towards the same area.

It was useful, after all, to have neighbors who weren't going to ask awkward questions if you accidentally transformed into a wolf or a parakeet in the backyard. Some supernaturals became developers specifically to take advantage of that tendency and need, which tended to result in gated communities in places that allowed such things.

Calgary didn't, but that hadn't stopped several cul-de-sacs becoming private, NO TRESPASSERS areas. The communities that were all supernatural ended up with community associations that were less than condo boards but more powerful than the usual block-party teams.

Like every condo board ever, however, they had their personality conflicts. And when the people involved in those conflicts were fae, shifters, and other supernaturals, well, things could get messy.

Which resulted in me sitting in the kitchen of one of the members of Calgary's tiny Kami community, watching an Unseelie and a shifter lay into each other over dog poop, of all things.

Juro Mori, our hostess, leaned against the wall with an amused smile as the two men argued. She was a petite thing, a second-generation immigrant from Japan, but she was also a rock spirit. If it came down smacking heads together, she was probably more capable of it than the werewolf or the will-o'-the-wisp arguing in her kitchen suspected.

"Let me get this straight," I interjected, hoping to cut the chaos down to a minimum. *"You"*—I pointed at the shifter—"are complaining that Davis here is letting his dogs crap all over your lawn, which is extra annoying here because you then have to deal with that smell in wolf form.

"Am I roughly correct?"

"Yes," Roger Aalmers ground out. The big Dutch werewolf spoke with a thick accent and was trying hard not to glare at the fae. "He is letting his *beasts* mark *my* territory."

That was...a very shifter complaint.

"And Davis is arguing that his dogs are doing no such thing, except when you, in wolf form, invite them onto your lawn to seduce them?" I asked, turning a sardonic eyebrow on the Unseelie.

A will-o'-the-wisp knew everything about luring, I supposed, even if my own family lineage of the type was of the "leading people *out* of the marsh" tradition. Davis looked uncomfortable, and Aalmers was just looking *angrier* at the accusation.

"Exactly," the Unseelie snapped. "He lures my dogs onto his land to have his way with them, and then blames *me* for it!"

"I have never pursued a dog while shifted in my *life!*" Aalmers growled. "This is ridiculous—what is so difficult about keeping your dogs off my damn lawn?!"

"The fact that you leave damn scent trails to bring them onto it!" Davis snapped.

This was frankly getting ridiculous.

"Do you mean to tell me, Mr. Davis, that you're incapable of keeping your dogs restrained on a leash?" I asked calmly. "Surely, one of the Unseelie has sufficient physical strength to keep a pair of German shepherds from wandering off where you don't wish?"

I looked from one to the other.

"I think it is reasonable, Mr. Aalmers, to ask that you no longer harass Mr. Davis's dogs, in exchange for Mr. Davis no longer allowing his animals on your property."

From Aalmers expression, I was judging correctly when I guessed that the shifter had been doing no such thing—or at least, not in the scale or manner that Davis was implying.

Davis snarled.

"I don't have to listen to this," he told me. "You're clearly biased— I'll take this up with Lord Andrell!"

"Over dog poop, Mr. Davis?" I said quietly. "I am here because you asked me to mediate. What you should realize is that by asking for *my* mediation, you agreed to the *Queen's* mediation, which overrides Lord Andrell."

I shook my head.

"We all know that this began with Mr. Aalmers complaining about your dogs crapping *anywhere* in the cul-de-sac," I pointed out. "That was unreasonable, and Mr. Aalmers has come down to you keeping them off his lawn...though I'll note that city bylaw calls for you to clean up after them everywhere.

"*You*, however, have made some rather extreme and unnecessary accusations through this discussion...and I see no reason to give any more credence to them than that," I warned him. "You asked me to mediate, and I believe we have reached a reasonable compromise: you keep your dogs off Mr. Aalmers' property, and Mr. Aalmers does not harass you or your animals."

What harassing there *had* been had probably been over Davis not cleaning up dog crap. Of course.

"But again, I remind you that you chose to accept my mediation," I told him. "And that my mediation cannot be appealed to the Seelie or Unseelie Lords of this city. I am neutral for a reason, Mr. Davis.

"Now." I checked the time. This had gone on for hours, but I still had time to make it to dinner. "Are we going to have a problem, or can we all be reasonable for once?"

8

THE HOSTESS from the restaurant ushered Mary and I into a quiet side room that didn't, so far as I could tell, officially exist. Talus was waiting for us there, along with his mortal lawyer and girlfriend Shelly Fairchild.

The slim auburn-haired woman was dressed in a light blue summer dress that was almost a perfect match for the light green one Mary was wearing. Summer sunlight streamed in through a window in the roof, rendering the artificial lights in the room unnecessary.

"It's good to see you," Talus told me as he shook my hand and quickly embraced Mary. "The addition of a new Court has all sorts of wrinkles."

"Agreed. I wish fewer of them could be personal," I admitted as I took a seat and glanced over the menus. "I'd love to get back to actually being able to take Mary on dates."

The adorable shifter next to me wrinkled her nose and sighed.

"What are those again? A type of fruit?" She shook her head. "The Shifter Clans are nervous, people. A lot of Clans have dealt with dual Courts, but no one here in Calgary has. Not on an institutional scale, at least.

"We've got a lot of twitchy Alphas, and twitchy Alphas are dangerous Alphas."

"And a new Unseelie Court is inherently prickly," Talus said with a sigh of his own. "That's part of why I wanted Jason to bring you, Mary. Partly, you *are* a friend and I did want to keep this mostly social, but I also wanted to get your feel of where the Alphas are.

"Like my uncle, I can no longer speak for all of the fae in Calgary," he reminded her. "But the Covenants we swore to are binding on Andrell. There will be official introductions later this week, once Andrell formally opens his new Court and invites everyone. Until then, the Clans will need to reach out to him through us."

"Which can only be awkward," I said grimly. "Wonderful."

"So, quiet channels are good," Talus told Mary. "You have my phone number. So does Enli, for that matter. Let him know that it may be easier to reach Oberis through me for a while as we find a new balance."

"What if you leave again?" she asked. Talus normally split his time between Calgary, Edmonton and Fort McMurray, handling the fae component of the operation that removed heartstone from oil sands production.

Neither Edmonton nor Fort McMurray even had a joint Court. The handful of fae across those two cities currently paid fealty to Oberis... which was going to be a headache pretty soon, I was sure.

"For now, I will be remaining in Calgary to help counterbalance our new friends," he told us. "Tamara will be taking over in Fort McMurray. She will be permanently located there now."

"Shouldn't she be signing on with Andrell?" I asked. There had been no Unseelie Nobles in Calgary before Andrell's arrival, which had left the Nightmare Tamara as one of the most powerful Unseelie in the city.

"Tamara's interview with Lord Andrell was apparently...fractious," Talus said carefully. "She requested the position in Fort McMurray, as an excuse to not have to officially join his Court. Several of the lesser Unseelie, while now technically under Andrell's protection, have made it clear that their Fealty is still owed to Oberis."

"From what I can tell," Shelly interjected, "this kind of thing is normal for the formation of a new Court. The fae, of course, do nothing simply and don't keep very good records."

"Why would we?" I asked with a chuckle. "We don't want anyone to know all of our secrets—not even ourselves."

"Or your employees," she noted. "You lot are annoying to work for."

"You love me," Talus objected.

"I do," she agreed. "But not necessarily as a *boss*, my dear. And your race has secrets and melodrama bred into their damn *bones*."

"She's got you there," I told the Noble. "We do. And this is exactly the kind of clusterfuck that brings out the worst in our people, Unseelie or Seelie alike."

"I know," he allowed. "You've met my new counterpart, Gráinne?"

I remember the grouchy Unseelie Noble.

"I have, yes."

"She hates you," Talus said bluntly. "I don't know why. Andrell seems to like you well enough, and the rest of the Unseelie Nobles don't give a damn about you beyond that you're supposed to be the formal mediator for conflicts between us."

"A role that I look forward to with bated breath," I snarked.

"Gráinne, Oberis, Andrell and I spent the afternoon closeted in private, going over all of the major files in play right now," he continued. "Everyone here knows we need to renegotiate the Covenants in Calgary. The Wizard's decision to dissolve his Enforcers leaves us in an imbalanced state. It's not a great time for a new Court...but it also means they'll want a say in those new Covenants.

"It's going to be ugly," he said quietly. "And in the midst of all of that, we have a rogue Pouka Noble, unquestionably Unseelie, causing havoc."

"She may have left," I suggested. "But...my impression is that everyone thinks she's going to come after me."

"Most likely," Talus agreed. "Andrell didn't say much about it today, but I got the impression from Gráinne that they don't like that you, a Seelie in their minds at least, are responsible for hunting Chernenkov."

I snorted. I was a *Hunter's* changeling, and the Wild Hunt stood apart from the Courts. Plus, since I was a Vassal of the Queen, I was again separate from the Courts.

Which didn't change the fact that I regarded myself as Seelie. My early encounters with the fae had been when everyone assumed I was a will-o'-the-wisp changeling, and *that* bloodline of mine was Seelie.

More importantly, however, I regarded Oberis as a friend and a teacher. Being neutral in affairs involving him was going to suck.

"They don't expect me to be neutral," I admitted. "They may not be wrong, but...I swore an oath and it's part of the damn job, little as I like it."

"I have faith," Talus replied. "But yes, that is their concern and, as you say, it is not illegitimate. It's also not *applicable* in this case, but you're going to have to fight for it. Probably when Andrell holds his open Court on Friday."

"What do you mean?" I asked carefully.

"I expect him to formally call on Oberis to strip the investigation from you," the Noble told me. "The counterargument is that you don't actually answer to Oberis and your investigation is independent, under the authority of the Queen and the High Court, but I'd prepare to lawyer up if I were you."

Another part of the job I hated. But given that we'd stopped a massacre already *this week*, it was pretty easy to remember why I did the job right now.

"I'll do what I must," I said quietly, feeling Mary sneak her hand onto mine. "I hope that's the last of the business for tonight?"

Talus chuckled.

"If you're ready to order, I'll flag a waitress," he promised. "And then we can discuss calmer things, like heat waves and merely *human* politics!"

9

THE REST of the week passed in a blur of training and meetings. Inga took over my mornings, which forced me to condense the inevitable meetings and duties of being a Vassal into the afternoon. It was an exhausting series of days, made no easier by continually watching out of the corner of my eye for a vengeful Pouka to materialize.

Friday morning, however, was the first time I actually managed to intentionally conjure a blow of Force. It was far from precise enough to knock the sword from the Valkyrie's hand. It was basically the same blast I'd thrown at Chernenkov the weekend before, but this time, I *knew* what I was doing.

Flinging Inga Strand into the air, however, allowed me to see just what had earned the Valkyries their reputation as flying warriors. Her own telekinesis caught her in midflight, correcting her stance and allowing her to drop back to the ground only a handful of feet from me, back in combat position.

"Good," she told me brightly. "That's even faster than I hoped. Can you do it again?"

I took a deep breath, focused on the sensation I'd just unleashed, and thrust my right hand toward her.

This time, she was waiting for me with a shield, catching the blow of telekinetic force and channeling it safely into the ground, but she was grinning.

"A beginning," she told me. "Crude, forceful, but a beginning. You will need to be more efficient with your energy—you don't have the strength to overwhelm my defenses, but you should at least be able to make me *sweat*, Jason."

"So, what, we get to that point?"

She chuckled.

"Exactly. Fire, Force, and Between, these are your Gifts, boy. They are powerful, powerful Gifts among the fae, and if you have the strength behind them that I suspect you do, you will serve your Queen well."

"What do you mean, 'the strength behind them?'" I asked.

"You are a changeling," she noted. "The type of child your people once abandoned in human homes to keep from being enslaved by your own kin. You *should* be weak. Your gift of Fire should barely suffice to light a candle."

"That's about where I was until recently," I admitted.

"And were your father a will-o'-the-wisp, that would make sense," she said. "However, you draw that gift from your grandfather, possibly one of the most powerful wisps I've ever met."

"You've *met* my grandfather?" I asked. I hadn't. I barely knew anything about my family beyond my mother.

"Met him, fought alongside him, dragged him out of half a dozen battles...failed to drag him out of his last one," Inga said quietly. "For a supposedly subtle type like a wisp, he didn't have it in him to walk away from a fight or someone in need. You remind me of him. And..."

She trailed off.

"And who?" I asked.

"That's neither here nor there," she told me sharply. "Your Gifts are strong, Jason, stronger than any changeling has a right to. That gives you an advantage, as your enemies will not suspect your strength until it's too late.

"You must learn to use them to their maximum efficiency, to use Force and Between to make up for the strength and speed your body lacks when compared to a Noble or a Lord."

"Last I checked, fighting Nobles and Lords isn't exactly in my purview," I noted.

She laughed at me.

"And what, pray tell me, Jason, is Maria Chernenkov if not a Noble?" she asked. "No, my boy, if you are to survive as a Vassal of the Queen, you must be prepared to fight any foe short of the Powers themselves...and if I could train you to survive fighting a Wizard, I would."

I shivered.

"I saw Kenneth MacDonald end a battle with a gesture and wipe the minds of three hundred men and women with a thought," I pointed out quietly. "I don't think fighting Wizards is in anyone's cards."

"No," she agreed. "Even Lord Calebrant, who was a Power in his own right, hesitated to challenge the Wizards."

I parsed that and paused. "Aren't all of the High Court Powers?" I asked.

"Mostly," she confirmed. "Not always. The Lord of the Wild Hunt and the Seelie and Unseelie Lords are... political titles, not ones of power. They are *usually* Powers, but Ankaris is not. Karos was close enough for anyone who *wasn't* a Power."

She shrugged.

"Karos willed Calebrant much of her strength at her death, which *did* make him a Power," she noted. "Calebrant..." Inga sighed and shook her head. "Calebrant didn't die in a way that made that possible."

"So, the Hunt doesn't fight Powers, then?" I asked.

She laughed aloud.

"My dear boy, *nobody* fights Powers if they can avoid it."

———

THAT CONVERSATION WAS STILL HANGING in my mind as I arrived at the new Unseelie Court. Before Mabona had insisted on my acquiring a vehicle, I would have had to arrive with Eric—my normal sources of rides for fae events were Talus and Robert, neither of which were options tonight.

My Queen, as per usual, had more than one string to her bow when she insisted I do something. Not only had the Escalade been needed for meeting Andrell at the airport, it gave me independent mobility without appearing to be beholden to the Seelie Court.

Andrell—or more likely, a scouting agent—had chosen the warehouse for the new Court with care. It was an older building in one of the smaller industrial parks in the northeast quadrant of the city, almost exactly the opposite corner of the city from the hotel Oberis's Court resided in.

Despite its age, however, it had an underground parking garage—what the Canadians around me called a parkade. Anyone paying attention might still notice the unusual parade of vehicles arriving at a warehouse on a Friday night, but we at least wouldn't have the blatant sign of a full parking lot at eight PM on Friday.

During Stampede week, especially, that would have stood out. The entire industrial park around us was dead, without a human to be seen as I maneuvered the wheeled boat into the ramp.

The guard standing at the entrance was Bryan Milligan, the Unseelie Gentry who'd helped us hunt Chernenkov, and he threw me a cheerful salute as he leaned into my window.

"It's a two-floor parkade," he told me. "Top floor has been reserved for specific VIPs; one of the stalls has your name on it." He pointed several rows over and I nodded my thanks.

Most of the time, old rules and tricks around fae and gratitude didn't apply anymore—blame Hollywood; it's as influential on us as anyone else—but at formal events like tonight, no fae would audibly acknowledge debt.

I found the sign, probably illegible to a human in the same position, and parked the big SUV. Whoever had been picking the stalls, I noted, knew perfectly what I drove—and what Eric drove. They'd carefully marked a new dividing line that turned three parking spots into two: one for my Escalade and one for Eric's Range Rover.

The gnome wasn't here yet, but looking at the space set aside for the two cars Eric had picked out for the city's neutrals, I couldn't help but chuckle.

No one would ever suggest it to his face, but it did rather look like the Keeper was compensating for his lack of height with size of vehicle.

I HAD no idea what the warehouse had been built to house. About all I could be sure of was that the lack of fridges meant it hadn't been food, which only narrowed it down to just about any variety of equipment or raw materials.

It had unquestionably not been built to house the mix of social event space, administration office, and royal audience room that made up a Fae Court...but then, few spaces were. The warehouse had originally been built with an office in one corner, and the lights flickering through the newly glazed windows suggested it was in use for that purpose.

The rest of the space had presumably been filled with racks upon racks of shelving and at least some internal dividers. All of that was gone now. Whether it had been removed by the previous owner or by the Unseelie was irrelevant, but its absence turned the warehouse into a single vast, empty space.

There was no carefully grown moss on the floor there. The ground was concrete, stained ebony-black with a combination of paint and magic. Massive swathes of heavy black cloth had been turned into curtains that covered the exterior walls, blocking sound from traveling either way. The massive artificial fluorescent lights had been upgraded, traded out for massive arrays of LED bulbs that neatly approximated the early evening sunlight outside.

Dark red cloth hung over what were probably folding tables laid out across the immense void of the floor, with speakers positioned carefully amidst a neatly designed pattern to make sure everyone could hear the speakers from the main stage.

And it was a stage, too. Not just the slightly raised dais that Oberis held Court from, but an honest-to-Powers four-foot-high stage built of black stone of some kind.

The whole effect was so goth, it *hurt*—but the fact that they'd turned an empty void into this in under a week was impressive. Like Oberis's Court, magic and Power had gone into building the space, but there were no glamors to it. What you saw was what was there.

For all its scope and scale, however, the room was over half-empty. I wasn't the last guest to arrive, but I was far from the first, and I recognized many of those present. A small contingent of Kami had taken over a table tucked away at the edge, chattering away in Japanese.

The Calgary Police Service officer Aheed Ibrahim, the patriarch of the city's only Djinni family, lounged at the back, nodding to me in recognition. We'd worked together once, and he was a *very* smart man.

Other representatives of Calgary's smaller supernatural communities were scattered around the room, but the two largest clearly matched sets of tables were for two groups: the Seelie and the shifters.

Lord Oberis sat rigidly straight in the center of the table where his fae were gathering, with Talus at his right and the city's other two Seelie Nobles, including Robert, in front of him. There were perhaps a dozen other Seelie, all Gentry or Greater Fae, with them—in a group of tables that could have held a hundred.

Even for me, it was hard to say who was insulting whom there.

The shifters had been given an equally large set of tables and were occupying a larger portion of it. Enli Tsuu T'ina, the Grandfather and Speaker of the Shifter Clans in Calgary, had made sure enough of his people came along to be respectful.

He was surrounded by the city's other seven Alphas, each of whom had brought an escort of their own. All told, thirty shifters—*not*, I noted, including Mary—were gathered. None of them were of Mary's power level, I realized. This was a collection of wolves and cougars and bears, the strongest of the shifters.

No one had come here expecting a fight, but everyone had brought a contingent *able* to fight. Most of the Unseelie members of the new Court, a good seventy people, were seated at the front of the room. Only Andrell and his Nobles were missing from the Court who'd called us together.

I hesitated for a moment as to where to sit. I *wanted* to sit with Oberis, but that was a violation of my neutrality. Instead, I crossed through the tables to an empty table sitting in front of the stage and took a seat. There was space for Eric and Tarva to join me there once they managed to get free of Friday night at a bar.

I would be neutral until and unless Andrell gave me a reason not to be. That was my job.

At least the Unseelie Lord was being a reasonable adult about the whole thing.

So far.

ERIC ARRIVED SHORTLY AFTER ME, in the middle of another pulse of various guests. He brought Tarva and Zach to my table and joined me while watching the others filter into tables across the room.

"The party is looking pretty empty," I noted under my breath.

"That's probably intentional," he replied. "Andrell wouldn't want to be outnumbered by the guests tonight...which is what makes *who's* missing interesting."

He flicked a stubby hand toward the front tables, where the Unseelie were gathered. "There's over a hundred Unseelie in this city. Where are the rest?" he asked. "Andrell will have kept a suitable escort with him for his grand entrance, but that's not forty-odd people."

Eric was right. It wouldn't take many more guests before the Unseelie were outnumbered by the people they'd invited to witness Andrell's inauguration. That...wasn't a good look for the new Lord.

"I know Tamara got out of town to take over Talus's role at Fort McMurray," I said. "But the rest?"

"At least a dozen are standing by their personal fealty to Oberis," Eric admitted. "They came to me to affirm that. The rest..." He shrugged. "Waiting to see which way the wind blows. Or playing all sides against the middle; that's not unusual for Unseelie."

Zach shifted uncomfortably, the young changeling as out of sorts at this type of event as I would have been a year before. I sympathized with him—a *lot*.

Hell, *I* was more out of sorts there than I was pretending. There was a reason I was hanging on to everything Eric was saying. There was a new layer of politics in my city, one that was going to affect me more than I liked, and I wasn't entirely sure I understood it yet.

The old Keeper, however, had seen all of this before. I was willing to be shown the way right now.

"So, what do *we* do?" Zach demanded nervously.

"We wait," Eric replied. "There's one more guest missing. Either he isn't coming, in which case Andrell has to wait to be *sure* because he's been dangerously insulted, or..."

A rustle of movement and sound rippled through the crowd, and Eric stopped in mid-sentence, turning in his chair to see who had arrived.

I turned with him, and I doubted I was the only one. The rustle of movement was *everyone* turning to see who had come in last, fashionably late, and drawn every other eye in the room. From Eric's comments, however, I wasn't really surprised.

Magus Kenneth MacDonald was *always* the center of attention in any room he was in. He was of only average height, completely bald, and seemingly unimposing in person...and yet. Today, he wore the formal robes of his title, an ancient Persian garment that predated the European colonization of North America by a millennium or two, over a modern business suit.

Even for me, that would have been painfully hot. I suspected the Wizard's clothes were enchanted past any such mundane concern. I could feel Power radiating off him from halfway across the warehouse, in a way that only my Queen had ever matched.

Two companions escorted him, but as the doors to the stairwell swung shut behind them they rolled back the hoods of their rain jackets to reveal completely featureless haziness instead of faces. They were constructs, not men, though their being this obvious was a message all of its own.

There were rules and protocol for where the Wizard, as a guest, should sit in this kind of Court opening. Being a Wizard, of course, MacDonald ignored them all. He and his constructs crossed to the

Seelie portion of the gathering, where he embraced Oberis with a swift kiss and took a seat beside his lover.

Kenneth MacDonald, after all, didn't need to worry about *appearing* neutral. If he wasn't neutral, well, there was no one else in the city who could make him be.

He was a Power, after all. For all intents and purposes, the average-looking man holding Lord Oberis's hand under the table was a living god.

————

IT WOULDN'T HAVE BEEN appropriate, of course, for Andrell to come out the moment the Wizard had sat down. On the other hand, no one was going to pretend too hard that he hadn't been waiting for MacDonald, so the lights dimmed slightly, and new spotlights appeared on the stage less than five minutes after the Magus arrived.

Andrell came out accompanied by the same four Nobles he'd had with him when I picked him up. He was smiling as he gestured, floating a microphone to his hand as he looked down over his guests.

"Good evening, everyone, and welcome," he greeted us. "Be welcome at the opening of Calgary's Unseelie Court. I know that it has been decades that Calgary's fae community has been run under a single Court, and the new structure will take some getting used to.

"Nonetheless, the divide between Seelie and Unseelie exists for a reason," he told everyone. "We have different cultures, different attitudes, and joint Courts risk confusion and conflicts that are not necessary.

"Like Lord Oberis's Court before us, we accept the existing Covenants of this city and acknowledge the authority of the Magus Kenneth MacDonald." He paused. "I do note that the Covenants speak of the Magus's Enforcers, who...do not appear to be a factor anymore."

He might have meant it as a joke, but discomfort rippled across the room. There would only be a few people in the room who hadn't lost friends in the conflict that had resulted in the dissolution of the Enforcers—and all of us had known Enforcers, if no one else.

There were no Enforcers left. Many were dead, and those who had survived had been stripped of their memories by MacDonald for their rebellion against him. An Enforcer might have been your dearest friend, but now they wouldn't even know you existed.

"My Court now stands as the point of contact for dealing with Calgary's Unseelie population," he finally said, resuming from a gap I didn't think had gone as he expected. "Justice and law for the Unseelie now come through me, as they have always done with Lord Oberis before. If you have conflicts with my people, come to me and we will see it made right."

He surveyed the crowd.

"I have arranged some light refreshment while we mingle," he told us. "I hope to meet with each of you personally before the night is out. We have much to discuss to lay the groundwork of what is to come. Our future together is bright, and we must all work together to bring it forward!"

———

THE SPEECH HAD BEEN SURPRISINGLY short, and the food and drinks carried around by manifested-glamor servers were surprisingly good for having been prepared in a warehouse. Soft music played in the background, and I could see people getting up and moving around to mingle.

There weren't that many opportunities for the supernaturals of the city to see each other at all. This kind of large formal cross-community gathering was extraordinarily rare. Looking around, I could see one of the Seelie Greater Fae in quiet conversation with the Djinni Ibrahim, while two high-ranking members of the Shifter Clan Fontaine were talking to the Kami.

Business wouldn't be concluded tonight. But many deals and projects would be *begun* tonight, even ignoring the projects that the quietly circulating Unseelie Nobles would be aiming to kickstart.

"Watch yourself," Eric murmured. "Andrell's heading our way."

We weren't the first table that the Unseelie Lord had gone to—but he definitely seemed to have us high on his list. He gestured as he approached, pulling an empty chair out for himself with a flick of Power.

"Keeper von Radach, Vassal Kilkenny," he greeted us. "I'm glad you could make it."

"We would be amiss in our duties if we didn't attend," I told him. "My Queen has charged me to make sure your setup went smoothly. May I assure her that things have gone well?"

"You may," he agreed. "Much of the groundwork had already been laid, obviously. We've been moving in this direction since Laurie's execution."

"You know the reasons for that," I pointed out. She'd betrayed us all, working with vampires and the rogue Enforcers to try and bring down the Covenants guarding the city and murder both Lord Oberis and Magus MacDonald.

Her execution hadn't been a choice on Oberis's part. Our law laid out worse penalties for what she'd done than that.

"I do," he agreed. "And so does the Unseelie Lord, but..." He shrugged. "We did not judge and, no offense to Lord Oberis, we cannot always be as certain of the judgment of a Seelie on one of our own."

"Her crimes were without question."

"They were," he agreed. "But not all cases are as cut-and-dried, are they, Kilkenny?"

"Nothing is ever straightforward," I agreed.

"Such as is the case with Miss Chernenkov," he pointed out. "That situation is messy, not straightforward. Given the arrival of my new Court, it could easily grow messier. I beg you, Master Kilkenny, to leave the investigation and pursuit of this Pouka Noble to us."

I smiled thinly. I was glad Eric had warned me this was coming—the Unseelie Lord was earnest, charismatic and friendly. He was also, frankly, more capable of defeating Chernenkov than *I* was.

But...

"Maria Chernenkov entered this city by stealth and murdered one of its mortal inhabitants," I reminded him. "She also had set up a chemical weapon attack that would have murdered dozens, if not *thousands* more.

"I hesitate to guess at her motivations," I continued. I could, if I wanted to, but this wasn't the place. "She has broken not merely fae law and not merely the Covenants of this city, but risked the Covenants of Silence that bind us all. Her fate is set in stone now, Lord Andrell, dictated by the High Court itself and delegated to me by our shared Queen."

I shook my head.

"Were the crimes any less or the orders any less clear, Lord Andrell, we might be able to come to an agreement," I told him. "But my orders from my Queen are clear: I am to hunt Maria Chernenkov. I am to *find* her, and I am to prevent her from murdering any more innocents."

"If she is Unseelie, then she is mine," Andrell told me.

"The Fae High Court has decreed her fate," I repeated. "She is no longer Unseelie, Lord Andrell. By our law, she is simply dead. It is my duty to make that law truth."

10

Somehow, Mary and I managed to squeeze Saturday off. We got to sleep in, lazily snuggle on the bed, and take advantage of our new vehicle to actually head out of town.

We were planning on a day trip out to a hiking trail we'd heard of near the mountains, but we were barely thirty minutes out of town before my phone started to ring. I glared at the black plastic and electronic block on my dash, and then looked at the number my car was saying was calling.

It wasn't one I recognized, which was odd. There were only so many people who had my number, and one of the advantages of whatever magical cellular network my phone—a gift from MacDonald—was linked into was that spammers didn't seem to find the number.

I let it ring again, and Mary sighed at me.

"You know you have to answer it," she told me.

I echoed her sigh and hit ACCEPT on the touch screen, keeping my attention mostly on the highway.

"This is Kilkenny," I said as sharply as my Southern drawl allowed.

"Mr. Kilkenny," a Middle Eastern-accented voice greeted me. "This is Detective Ibrahim. I apologize for interrupting your weekend, but, well…someone interrupted mine and now I get to pass the pleasure onwards.

"I've been called to a homicide site in the Northwest. It's…messy. The officer who called in used to work with the Enforcers, but she didn't know who to talk to. Given what I heard about the Stampede incident…I believe this one may be yours."

Fuck.

"Ritualistic cannibalism, horse-related facility, people who should have been there had a sudden sense of dread and didn't show up?" I reeled off instantly.

"Three out of three, though 'ritualistic' may be stretching it," Ibrahim told me. "If you can get here in the next hour or so, I can keep the scene uncontaminated until then, but that's as long as I can put off Forensics without making it obvious I'm playing games. And I have no intention of getting in trouble on your behalf. Not for free, anyway."

I sighed.

No Djinni ever did *anything* for free.

"What do I owe you for the warning?" I asked.

Ibrahim was silent for several seconds.

"Normally, I'd say this was covered by the spirit of what the CPS pays me for, if not the letter, but given this scene…" He snarled wordlessly. "I'll take payment in blood, Mr. Kilkenny. When you track this bitch down, you kill her for me, you hear me?"

"I hear you," I agreed. I looked over at my passenger, to find Mary had already pulled up her phone and had the best turn-off and route back to northwest Calgary on it for me already. "We're out of the city, but I think I can be back in the limits inside twenty minutes. Where do we need to meet you?"

———

IBRAHIM'S ANGER had warned me that there was more than just the usual grotesqueness going on, but I still wasn't quite ready for just how bad the situation actually was. The stable he'd directed me to was a small facility on the outskirts of the city. The sign said that they were expecting a Girl Guides of Canada event the coming week, which was my first warning of how bad it was going to get.

This wasn't the kind of stable where rich kids put up their horses. This was the kind of stable that was run as a labor of love by horse people, to make sure that children who could never afford a horse of their own would have the opportunity to come riding and take lessons at least a few times in their life.

A single marked police car blocked the entrance to the stable, a smoking policewoman sitting on the hood. She saw me and Mary approach, gave us a single glance-over, then sighed and took a drag on the cigarette.

"You'd be Ibrahim's *friends*?" she demanded.

"Yes," I said quietly.

"If I find out you had anything to do with this, I don't care if you fart fireballs, I will see you rot for it," the woman told me. "And that's if I can't find a reason for you to be 'shot resisting arrest.' We clear?"

"I understand," I told her levelly. If the situation was as bad as I thought, I sympathized. The people who kept supernatural shit under wraps didn't get a lot of information. The deal was pretty straightforward: we made sure no one in their family died of cancer or similar bullshit we could prevent, and they helped us keep things quiet.

She waved us through, pointing toward a specific outbuilding. It wasn't like we needed the directions. From the moment we'd got out of the climate-controlled Escalade, Mary and I had been able to smell the blood.

As we got closer, even I could begin to distinguish between human blood and horse blood. This was looking worse by the minute.

Approaching the door, however, we both paused. I looked at Mary and smiled wanly.

"We're both trying to think of an excuse to make the other stay outside, aren't we?" I asked.

"Yeah," she admitted, shaking her head. "This isn't going to be pretty."

"No." I sighed. "Let's go."

The door swung open easily and the smell got *worse*. The building had been a prep stable, where the kids would learn how to groom and saddle the horses before they rode them out. If there was a mercy, it was that there'd only been three horses in there when Chernenkov had arrived.

It was hard to tell, though, and I swallowed my gorge as I stepped carefully into the mess, using every aspect of my inhuman nature to control my reflexive reactions.

"You're here," Ibrahim told me, his voice flat. "Is this what you were expecting?"

I closed my eyes for a minute, forcing myself to focus, then opened them again and looked around.

Three horses. Each had had a kid grooming them. All three had been girls, early teens from the looks of them. The teacher hadn't been much older, maybe twenty.

It was hard to say. All four girls had been torn open, their torsos ripped into by a *creature* seeking the most delicate parts. The horses appeared to have been killed out of sheer perversity, with one ripped completely apart but only a few chunks of flesh appearing to have been taken from the others.

Life force and mass alike had been consumed, fueling Maria Chernenkov's return to physical form after I'd destroyed her last body.

"It's worse," I admitted. "Last time, she'd only killed one."

"She was hungry, apparently," Ibrahim snapped. "Is there anything here that can help you, Kilkenny?"

I swallowed hard, restraining my urge to vomit again.

"I don't know," I admitted. "Give me five?"

"I can't give you much more," he told me. "Forensics is wrapping up at their last site as we speak. They'll be here soon."

"Okay," I said. "I'll find what I can."

———

FIVE MINUTES in the gore-soaked stable was enough for a lifetime. *Several* lifetimes.

It also didn't tell me much that I couldn't have guessed at first glance. Maria Chernenkov had used one of the three horses as an anchor for her spirit, literally ripping herself out of its guts and consuming much of its mass to fuel her initial return.

She'd then killed the children and their teacher with telekinetic force before they'd even reacted, and finished off the horses to stop them raising a ruckus while she set to her meal.

All of this had occurred that morning, about six hours before. Her fear aura had kept the scene uninspected until whoever had called the cops had finally come in.

Stepping out into the sunlight didn't help much. To my inhuman senses, the whole area still reeked of blood.

"They were just kids," I said to Ibrahim. "Fuck."

"Yes," he agreed. "And this is one of yours, Kilkenny. You'll forgive me if I'm angry."

"What's to forgive?" I asked. "If you'd asked me this morning, I would have thought I couldn't get more determined to bring this lunatic down. I would have been wrong."

"Good. Because if *you* don't, sooner or later, one of these regular cops is going to end up trying. And that will only add more death to the list."

"I will stop her," I promised. "We didn't know she could survive being shot with cold iron and incinerated. Now we do."

"And your new political landscape will not interfere?"

"Andrell tried, but the High Court has issued their order," I told the Djinn. "Death. And with me the executioner."

I shook my head.

"Normally, I dislike it when they try to make that part of my job, but this time...this time, I may even allow myself to enjoy it."

"Don't," Ibrahim suggested. "It's a bad plan, however much it seems like they deserve it. Trust me."

"Did you learn anything I didn't?" I asked after a moment. "Right now, I'm pretty sure who did this, but this area is too much of a mess of scents for us to follow her from here."

"Officially, we're still digging," he told me. "Unofficially, the teacher drives her dad's car to this on weekends." He passed me a printout with an address and a license plate. "There's no way she went to the address, but we can track the car."

I *really* didn't want to involve the mortals.

"If we get the CPS looking for the license plate, can you keep them from jumping her until we get there?" I asked softly.

He sighed.

"That *is* a violation of my oaths," he pointed out. "I have a few tricks I can pull, but they'll require me to go after her myself."

"No offense, Detective Ibrahim, but better you than your colleagues," I reminded him. "If you can stop her without me, I'm not going to complain—but if you find her, call me.

"She's my problem, not yours, and the last thing any of us want is her facing down with a Tac team that doesn't know what they're fighting."

The sound of engines announced the arrival of the Forensics team, and Ibrahim nodded with a sigh.

"You're not wrong," he admitted. "I'll send out the call and I'll let you know when we find her. Now get out of here."

11

OUR PLANNED DAY out at the mountains was officially wrecked. I drove away from the stable in a random direction and pulled us into a mall parking lot to try and catch my breath and emotional equilibrium.

Mary didn't look much better than I did. We were both shaky with shock. The car at least didn't smell of blood, a small mercy as we gripped each other's hands tightly and tried to calm ourselves.

"We need to eat," she finally concluded, always the sensible one. "Or, at least, I need to eat and you probably should."

I squeezed her hand in agreement and gestured to a chain restaurant across the parking lot.

"That work?"

"That works," she agreed.

"I'll need to drop you off at home after," I told her. "I'm going to need to be on call now. Shouldn't have expected to be able to get out of town with this bitch on the loose."

"I know," Mary agreed, squeezing my hand back and opening the car door. "Drop me at work, though. I need to fill Grandfather in on all of this—and I can get home from there."

Part of me wanted to argue that Enli didn't need to know, that this was an internal fae affair...but the Covenants of Silence didn't give me that option. Once Maria Chernenkov started becoming a threat to the secrecy of the supernatural, she became *everyone*'s affair.

Even if it was my job, in particular, to deal with her.

"Okay," I told her. "I'm sorry."

"For what?" Mary asked with a shake of her head. "You did everything in your power to stop her. We don't expect our enemies to be nearly immortal, Jason. We deal with them with the tools we have."

"And that wasn't enough," I replied. "And now four more innocents are dead."

"Yes," she said flatly. "But that's not your fault. That's on her. We just have to make sure it doesn't happen again."

"Agreed."

"And we need to eat," she repeated, stepping out of the car. "Before your overcharged metabolism crashes you into a calorie deficit from stress!"

I forced a laugh and joined her outside the SUV. There were some surprisingly mundane disadvantages to being more than human.

———

MARY GAVE me a quick kiss and slid out of the Escalade's passenger seat into the mostly empty parking lot outside the small suburban office in Calgary's Northwest quadrant. There was nothing to distinguish the modern-looking six-story building from any of a hundred similar small offices across the city. Indeed, the bottom four floors were a normal mix of accountants, realtors and lawyers.

The top two floors, however, were the new home base for Calgary's Shifter Clans. The Lodge, their equivalent to the Manor, was still a sports bar in the northeast, but Grandfather had decided that he wanted to separate his role as Speaker from his role as Alpha of the Tsuu T'ina Tribe's shifters.

He'd built an equivalent to the Fae Courts, the Speaker's Hall. His people could find him here and present their requests and concerns—and the other signatories to the Covenants, like the fae, could find him to present their concerns.

It also meant we weren't showing up at his house, as we'd done when Tarvers Tenerim had been Alpha. The intrusion had been worth it to the Tenerim Clan, but Grandfather wanted to keep the Speaker-ship separate.

That meant the office was busier than most such buildings on a weekend, and I could spot the pair of loitering werewolves providing security. I met their gazes and they gave me informal salutes.

I returned the gesture and then looked at the SUV's touchscreen with disfavor as my phone buzzed again. I considered it for a few moments, and then poked at some random buttons until it finally disgorged Ibrahim's text.

Found the car. Abandoned just off 16th Ave. I'll be there to check it out in ten. Meet me?

He finished with the address. I could be there before he was if I pushed it—even faster if I stepped Between, but if the car was abandoned, it wasn't that urgent.

I'll be there, I sent back, and then pulled the SUV into gear.

Duty called.

———

I ARRIVED to find Ibrahim's unmarked police car parked in one of the more rundown alleys I'd yet seen in Calgary. The Djinni was leaning on the hood of the black car, glaring at a powder-blue sedan with utter distaste.

"I don't smell blood," I told him as I got out of the SUV. "So, I'm hoping there's no corpses this time?"

"Not yet, anyway," he confirmed. "I guess she wasn't hungry again. Apparently, the car's usual driver didn't fill up the tank before driving to work this morning. Our friend Chernenkov ran out of gas and decided to ditch the car rather than try and buy more."

I nodded and crossed over to the car, looking it over. There was nothing about the vehicle to stand out from a million other sedans like it across North America. Certainly, there was nothing to suggest that its "usual driver" had been viciously murdered this morning.

"Well, you're the detective," I pointed out as I circled the car. "Any-thing useful?"

"She dumped the car rather than buy gas," he repeated. "So, she has no cash. There were enough clothes and such at the stable that I doubt she's running around naked, but she's wearing riding gear—if it weren't for Stampede, she'd stick out."

"And Stampede is over tomorrow," I noted. "But she'll find new clothes by then."

"Almost certainly." Ibrahim shrugged. "The car has no GPS or maps, so if she was navigating, it was by phone—and all four of the phones the girls at the stable had are still there. We checked."

"So, no money, no phone, nothing." I shook my head. "She almost certainly has a stash somewhere. Backup supplies, even if she wasn't planning on getting blown up."

"I find most people don't plan on exploding, but bug-out bags are useful. She would have been headed for one, you think?" the cop asked.

"I would have been," I told him. "The question is: how well could she navigate the city? We don't know how long she's been here."

"Long enough to get five thousand liters of chlorine into a place that's supposed to have a hundredth of that," Ibrahim noted. "It's a shame that all got blown up; tracking it would have given us another avenue to find her."

"No luck at all with that?" I asked.

He shook his head.

"There's only so much I can do for free, Kilkenny," he noted. "That info's worth money."

"Right." I grabbed a loonie from my pocket and tossed it to him. "Enough?"

He chuckled bitterly.

"Some day, my friend, you are going to actually want something from me that will cost you for real," he noted. He pocketed the coin, not even enough to buy a coffee these days.

"We've got a forensic audit team ripping apart the books for the Stampede and that stable, trying to sort out when and how that chlorine got there, but that kind of tracking can take months," he warned me. "The info's cheap because it's worthless. By the time the auditors find a trail, Chernenkov will have left us a trail of blood across half the damn city."

"I will *not* let that happen," I replied. "Whatever it takes."

"Good." He shook his head. "I've done all I can for now, Kilkenny. We'll haul the car in, get it back to the girl's family. Little enough solace *that* will be. I don't know what to do from here."

I studied the ground around the parked car. Hard dirt, no tracks… but also no rain to wash away scent. Ibrahim and I were on about the same tier for senses: we could smell things no human could, but we couldn't really track by scent.

My girlfriend, on the other hand, knew people who could.

"I think I do," I told him. "Can you hold off on collecting the car for a bit? I need to call in some favors, and I'd rather we mess up the area as little as possible."

———

IBRAHIM RETREATED out of sight and out of mind as I waited for my call to have results. I was impressed at the speed, to be honest, as a massive black pickup truck roared up in less time than it had taken me to respond to Ibrahim's call.

Barry Tenerim was the first out of the truck, a Clan Tenerim werewolf, a cousin of some kind to Mary. Two more werewolves followed, one of them turning back to help Mary down out of the extended-cab truck. A true work vehicle, it managed to make my Escalade look like a pampered poodle next to a grumpy Rottweiler.

"Mary tells me you need someone tracked," Barry told me. "I don't need to tell you what Tenerim owes you. Our skills are at your command."

Unless I missed my guess, the three burly young men who'd arrived with my girlfriend had been the "brute squad" that Tarvers Tenerim had brought to the raid where he'd died. My intervention had stopped them picking a fight they couldn't win…and then I had killed the man who'd killed their Alpha.

I was reasonably sure Clan Tenerim wouldn't go to war on my say-so. I wasn't sure how far short of that the debt they regarded themselves as owing me stretched.

"You know about the mess with the Pouka," I told Barry. "She showed up again this morning. Killed four innocents and stole a car."

I pointed at the blue sedan.

"She ran out of gas and dumped it here, but I'm guessing that she was heading for either a safehouse or a supply cache. She was on foot from here—and I need to know where she went. *My* nose isn't good enough to track a shapeshifter through the city, but..."

"But you know werewolves," Barry said with a grin as Mary smiled past him at me. "*Urban* werewolves. There is *nothing* we can't track across the city."

"That's what I was hoping," I told him. "You find the bitch, I'll put her down."

Barry snorted.

"If you think you're getting into a fight and we're just going to stand there and hold your coat, you've got another think coming," he told me. "Shall we hunt?"

Something in his phrasing ran *right* down my spine, and a part of my soul I rarely recognized as being present woke up with a vicious hunger.

There was a reason, after all, that even as a changeling, I was still acknowledged as a *Hunter*.

"I have some specific gear in the car for when we catch her," I told him. "Let me grab it. Then, my wolven friends, you are quite correct.

"We shall hunt."

12

MARY TOOK my SUV and one of Barry's burly companions took his truck, moving the vehicles away from what would soon be a CPS crime site as the other two werewolves and I went after the scent.

Barry started by squatting down next to the stolen car, breathing shallowly as he inhaled. I waited, hopefully patiently, as he picked up the scent. After a few moments, he turned back to me and grinned.

"Got her scent," he told me. "Shall we?"

I gestured for him to lead the way, falling in behind him as he took off at a brisk walking pace.

It was warm weather. Too warm, really, for the rain jacket I was wearing over my T-shirt. I didn't trust the skies, though, with the rain we'd had lately—and it made a good cover for the revolver in the shoulder holster and the package of cold iron spikes.

"Any idea where she was headed?" I asked Barry after a minute or so.

"South," he said. "Otherwise..." He shrugged. "Half the city is south of here, Jason. I can only follow the trail a few meters at a time."

The polite request not to be an idiot was silent, but I heard it anyway. My two werewolf companions knew what they were doing. I was there for when we reached the end of this hunt—and if I happened to pick up some tips and tricks on the hunting along the way, that was an extra benefit.

The trail led us deep into the neighborhoods just north of downtown, separated from the skyscrapers by a river and a hill. After ten minutes, I realized we were starting to approach my own apartment and began to get a bit nervous.

There was, as Barry had pointed out, no point in asking the werewolves if she'd been heading there. They were following a scent, not predicting where she was going.

Finally, however, they stopped in front of one of the small older homes that filled the area. Unlike most of the houses around us, this one hadn't been renovated at any point and looked rather rundown, showing every year of its probably sixty years or so of existence.

What qualified as "old" in Calgary could still make me chuckle at times.

"She went in here," Barry told me, studying the home from the sidewalk, then shaking himself like a big dog. "Let's keep moving; eyeing the place is way too obvious."

We looped the block, settling in to study the house from a distance.

"Yeah, no continuation of the scent," my werewolf friend noted. "She went in that house and didn't leave on foot. Karl?"

"Yeah, boss?" the second werewolf asked.

"Check out the alley behind the house," Barry instructed. "I'm *guessing* she's either in there or had a car stashed here, but she could have snuck out the back and we just missed the scent when we looped."

"Will do."

Karl disappeared back along the street while Barry and I continued to watch the front of the house.

"No way to tell if she's still there," I said grimly.

"Unless Karl finds her scent out back, no," he confirmed. "I'll bet biscuits to dollars there's no vehicle parked out back, either. That might be because there never was a car—or because she left in it."

He shook his head.

"*I* don't have the authority to bust into a human home on my own say-so, Jason," Barry pointed out. "Won't stop me if you, say, see the bitch through the windows, but breaking and entering is outside my purview."

I chuckled.

"There's an open question whether or not I have that authority with the mess with the new Court," I admitted. "But my orders are clear, and that means I have *sanction* even if I don't have authority."

The werewolf grinned evilly.

"So, anyone who wants to argue can take up with the scary lady who may as well be a goddess?" he asked.

"Exactly," I confirmed, pulling out my phone to check the time. "It's Saturday. The area is probably as empty as it's going to be before work starts on Monday, so I figure we call in Mary and Evan to have the vehicles on hand.

"And then we go kick down a door."

————

IT SAID everything about the attitude of the shifters I worked with that both Mary and Evan exited the vehicles openly armed. My girlfriend *had* been wearing a rain jacket, but she'd left that in the Escalade, making the shoulder holster for her ugly little Czech machine pistol very visible.

Evan, on the other hand, was carrying a black police-issue shotgun with a long box magazine that made it resemble an automatic rifle. It might have been overkill...except that I could tell Mary's gun was loaded with cold iron and Evan's wasn't.

"Are we good, or does anyone need to grab any more artillery?" I asked dryly.

"We don't have any cold iron ammo in the truck," Barry admitted. "Claws are probably our best bet from here."

I shook my head—but I also tossed my raincoat in the SUV and grabbed the spare speed loaders for my revolver. My Gifts of Fire and Force were probably more useful against Chernenkov, but the cold iron-tipped rounds in the .38 Special would be useful against anything else.

The street was quiet enough. As quiet as it was likely to get in the midafternoon on Saturday, anyway. I could see cars down the road and a few pedestrians, but no one close enough to see what we were doing.

"Okay. With me," I told them all.

I strode across the street, trying to at least look like I was moving with purpose and not plotting anything furtive or covert, and walked up to the door of the house Chernenkov had entered. The door was locked, and I studied it for a moment.

Talus or Inga probably could have picked it with their minds, but they'd had access to their Gift of Force for decades or more. I'd only realized I had it a week ago. I could probably break the door down or shatter the lock with Force, but...well, I had been practicing with my fire, too.

With a gesture and a flick of concealed green flame, I cut the bolts and pushed the door open. We were now officially breaking and entering, as far as mortal law was concerned.

Not that mortal law was high on my mind as I stepped into the old home, drawing the iron-loaded revolver. The main entry was empty, and I moved aside, letting the shifters follow me in and sweep the floor.

"There's no one here," Barry reported grimly. "But take a look at this."

I followed his gesture and saw the small business license half-concealed near the main door. It listed a numbered company, a maximum number of occupants, and a section of the Innkeepers Act.

"Vacation rental," the werewolf continued. "If they had this much paperwork in place, probably before the internet made it easy, too."

"But she probably booked it over the net, somehow," I noted. "Follow the scent, Barry. I doubt this isn't a dead end, but let's see what we can find."

I took a picture of the business license and emailed it to Shelly Fairchild, Talus's mortal girlfriend and lawyer. If anyone could get anything useful out of that, it would be her. That side of things was better left to, well, humans.

"The place is covered in her scent," Barry said after a few minutes. "Mostly old, though. She was staying here before the whole mess at the Stampede. Freshest scent...from today. She came in the front door and went straight upstairs."

I gestured for him to lead the way and followed him onto the second floor. There were two bedrooms upstairs, one of which was undisturbed and one of which looked like a hurricane had come through. Barry stopped in the door, inhaling sharply and then shaking his head.

"Take a look," he told me.

The bedsheets were...well used. From everything, I would guess that the mussed-up sheets and the discarded lingerie were from before I'd met and burnt Chernenkov. She hadn't spent her last night alone, that was for sure.

From the lack of blood, her partner had even survived the experience.

"One other scent, missed it downstairs," Barry said carefully. "Stronger here, for obvious reasons. Male. *Fae.*"

"Damn." That shouldn't have been unexpected—the woman had managed to sneak about five thousand liters of a poisonous gas into my city. She hadn't done that on her own. That the partner was fae wasn't really a surprise, either.

Pouka weren't known for regarding humans as anything other than a source of protein.

"That suitcase"—Barry pointed—"had guns and cash. Quite distinct smells, those two," he noted.

"So, she got here, grabbed clothes, guns and money, then left, I'm guessing?"

Barry sighed.

"Yeah, scent went from the stairs to the backdoor, to the parking spot. Since we didn't have her scent leaving, she had a car."

"Couldn't have gone for a motorbike, could she?" I half-jokingly bitched. Chernenkov wouldn't have been expecting me to bring urban werewolves to bear on tracking her, but scent was a tool available to fae, too. A motorbike rider *could* be tracked by scent.

I shook my head, looking around the room with its three wide-open suitcases and lack of answers.

"I guess I go through everything," I told Barry. "Don't think I need you for that. You've been more helpful than I hoped, to be honest."

This wasn't much, but it was a starting point.

"We owe you, Kilkenny," he told me. "And even if we didn't, you take good care of Mary." He chuckled. "And if I said that where she could hear me, she'd *hurt* me."

"I have *very* good ears," a familiar voice shouted up from the ground floor. "You're lucky you're being helpful!"

"You have your own business, I'm sure," I said. "Not least, apparently, hiding from my girlfriend. I think I've got it from here."

He punched my shoulder gently.

"All right. You have my number—don't hesitate to call if you need muscle, guns or money."

I laughed.

"Barry, I have my boss for at *least* two of those," I told him. "But I appreciate it. Thanks."

———

MARY and I turned the vacation rental upside down for the next few hours, hoping to find some kind of sign of or information on our prey.

Finally, as the road outside began to fill up with people returning from their weekend excursions—tomorrow was the last day of Stampede, after all—we sat down in the kitchen and compared notes.

"Well, I now know her bra and underwear size and that she likes black and lacy at multiple layers," I concluded. "I'm guessing she took a couple of sets of clean clothes, and I *think* there was at least one more suitcase that's missing, but that's it."

I shook my head.

"If there was any useful paperwork or ID or *anything* here, she took it with her," I said. "Did you find anything?"

Mary snorted.

"I can probably identify both her and her lover by scent, which may come in handy later," she told me. "Right now?" My lover shrugged. "About the same as you. I can tell you she likes Starbucks and had packed the freezer with meat. No receipts in the garbage to find a credit card or anything."

We could probably get a DNA sample from upstairs, but that wasn't going to help us. It wasn't like Oberis had a database of the DNA of the fae in the city. Mary's memory of the scent was probably more useful than anything we'd get from that.

"If it's a rental, the neighbors are probably used to seeing strangers come and go, but we should probably clear out regardless," I said with a sigh. "We're not getting anything useful here. Shelly may have more for us by Monday, once she can get into the legal records."

"I was hoping for more," Mary admitted, and I nodded my agreement. "This...*woman* needs to die."

"We'll find her, love," I promised. "She will pay for those girls."

I didn't even know how many people Chernenkov had killed. It was at least theoretically possible that she'd spent her life up to this point eating cadavers and such as most "reformed" feeders did. Somehow, however, I didn't think that was the case.

"There was another fae here, Jason," Mary reminded me. "I'm guessing that's trouble?"

I nodded, considering.

"If they're Seelie, Oberis will hand them to me on a silver platter once we find them," I said grimly. "If they're Unseelie..." I shivered. "We may need more than your nose to identify them before Lord Andrell will turn them over."

"And if he refuses to turn them over?" she demanded. "Are you going to let what they did stand?"

"Mary...love...we don't *know* that her lover was involved," I pointed out. "I'm pretty sure Andrell will at least let us interrogate them if we can finger an Unseelie lover of hers."

"And if he doesn't?" she repeated. "Are you telling me that your fae politics may help this *bitch* escape?"

"No," I said levelly, rising from the table and looking around the room. "But I have to at least *attempt* channels before I go over Andrell's head. He's going to be here for a while and I have to work with him.

"So does Grandfather, for that matter," I reminded her. "Let's not start any wars until we have to."

She sniffed a half-acceptance at best, but she rose and took my hand.

"That's fair," she allowed. "But trust me, Jason—if the shifters start thinking we have to take Chernenkov down ourselves, we *will*—and fae inter-Court politics won't stop us."

"If it gets that bad, you know I'll be there," I said quietly. "I'll work with Andrell until he gives me reason not to, but she doesn't walk away."

The consequences of that could be...messy for me. But we were going to catch Maria Chernenkov.

13

"I'm sure no one is surprised that the numbered company that owns the property is a holding company," Shelly told us at lunch on Monday.

Sunday had been frustrating, a mix of my usual duties and running around the city chasing any tiny hint of the Pouka's whereabouts. Now Eric and I joined Talus and Shelly for lunch in a skyscraper conference room. I wasn't sure what service had catered the food, but we had an amazing view out over the half of downtown shorter than the building Shelly worked out of.

"Numbered companies have owners, don't they?" I asked. "Isn't all of that public record?"

"It's complicated," the lawyer said with a sigh. "Look, Jason, a good three-quarters of what I do is obfuscate ownership records to make sure no one realizes that the fae in Calgary exist. There are, at my best guess, about fifteen lawyers in the city taking care of that for the various supernaturals—we are, in this day and age, the most essential interface you lot have with the mortal world."

She took a sip of coffee.

"Across North America? The various supernaturals probably employ ten or twenty *thousand* lawyers, primarily for the purpose of hiding money and assets so they can't be traced back to them. Add to that the corporations and celebrities and wealthy mortal individuals doing the same thing, there is an entire *industry* occupied in making sure that those 'public records' are almost completely opaque."

Shelly tapped her laptop.

"Whoever set this one up? They're better than I am. I lost the ownership trail somewhere in *Cuba*. I'm sorry, Jason, but even the Airbnb records are a wash."

"Let me guess: booked through a numbered company?" I asked.

I wasn't sure how much most people could access from internet sites, but I was prepared to bet a lot that Shelly could access more.

"Not even. Unit was blacked out for all of July—unusual, since Stampede is when most locals running vacation rentals gouge *everyone*."

"So, our Pouka is related to whoever owned the building," Talus concluded with a sigh. "Does that help us at all?"

"I think it's a safe assumption the building is owned by a supernatural, probably a fae, given what Jason's shifter friends smelled," Eric noted, the gnome diffidently chasing the last of his french fries around his plate.

"Still not much use, though," he concluded. "I can poke through my records—no fae outside Calgary should have been buying property in the city without letting me know."

"How much do they tell you?" I asked. "We know the Unseelie have to have been acquiring new properties."

He snorted.

"That they're here, really," he admitted. "Our people don't go in much for giving away our secrets; you know that."

I nodded. At some point, I might manage to find out who my father was, for example.

"So, we have nothing?" I said slowly. "Just half a dozen dead people, a gas bomb, and a murderous fae somewhere in the city?"

"She may have left," Shelly pointed out. "If she knows you're hunting her, well...*I* wouldn't want to be hunted by a fae."

"If she has any friends at all, she's probably sure she can take me on round two," I admitted. "Remember that I'm still a pushover by her standards."

"Plus, Jason here burnt her to ashes and forced her to rebuild herself from her shadow," Eric added. "And she's both Unseelie and a Pouka." The Keeper shook his head. "Sorry, Jason, but she's not leaving this city until you're dead—or she is."

"Being hunted by psychotic Unseelie is always the best way to make me feel loved," I quipped. "Any ideas on what we can do until she finds me?"

I got a series of uncomfortable looks in response, and then Talus sighed.

"You have to talk to Andrell," he told me. "He may be able to pull something from our research, and, well, you have to talk to him anyway."

"I know," I admitted. "I can't meet with the Seelie on this and not the Unseelie." I shook my head and checked my phone. "I sent an email this morning," I noted. "Still sorting out details, but I believe I'm having dinner with Andrell and Gráinne tonight."

I knew my responsibilities. No one was going to be particularly shocked if I had some favorable feelings towards the Seelie Court that had always been here, but as a Vassal of the Queen, I *had* to be neutral.

"Good," Eric said. "It's a careful balance we have to walk, Jason. Harder for you, I suspect, than the Keepers—my duties are less active than yours."

"Unless the Unseelie know something, though, unfortunately all I can suggest is that you keep your eyes open and carry on as normal," Talus told me. "There's not much else you can do.

"She's going to come at you sideways, from where she thinks you're vulnerable. I don't know what she's going to think your weak spot is...but that's because I know you."

I snorted.

"And my actual weak spot is probably me?" I admitted. "I had Robert and two Gentry with me last time I fought her. I can't take her head-on. If she comes at me..."

"You'd better find a way to take her head on, then," my friend told me. "Whether that's one of Eric's toys or training or *something*. I'm guessing the Queen sent you the tools to take her *out*, but you'll have to take her *down*."

The Keeper looked at me and shook his head. Unlike Talus, he knew Inga was there and training me, which should help, but he was also the best source I had for enchanted gear.

"Give me till morning to think about it and put out some feelers," Eric said. "I don't have the gear to hand to forge anything new quickly, but I might be able to beg or borrow something useful."

"And I'll see about staying alive that long," I said with a sigh.

————

ONE OF THE sometimes-frustrating aspects of my job was the occasional reminder of ways my background made me bad at it. I'd grown up the son of an untenured university teacher in the United States. We hadn't been poor, precisely, but money hadn't been easy to find, either.

My adulthood after discovering my fae gifts and prior to ending up working for the Queen had been an extended period of glorified homelessness, bouncing from city to city and Manor to Manor, abusing the tradition of succor as hard as I could.

Now I had access to resources beyond my wildest dreams. Not only did Mabona pay me quite generously, but her attitude toward expenses was...cavalier at best.

I was relatively sure the black credit card I'd been given for work expenses had a limit, but I'd never hit it—nor had I ever put enough charges on it to even get a blink from the accountants in Ireland who paid it off like clockwork every month.

Invoices sent to the address of the toy manufacturer I theoretically worked for got paid without question. I could probably have had memberships in any golf or private club I wished, but the thought had never occurred to me.

As a uniformed waiter escorted me to a private room in one of Calgary's most exclusive downtown business clubs, it was clear that that *had* occurred to Lord Andrell. The man opened the door to the room and ushered me in with an actual *bow*.

Where did they even *find* that big of a suck-up in this city?

"Master Kilkenny," the room's sole occupant greeted me in her soft Irish accent. Gráinne wore the same style of black business suit she'd worn when she'd arrived in Calgary, cut to show off the Unseelie Noble's tall, athletic figure and allow for a full range of movement.

"Lord Andrell will be here shortly," she promised, gesturing to the table. "Please feel free to peruse the menu while we wait."

"Of course."

I took a seat across from her and studied her for a few moments.

"If you don't mind my asking, Ms. Gráinne, what brings you to Calgary with Lord Andrell?" I asked. "It seems quite the distance to pick up and move on a whim."

"Perhaps, but the whim was not mine," she pointed out. "My family has served Andrell's family for generations. I swore personal Fealty to him when I was twelve, Master Kilkenny. The bonds of the old Fae Nobles and Lords are...special. Not something I'd expect an American-born changeling to understand."

She didn't even *pretend* she wasn't insulting me, but that was fine. I wasn't under the impression that Gráinne liked me, after all. And if she was an old-school retainer of a Noble line...damn. Andrell came from blood so blue, it glowed in the dark, even for fae.

Most Lords came from families of Lords. Those families occasionally produced Nobles, but they tended to produce at least one Lord or Lady every century or so. Most of those families, in turn, had families of traditional retainers.

But those families were usually Gentry or Greater Fae. Only the oldest and most powerful bloodlines had entire lineages of Vassal Nobles.

That was normally restricted for Powers like the Queen or the Lord of the Unseelie.

Before I could respond to her implied put-down, however, Andrell himself swept into the room with a second Unseelie Noble in tow.

"Apologies for my being late," he told me. "We are still learning the city's traffic and, well, it was different last week."

His grin was disarming and cheerful, setting me at ease as I leaned back and chuckled with him.

"Stampede creates its own kind of chaos, I'm told, but it clears other areas of the city up as well," I agreed. "Even we are limited by the mortal habits, I suppose."

"Indeed." Andrell pulled open the menu, studying it. "I don't suppose you have a recommendation?" he asked. "We bought the membership, but I haven't eaten here yet."

I coughed delicately.

"I've never eaten here myself, but steak is usually reliable in this city," I told him. I opened the menu myself and tried not to visibly blink at the prices. The Unseelie Lord was unbothered, but the man would probably think my entire annual salary was petty cash.

"This is true, this is true," he agreed with that charming grin. He rang for the waiter and smiled up at the man as he entered.

"Four of your filet mignon, medium, with the side of the day," he ordered crisply. "Bring us a bottle of the house red and make sure to buzz before entering; our discussions are with regards to some confidential business matters."

The waiter seemed completely unfazed, simply nodding with what I suspected was a fake smile, and letting himself out of the room.

"Now, Master Kilkenny, what can Calgary's Unseelie Court do for you?"

———

AFTER I'D BRIEFED the three Unseelie on the weekend's events and everything I'd learned, the food arrived. The timing was pretty much perfect, allowing us all to dig into the unsurprisingly excellent steak while Andrell digested what I'd told him.

"Do you have the ownership information that Talus's lawyer extracted?" he finally asked. "The timing, unfortunately, makes it look like this rental was picked up as part of our portfolio acquisition here. We used a firm with a solid reputation in Unseelie circles, but if this Pouka had the right connections…"

"She'd have been able to piggyback on your own acquisitions," I agreed. I slid a USB stick across the table. "Ms. Fairchild was kind enough to provide a copy of her research. I was hoping you'd be able to pass it on to your lawyers and see if you can trace it back."

"I will see what they can do," he promised carefully. "I wish we had something more solid to go on, Master Kilkenny. This whole situation reflects poorly on my new Court and creates tension I'd prefer not to be dealing with."

"Trust me, my lord, I far prefer my job to involve resolving petty squabbles between members of the Courts," I told him. "This is the first time the High Court has handed down a death sentence for me to carry out. It's not a pleasant order."

"Few things that end up involving the High Court itself are," Andrell agreed. "At least if this Chernenkov leaves, she becomes another city's problem instead of ours."

"She strikes me as the type to be vengeful, unfortunately," I replied. "The only lead I have right now is that she has a fae lover somewhere in the city, tied to that property. My shifter allies assure me they can identify him by scent."

Andrell snorted.

"We'd trust the opinion of shifters on that?" he asked.

"I would," I said flatly. "Calgary's Clans have earned that respect from us, Lord Andrell—with blood and fire."

He made a mollifying gesture but still seemed unimpressed.

"Even if they could, I hesitate to condemn anyone merely on association," he told me. "I'm sure Oberis would agree with me in this, but I don't see having known the woman as a crime!"

"The evidence suggests that whoever she 'knew' helped smuggle in a chlorine bomb that could have killed hundreds, creating a level of chaos that would only have complicated all of our lives," I pointed out. "He may not be guilty of her crimes, my lord, but if I can identify him, I *will* claim the authority of the High Court to interrogate him under a Lord's truth compulsion."

I liked Andrell well enough, for all that his right-hand woman was treating me like something she'd found on her shoe, but his priorities were not my priorities—and we both answered to the High Court.

"That would be...reasonable," he allowed.

Before I could say anything more, my phone buzzed with an incoming text. That was...odd, given that all of my notifications were turned off. I sighed in suspicion and pulled the device out.

"Excuse me, my lord," I told Andrell as I studied the screen.

Kilkenny. Attend me at your earliest convenience. KM.

"The Wizard," I said aloud in unfeigned surprise, swallowing hard. When a Power said "earliest convenience," that meant, well, *yesterday*.

"I apologize, Lord Andrell," I told him, "but my Queen's alliance with Magus MacDonald requires me to respond immediately. He seeks my presence."

There were no *good* reasons for the Wizard to want to talk to me.

"Of course," the Unseelie conceded instantly. "When Powers call, we 'lesser beings' have few choices.

"I appreciate the briefing, Master Kilkenny, and the data. I will let you know what we learn."

14

A BOUNCING blue light guided me through the garage under MacDonald's tower to a designated parking stall. The underground structure was empty this late at night, allowing the Wizard's magical guide to play along.

Though, given the Wizard's abilities, I wouldn't have bet against the blue light only being visible to me. I'd never yet been led astray by assuming that MacDonald was functionally omnipotent, though assuming his *omniscience* had proven dangerous.

He had, after all, missed that his own followers were betraying him.

The first actual surprise came when I stepped out of the Escalade to find someone waiting for me. My greeter wasn't a magical light or even a construct but a small woman, perhaps an inch or so over five feet, wearing a face veil.

The moment she moved toward me, however, I knew what she actually was and bowed my head slightly as I greeted her in halting Vietnamese. No human moved with that speed and grace—and only one supernatural averaged five feet tall while covering their faces.

The goblin's eyes flashed in surprise as she returned the greeting, then continued on in a liquid stream of Vietnamese.

"Sorry, Theino taught me a greeting, but I suck at languages," I admitted to her with a smile. Theino was the Speaker to Outsiders of the goblin colony in Calgary, a collection of Vietnamese refugees under Talus's protection. I'm just too American, I think."

She nodded and inclined her head.

"Of course," she said. "I am Lan Tu, daughter of Trai, son of Krich."

Krich was one of the original goblins who'd evacuated to Calgary during the Vietnam War. I'd met him, and Lan Tu was the second of his grandchildren I'd met.

"I didn't expect to see any of the colony here," I told her.

She shrugged delicately, a smile glinting in her bright blue eyes.

"We need work, and it's hard for us to find mortal employment," Lan Tu noted.

I nodded my understanding. The veil, after all, was in place to cover inch-long ivory tusks.

"The Magus sent me to bring you upstairs," she continued. "If you would follow me, Lord Kilkenny?"

I chuckled.

"I'll follow," I promised. "But don't call me Lord. I'm not owed any titles, and that's a dangerous one among my folk."

"As you wish, Mr. Kilkenny," she conceded with a bob of her head. "My father's father and cousin would be...hurt if I did not show you proper respect. You are a friend of the colony, after all."

There were worse allies to have. Goblins might be small, but they were fast and strong—and every goblin in Calgary had been trained in fighting dirty by ex-Viet Cong commandos.

———

LAN TU LED me into the elevator and produced a key from inside her sleeve. Inserting the key, she tapped a sequence of three buttons on the control panel, then withdrew the key and let the doors close as she began to hum gently.

Exiting on the top floor, I was unsurprised to see that the top floor of MacDonald's tower had been completely renovated since my last visit. At a minimum, much of the three floors of the office building that made up the Wizard's home had been shot to pieces during his Enforcers' revolt.

The reception area still recognizably had the same bones as when I first arrived in Calgary but the walls, floors and furniture had all been replaced with new marble and steel pieces.

Instead of the semi-open plan of the old layout, security doors with concealed armor blocked access from the lobby, and I noted the slot in the ceiling that likely contained a bulletproof shield to protect whoever was holding down the reception desk.

The "woman" sitting behind the desk right now, however, was a construct. Few mortals would have been able to tell, but I'd had extensive encounters with the Wizard's magical simulacrums by now. I could feel the presence of others, as well. Invisible or otherwise concealed, those constructs would appear only in response to an active threat.

A single veiled goblin in a business suit stood in a back corner, watching us enter with level eyes. From the way he leaned against a decorative cabinet, I suspected the cabinet probably contained at least one variety of heavy weapon—and I wouldn't have been surprised to learn it included guns and magical blades carefully designed to counter each of the supernatural races.

"Mr. MacDonald is waiting for Mr. Kilkenny in his office," the construct told us cheerfully as we approached. "You can take him right in, Ms. Lan Tu."

Lan Tu gestured for me to keep following her, and the second goblin stepped over to press a key card against the reader on one of the doors. The heavy security door clicked open and Lan Tu opened it for me.

I could guess, roughly, what the armored panel pretending to be a door weighed. If I hadn't already known just how strong the goblins were, the ease with which the tiny woman leading the way swung the door open would have warned me.

MacDonald's office was just down the hall, in the exact same place as it had been before. The hallway back there had been refloored and the walls repainted but was otherwise unchanged—until we reached the Wizard's office itself.

The walls around the door had been completely replaced, likely due to the previous walls no longer existing, and the plain door that had opened into the office had been replaced by a double door planed in what appeared to be one-way mirrors backed in bulletproof glass.

The doors were almost certainly magically reinforced as well, but the one-way mirror provided a surprisingly mundane way for MacDonald to see who was coming while remaining unseen himself.

As we approached, the doors swung open of their own accord. I heard the whir of small motors as they moved, showing again that MacDonald saw no reason to use magic when technology could serve.

"Come in, Mr. Kilkenny," he ordered calmly. "Thank you for bringing him up, Lan Tu. Tell Skavrosh that you two have the rest of the night off. We have no more visitors scheduled, and the constructs can handle security."

"Yes, milord. Thank you, milord."

Lan Tu bowed and retreated as I stepped into the office. Kenneth MacDonald stood next to a floor-to-ceiling window, looking out over the city from his plain-seeming office. It hadn't changed much, and I suspected that the furnishings of MacDonald's office probably hadn't changed in a century or two. The computer equipment was new, but the desk could well pre-date the arrival of Europeans in North America.

The looming hunk of black oak certainly *looked* the part, anyway.

"Join me, Kilkenny," MacDonald ordered. He hadn't looked at me yet, but I knew how this game worked. I crossed over to join him in looking out over the city.

"You summoned me, Lord Magus?" I asked carefully.

"I did," he allowed. "It seems that you have once again found your-self at the center of quite the storm. Tell me, Mr. Kilkenny, when *did* you plan on telling me about the chlorine bomb at the Stampede?"

I swallowed. Briefing the Wizard honestly hadn't crossed my mind. He might not be omniscient, but he still had the Sight—and the people we'd used to clean it up reported to him.

"We presumed you knew already," I finally admitted. "There was no intention of hiding it from anyone in the supernatural community."

"Indeed." He continued to study the city. "We all learned last winter that my Sight is not as pervasive as I and my brethren would perhaps wish. Your kin have always had ways to block our Sight, but thanks to the betrayal of my Enforcers, the knowledge of several *other* methods has spread far more widely than we would prefer."

I hadn't known that. I didn't *want* to know that.

Or, perhaps more accurately, I wished that wasn't the case. MacDonald, at least, was an ally. The better he could see, the safer my city was.

"So, you didn't know about the bomb," I said levelly.

"Mr. Kilkenny, do you really think so poorly of me that you think I would have let an attempt to poison *hundreds* of innocents pass without intervening?" he snapped. "An individual Pouka who may or may not have killed? That is a problem for the fae to deal with.

"A planned mass murder carried out by a supernatural? That I could not have let pass. Except I *did not know*."

The very average-looking man next to me had the Sight to understand and comprehend almost everything happening in the entire city. It was in his power, so far as I could tell, to obliterate the entire city with a word and a thought.

That my enemies could frustrate that being's Sight and hide from his power was *terrifying*.

"I hadn't thought that through," I admitted. "We assumed you'd left it to us as our problem."

"I probably would have," he agreed. "But I would have at least told Oberis about the bomb."

I nodded. That made sense. That kind of warning would have been enough for us to go in with a far larger force and better safety measures. If we'd known the bomb had existed, we could have reduced the actual threat to near-zero.

"I can brief you if you need it," I said quietly. "I'm about as well informed as anyone on this file."

"Your file," he agreed. "Your headache, per the High Court. So, what are you going to do about it?"

"We found where she was staying and are trying to track the ownership back," I explained. "If we can find her, we'll move against her. Otherwise..." I sighed. "Otherwise, I currently don't have any better option than to hang myself out as bait and hope she comes for me."

"Is that a fight you can win yet, young Kilkenny?"

I blinked. That question was…not the one I'd expected.

"I don't know if it's one I'll ever be able to win, not in a fair duel, anyway," I admitted. "We have some irons in the fire to even the odds, but I'll need those."

He chuckled, and I wondered what I was missing.

"I owe you a boon, Kilkenny," he said quietly. "To forge you arms and armor of orichalcum or, indeed, to carve the same runes I gave my Enforcers upon you, would meet that boon. If you desired."

I shivered. Few among the fae could claim *anything* forged by a wizard. Most of our orichalcum—an alloy of gold and the heartstone extracted from the oil sands—artifacts were forged by gnomes like Eric. MacDonald's Enforcers had been marked with tattoos in the same metal, augmenting their physical capabilities and giving them mystical gifts many supernaturals couldn't match.

Of course, I wasn't quite sure just how much power MacDonald would wield over those arms or those runes, so I slowly shook my head. My Queen would *not* approve, tempting as the thought was.

"I would…prefer to reserve that boon for a greater cause," I told him. "I will call upon it in time, Lord Magus, but I think we have the means to handle this creature ourselves."

"You are probably correct," he confirmed softly. "I do not think this Chernenkov knows what battle she has picked."

"I don't think she picked it. She's mostly just angry at me for killing her."

The Wizard chuckled again.

"That is…generally an upsetting action. But if she was wise, she would not choose this war."

I snorted.

"I am very young, as you say, Lord Magus," I pointed out. "And a quarter-human. If she was picking her enemies, I think I'd be too weak for her radar."

The Wizard seemed amused.

"This is true, perhaps," he allowed. "You will be fine, I think. But do not forget that boon is owed, young Kilkenny. Your past and blood-line guarantee you battles to come beyond this one."

"It seems everyone knows more about both of those than I do," I said dryly. "Is there any help you can give me short of the boon? This Pouka is dangerous, my lord."

"She is," he agreed. "Not least because she is concealing herself entirely from my Sight. I believe she remains in the city, but I cannot find her. I have tried."

I looked out over the twilit city beyond the window.

"I'd guessed," I admitted. "But it would have been damned helpful."

"What I can tell you, Jason, is that there are more games afoot than you can see," MacDonald warned me. "I cannot say much more; there are things I am bound by oaths not to speak of. But..."

He paused, clearly considering what he could say.

"Others are less bound," he finally concluded. "Ask the Valkyrie about the Masked Lords, Jason Kilkenny. She can give you some answers I cannot."

Of *course* the Wizard knew about Inga.

"I will listen to your advice," I told him. "Thank you."

He waved dismissively.

"If you learn of more bombs in my city, please do me the courtesy of letting me know as soon as you can," MacDonald told me. "Otherwise, well...know that I am watching."

I wasn't sure if he was even *trying* to be reassuring.

15

THERE ARE STRANGER ways to wake up in this world than by being nuzzled by a purring lynx that is also your girlfriend. From the smell of freshly brewed coffee wafting through the apartment, Mary had already been up and about and had decided to come back to bed to cuddle.

As a cat.

I laughed and scratched behind her ears, earning me an even louder purr and a headbutt before the dark gray cat with the red markings shimmered and transformed into my redheaded girlfriend. She was barely half-dressed, and for a moment, the coffee was the *second* most tempting thing in the apartment.

"I've got to get going pretty quickly here," she said regretfully after we kissed. "The heartstone shipment is coming in today, and I'm playing clerk for our portion of it."

The Covenants that ruled Calgary—and Edmonton and Fort McMurray, for that matter—declared that each signatory received a portion of the heartstone extracted from the oil sands. Since one of the uses of the material was to infuse it into silver to create Shifter's Bane, the Clans destroyed most of their portion.

Though that thought brought a new problem to mind, one that was almost certainly going to involve me by the end of the day. The Covenant didn't mention Andrell's new Court. Right now, all of the Fae's portion of the heartstone went to Oberis's Court, providing much of the wealth and influence that allowed Calgary to wield an outsized influence in the supernatural world.

"Andrell is going to try and claim part of our portion," I said aloud with a sigh. "That is going to be a *headache*."

Mary winced.

"That's going to be an entertaining shit show if it happens while everyone else is around," she noted. "I'll text you and Eric if he shows up. Some warning can't hurt."

"Appreciate it, love," I told her, stretching as I got out of bed. "The coffee smells fantastic."

She grinned at me and pointed to our dresser, where two steaming cups were waiting on a plastic tray.

"I've got enough time to sit and drink a cup with you," she told me. "What's your day looking like?"

"So far, a slice of paradise," I replied as I grabbed the coffee and kissed her on the way. "I need to meet with Inga and continue training this morning, then this afternoon I get to go back to being conflict arbitrator."

The truth was that I kind of *liked* that part of my job. Much more than the parts that involved killing people, anyway. Most of the problems I had to resolve were relatively low-key; they just crossed the lines of supernatural communities.

I honestly felt like I was making a difference every day and I didn't have to kill people. I couldn't complain.

Getting to drink coffee in the morning with my half-dressed girlfriend was a nice bonus, too.

"Intra-fae this time, I'm guessing?" she asked.

"Yeah," I confirmed. She knew not to ask more. If it involved the shifters, I could tell her some things. But fae affairs stayed fae affairs. That was part of how our world stayed secret.

Mary sipped her own coffee and sat next to me on the bed, pressing her leg against mine.

"Learning a lot from Inga?"

"Yeah." I shook my head and gestured, floating the coffee tray onto the bed next to us. "It's weird to be able to do that," I admitted. "I always envied the fae Nobles that gift."

"I envy *you* it now," she pointed out, though she kissed me to soften the point. "You seem more nervous than usual about the training."

"Yeah," I admitted. "I spoke with the Wizard last night. He was... enigmatic, as always, but he told me to ask Inga about something."

Somehow, I guessed that these "Masked Lords" were exactly the kind of fae business I shouldn't discuss with my shifter lover.

"The Wizard told you to ask someone *else* a question?" Mary asked.

"Yeah. I think he felt he didn't have the right to share the information...but that I needed to know."

She wrapped her arm around my waist and leaned her head into my shoulder.

"If the Wizard thinks you need to know, you need to know," she told me. "Wizards play games, but...MacDonald is generally a good guy."

"Agreed." I leaned my head against hers. "Which means I should probably get going myself. And you may be late if you don't start getting dressed...and *not* because getting dressed will take you too long," I concluded with a wicked smile.

———

WORK CREWS HAD BEEN VISITING Inga's dojo intermittently over the last week and it was starting to look less like a business that had died and more like a business that was about to be reborn. A new sign, VALKYRIE MARTIAL ARTS, had been added above the door, and new glazed windows had replaced the boarded-up wreckage.

A neatly printed sign announced that the studio would be opening at the beginning of August and gave an email address for expressing interest in classes. Inga Strand, it seemed, was planning on staying for a while.

Today, however, the locked door gave way to the key she'd given me, and I entered the room quietly.

My stocky blonde teacher stood alone in the middle of the hardwood floor, wearing a short-skirted tunic and a Kevlar-and-chain-mail battle vest. Her silver sword floated to her right, and a pair of ugly-looking modern combat knives floated to her left.

All three blades were moving in the air, a flickering pattern I could barely keep track of. The knives were mainly moving defensively, flashing through a kata of floating parries, at the same time as the silver longsword flickered around in a series of mixed offensive and defensive movements.

After a few moments, darts of silvery-blue fire added themselves to the chaos. The gaps between the blades were filled with flashes of light as Inga's kata expanded into a defensive sphere that I knew I couldn't get through, even *with* her training.

That was the difference between someone with a few months at best of using their gifts and someone with *centuries* of experience. At this point, I probably qualified as Greater Fae and could, at least, fight most Greater Fae on an even playing field.

But Inga Strand *also* qualified as Greater Fae and, from what I could see, could probably fight many *Lords* on an even playing field.

I waited for her to finish the kata, taking a seat at the side of the dojo as she worked through the motions and spells, then gave her a small wave as she turned to face me.

"Ah, Kilkenny," she said briskly. "You're early."

"One tries to be punctual," I replied. "And sometimes it helps in reminding me just how much I have to learn."

Inga chuckled.

"I was taught by two separate Lords of the Wild Hunt," she reminded me. "And I have trained the Wild Hunt for centuries. There is much you have to learn, child, but you have time."

She wasn't wrong. Even as a true changeling, a half-blood, I could have expected about a century and a half of healthy life. As a three-quarters-blood, I had a reasonable shot at over two centuries. Possibly longer, depending on just what my father had actually been.

"Are you ready to begin?" she asked me.

"I am, but I have a question for you first," I told her. "A...wise friend, let's say, told me that there were more games afoot in Calgary than we'd yet seen. He told me to ask you about the Masked Lords."

The blades had still been in the air, gently floating toward the bench where Inga was probably intending to leave them. At my question, the spell snapped, the knives and sword plummeting into the hardwood floor as Inga half-instinctually summoned a defensive shield around herself and cursed.

"That...that is not a name one who is not Hunt or the High Court should know," she told me, her voice very, very cold. "It is not a name we speak lightly."

"MacDonald told me to ask you," I admitted.

"The Wizard," she hissed. "Of course. They know many secrets. It is rare, though, for them to betray the secrets of others even this much." She shook her head. "I'm surprised, though. Did Mabona not tell you about them?"

"She did not," I admitted. "All I know is the name."

"Then it seems I have a story to tell you," Inga said with a sigh. "It is not my place...but if the Wizard believes the Masked Lords have reached here, then you *must* know."

———

INGA LED me into her office and fussed with the coffee machine for several moments. I suspected she was as much trying to marshal her thoughts for this conversation as to make coffee, but I took a seat by her desk and waited quietly.

"I'm surprised you never heard the name before," she finally told me as the pot starting hissing. "The Masked Lords were a problem back when Mellie Kilkenny left Ireland. Not my place to say if they were part of why she did, but there was a lot of blood shed that year. She wouldn't have been the only one to leave. Especially not the only *pregnant* girl to decide her babe was better born on a different continent from the High Court."

"The High Court?" I asked.

"Yeah. The Powers were the target of the whole mess, the closest thing the fae have seen to a serious civil war in a few centuries." She shrugged. "The Seelie and the Unseelie posture and cause havoc every few years, but it's been a long time since anyone fought anything resembling a real war.

"The Troubles in Ireland were cover for a lot of bullshit in the supernatural communities, but Ireland was always one of the strong-holds of the fae and the home of the High Court. So, when a bunch of Nobles and Lords decided they were going to take over, they came to Ireland."

"Take over?" I asked. "The High Court are *Powers*. Who goes gunning for a set of nine demigods?"

"Someone who's found a way to kill a god," Inga said quietly. She was silent for a few moments as she poured the coffee. She studied the cups for a long moment, then produced a bottle of whisky from Between and added a generous dollop to both cups before handing me one.

"We believe they were all Fae Lords," she noted. "But we have no way to be sure. We don't think they were all Seelie or Unseelie; the Masks seemed distributed across the usual lines. It's *possible* some were merely Nobles or Greater Fae, but the very thing that names them made it impossible to tell."

I took a sip of the coffee and managed not to grimace. The alcohol was harsh and raw—and the coffee was terrible, too.

"They wore masks?" I asked. "Why would that stop the Court identifying them?"

"They wore masks, yes," she confirmed. "Leather-lined, orichal-cum-enchanted, *cold iron* masks. No magic of the fae could penetrate those masks to identify the men and women under them.

"They had designed a ritual that called for twenty-one participants and mustered all of their power into a single strike. It was an assassin's tool, mostly...and it worked."

"They killed Powers," I said quietly.

"The Lady of Autumn. The High Keeper. The Lady of Summer," she reeled off sharply. "They ambushed and murdered three Powers of the High Court. They also assassinated lesser lords and Nobles who defied them. The Irish Courts ran with the blood of the fae, loyalist and traitor alike."

"Why wasn't the Hunt called?" I asked. It was the job of the Wild Hunt, after all, to protect the High Court.

"Because Calebrant and Mabona were fighting," Inga said sharply. "He was her Vassal once, and she imposed on the relationship more than she should have, so Calebrant had not attended the High Court in over a decade.

"We knew of the conflict, we'd been involved, but the High Court are bound to their secrets. We did not know any of the Powers had fallen—until the Masked Lords came for Mabona herself."

"And Calebrant had been her Vassal," I concluded. If Mabona was attacked, I would know. If she summoned me, I could walk Between to her side from anywhere in the world. She had other Vassals in the Hunt, I knew that, but if Calebrant himself had once been sworn to her...

"We rode," Inga said simply. "Mabona had been wounded, but she was cleverer than the Masked Lords allowed for. She escaped the brunt of their blow, and her home had become a pitched battlefield.

"And then we arrived. The Masked Lords couldn't fight *two* Powers, and Mabona was already wounded and hiding."

She shrugged.

"Calebrant killed...half of them. Maybe more. But they killed him. We destroyed their followers...but at least ten of the Masked Lords escaped.

"They killed four of the Nine Powers of the Fae High Court, Jason Kilkenny," she told me quietly. "And we have *never found them*. From the power they brought to bear, they walk among our highest echelons, but the Masks concealed them.

"Twice since them, Masked Lords have appeared to challenge Courts and cause trouble. Unidentified, unidentifiable. We don't know their goals now; we don't know their intent.

"But if the Masked Lords have stretched their reach into Calgary, then the Wizard's warning must be heeded," she said flatly. "You must tell Mabona, Jason, and we must redouble your training."

"My training?" I couldn't fight these Lords!

"You stand in the Queen's stead here. If the Masked Lords are plotting anything here, you will fall into their crosshairs," she warned. "We must prepare you to at least *survive* when they come for you."

Because I'd needed *more* headaches this summer.

16

AFTER INGA HAD SMASHED me into paste and forced me back together again, teaching me how to fight with telekinesis, I set out for my meeting. I could only barely use a sword in my *hands*, and she was making me duel her with the sword held in my mind.

Today, I was actually meeting people in an office. It was a suburban building across the parking lot from one of the city's midsized malls, full of accountants and doctors and dentists.

One of said accounting firms was only tangentially what it claimed to be, an entire floor of administrative affairs dedicated to the various bits and pieces of business required to keep the fae community in the city running.

We couldn't, after all, use regular tax accountants or lawyers or anything like that. Even the new changeling at the Manor, Zach, had bank accounts and registration with a firm like this one. My understanding was that there were three in the city, all reporting to Oberis's Court.

Which, of course, created the problem that resulted in my being here, and I studied the four people sitting across from each other in the room.

I knew George O'Malley, one of the Gentry who'd come down from

Fort McMurray to help deal with the vampires MacDonald's Enforcers had infiltrated into our city. He'd fought by my side and was, generally, a sensible soul.

The Unseelie seated across from him was barely an acquaintance to me. Dubhán McNeal was a gnome, one of the Unseelie breeds of that kindred, with dark eyes and an oddly metallic black tint to his skin.

The two humans in the room were senior administrators of the accounting firm, both looking entirely uncomfortable with the current state of affairs. Meine Masters was an older woman with graying hair and a sallow tint to her skin, heavier than was healthy for a mortal but with sharp green eyes.

Her companion, Jiang Kuang, was a younger Chinese man. His eyes seemed vaguely unfocused, almost as if he wasn't paying attention...but he was Masters's senior-most manager, which meant he was definitely no idiot.

"I do not understand," he began when we were all seated, in a notable Chinese accent, "why you are requesting these changes. We have served your Court successfully for over a decade without issue, and now you demand that we change everything.

"I do not understand," he repeated.

"The problem, Mr. Kuang, is that you have served a *Seelie* Court for over a decade," McNeal said harshly. "And while that was not through any choice of yours, it means that we would prefer to remove the various Unseelie accounts from your company and place them with a new entity."

"Any firm such as ours that functions in this city has only worked with Oberis's Court," Masters noted. "Have you brought your own accountants and lawyers, Mr. McNeal? What plan do you have once you've taken your accounts away from us?"

The gnome looked uncomfortable.

"That isn't for me to say," he admitted.

"By which you mean you have no idea," Kuang snapped. "If your new masters have brought such an organization with them, fine. We will transfer the accounts as requested. The contracts we've signed, however, do not allow us to simply abandon any of your kindred."

"And we are far too familiar with both the myth and the truth of the fae to lightly break our contracts with your people," Masters added. "I do have a compromise to suggest."

"Listen to her, McNeal," I told the gnome, my tone light. It might not have sounded like a command, but everyone in the room knew what I meant. "Ms. Masters is more familiar with how the interface firms work than any of the fae in this room, isn't she?"

"I suppose," McNeal allowed. "What would you suggest, Ms. Masters?"

"There are several interface firms in Calgary, but we have all worked with the joint Court to date," she told us. "What we can do, however, is divide the accounts and set up internal soft and hard firewalls. My firm has two floors here. We can split our databases, files and staff between the two floors and set up different security cards etc. for each floor.

"With those internal firewalls in place, the people working for Andrell's Court will have no information on Oberis's Court and vice versa. That will allow us to meet the needs of the Unseelie Court without leaving anyone high and dry, until we can set up a separate firm."

Of course, being the first firm in Calgary with that setup would benefit Masters dramatically. Nonetheless, it was a good idea.

Before I could say anything, however, my phone buzzed with a sharp sequence of vibrations I'd only felt it go through once before.

"Excuse me," I said swiftly, pulling the device out and staring at it. The code flashing on my screen was one I'd only seen when we installed the app—an emergency alert from Mary.

"Ms. Masters has an excellent suggestion, but I'm afraid *my* time has been overridden," I told them all. "My apologies, but this meeting is suspended until a later time—can you have your people arrange something, Ms. Masters?"

"I—"

I never heard the end of her response. The alert told me where Mary was and I was already stepping Between.

———

MARY MIGHT HAVE HATED the way Clan Tenerim regarded her and her brother as weaklings in need of protection, but she accepted enough of its truth to have an emergency alert on her phone. What she missed, I suspected, was that as one of Tenerim's administrators and armorers, she was also *important* to the Clan.

Barry had added the receptor app for her emergency alert to my phone a while back. While *he* hadn't mentioned that to her, I had. There were secrets I had to keep from my girlfriend—that I had access to the emergency alert she could trigger didn't strike me as one of those.

The alert gave me the GPS location of her phone, nearly on the opposite side of the city from me. My phone couldn't pick it up from Between, but I *could* cross the entire city in under five minutes by traveling Between.

I emerged from the chill of that other place into the blazing July sun and the smell of smoke. I stood in the middle of a deathly silent suburb, looking at the wreckage of a taxi that had been T-boned by a black pickup truck.

The taxi driver had clearly tried to crawl clear of the wrecked vehicle…and then someone had slammed an axe into his head. Bullet holes marked both vehicles, and a second body was sprawled backward over the tailgate of the pickup.

The chill silence told me I was no longer in the right place. I could see Mary's red-cased phone lying on the ground, but there was no sign of her. Whatever battle had started here was continuing elsewhere— and I strained my hearing to the limit to try and pick up *anything*.

Mary's little machine pistol had a *distinctive* sound, one I could identify even at this distance as it echoed in the quiet neighbourhood. I did what any good boyfriend would do: I ran for the sound of her gun.

Skipping Between every few steps, I covered the nearly two kilometers she'd fled in moments, emerging behind the pair of men advancing down the back alley of the strip mall they'd pinned Mary against. She wore a navy-blue business suit, the blazer flung open to expose the empty concealed holster against her shoulder where the Czech-built machine pistol normally lived.

A third man was sprawled on the ground where I emerged, and

this time, I was close enough to feel the cold iron in the bullets that had killed him. Mary was *not* playing around—and her hunters were fae.

They hadn't heard me arrive, and a whip of flame tore the ax from the leader's hand as he charged at my lover. He had enough time to curse and start to turn before Mary shot him in the head. The last attacker lunged at her with a bloodcurdling yell.

I caught him with Force, his ax only inches from Mary, yanking him back toward me and away from her. He spun in the air, a red baseball cap flying from his head and revealing a *different* red cap underneath it.

One that was part of his skull and dripping with fresh blood.

I slammed the redcap to the ground in front of me and glared at him.

"You have entered this city without announcement and attacked a supernatural ally in public," I hissed at him. "Explain yourself!"

"I serve—"

His head exploded, a cold iron bullet smashing through from above as a sniper opened fire.

"Jason!" Mary shouted, but I was already moving.

A second and third bullet slammed through where I'd been standing—but then I reached Mary, scooping her up into my arms and stepping Between as more gunfire sounded.

The last thing I heard before the chill silence of a strange reality took us was the distant sound of sirens.

Someone had called the cops when the shooting started—and while barely minutes had passed since I'd received the alert, Calgary's police were *fast* on the draw.

———

"ARE YOU OKAY?" Mary asked me the moment we were clear, and I chuckled softly.

"I'm fine," I told her. "I'm more worried about you."

"*I'm* not the one wearing brains and blood!" she snapped, and I looked down.

Between didn't have a visible sun. It was always lit with a strange diffuse glow that showed everything clearly. Right now, it was clearly showing the splatter pattern from the redcap's skull. The bullet had clipped my clothes—I hadn't even *noticed* that—but none of the blood was mine.

"That's all the redcap's," I told her. "What happened?"

She sighed, looking around Between and shivering closer to me. "Can we get out of *limbo* first? I need to call Barry."

I nodded and *stepped*, delivering us back to the car accident. Mary gasped again and grabbed her phone.

"We should move still," she said. "I hear ambulances, thank the Powers."

I nodded, and we slipped down an alley, away from the approaching mortal help. None of the redcaps were savable, and we'd make sure the coroners didn't mention the oddities of their anatomy.

Sadly, the taxi driver was beyond helping as well. He hadn't asked to get dragged into this.

"We'd finished the meeting," Mary finally said, tapping out a text on her phone as she leaned against a fence. "I'd arrived with Grandfather, but he was going to meet the Fontaine Alpha for lunch. I grabbed a taxi back to the Tenerim Den and...well, you saw what happened to the poor taxi."

She shivered again, hit SEND on her text and put her phone away to meet my gaze.

"They hit us in the middle of the road. I'm guessing the woman driving was Chernenkov, but the four assholes in the back were new. Given the current politics, I was carrying cold iron rounds...and I switched after the first bastard axed the driver and got back up after I shot him."

Redcaps *could* soak their hats in animal blood to sustain their life. That was, as I understood, how all accepted members of the Unseelie subspecies survived. This quartet, though...

"Chernenkov produced a big ugly gun after I killed the first one, and I decided that being somewhere else as a cat was a damn good idea," she told me. "Turned out that the...redcaps, you called them? They are *damned* fast."

"Yeah," I said quietly. "And murderous, even when they're *behaving*."

She shivered again.

"I noticed. They tracked me despite Shifting and pinned me against the back of that strip mall. No one saw enough to call the cops until I started shooting—and then you arrived. Thank you for that."

"You'd have been fine," I told her. It was even mostly true—she was fast enough to swap out the ten-round magazines in her machine pistol while the bastards were closing. She'd probably have been hurt, potentially badly, but she'd have taken both the redcaps on her own. She would have been fine.

Until Chernenkov shot her in the head with the sniper rifle, anyway.

Her phone buzzed and she checked it.

"Barry is almost here," she told me. "GPS is guiding him to my phone. What do we do now, Jason?"

"I don't think our Pouka friend realized you were a shifter," I replied. "They weren't ready for you to turn into a lynx and run."

And if Mary hadn't Shifted...she'd be dead. Maria Chernenkov had gone for what she thought was a weak point. She'd been wrong, thank the Powers.

"But we know where she was, which means Barry can track her again," I told her. "And this time, I *know* where her damn car is. She isn't going anywhere in *that* truck."

"What about the redcaps?"

"I'll talk to Eric," I promised. "He'll make sure they get dealt with safely...and see if we can work out when they snuck into the city." I shook my head. "There *aren't* any of those fuckers in Calgary, new Unseelie Court or not.

"We'll find out where they came from, and *that*, my love, will give us another angle of attack. She may have thought she was coming at us sideways, but all she's done is show more of her hand."

"Funny. Because I still feel like I came pretty close to getting gutted with an ax," Mary said sharply.

"Nah, you had them in hand," I repeated. "Anybody *smart* knows never to corner a lynx!"

The arrival of Barry's truck cut off the conversation there.

17

THE BIG WEREWOLF hopped down from the pickup truck and wrapped his cousin in a tight embrace.

"I'm glad you got here in time, brother," Barry told me. "Sometimes, it takes way too damn long to get out to the truck and get moving." He shook his head. "It's nice to have a friend who can *teleport* to the right place."

"I wish it was that fast," I admitted. "If Mary wasn't able to take care of herself, I wouldn't have been here in time."

"Which he did," Mary insisted, taking my hand firmly. "Even if he's determined to pretend I'd have been fine, we both know I would *not* have been able to get away from the damned sniper."

Barry shook his head.

"Just what have you been dragged into, Clan-sister?" he asked softly, looking over at me.

"Fae politics, I'm afraid," I admitted. "And some additional bullshit around this Pouka. I thought she was alone, but..."

"Then she brought thugs?" the werewolf asked dryly.

"Redcaps," I said. "About as stereotypically 'thug' as fae get. Murderous half-feeders with an attitude problem. There weren't supposed to be any in Calgary, so she brought in outsiders." I sighed.

"Sadly, I think a lot of redcaps live down to the stereotype by working as muscle for hire."

"So, she imported hired muscle. I guess we saved her some money," Barry noted.

"I want her, Barry," I said flatly. "If we find her sniper perch, can you track her?"

He bared his teeth.

"You're a Clan-friend and a personal friend," he told me. "And you're Mary's boyfriend *and* this bitch has killed too many innocents—and she came at Clan Tenerim. This isn't a favor anymore, Jason.

"This is Clan business now, you understand?"

I nodded, sighing again. That had its advantages, I supposed, but I didn't want to drag the Shifter Clan into this.

"She's Unseelie and she's terrifyingly powerful," I warned him. "This isn't a fight Clan Tenerim wants to take on. I want your help, Barry, not to add to Tenerim's graveyard."

He and Mary both growled at me in perfect sync.

"This is Clan business," Barry repeated. "Clan honor. Clan blood. By blood and steel and heart, you are *ours*, Jason Kilkenny. Do you understand me?

"She came at you, and we let it go because you have your own fights and politics. But now she came at Mary *and* you, and the Clan won't let that stand. *Can't* let that stand."

I inclined my head in acknowledgement. I should have known better than to underestimate just how highly Clan Tenerim valued the fact that their last Alpha had declared me Clan-friend.

"I understand," I told him quietly. "I owe your Clan as much as you owe me. I would not drag you into this fight, but I need your skills."

"Good," Barry said. "Because with Mary by your side, this was always going to be our fight."

———

THE COPS WERE all over the strip mall when we returned, the bodies of the redcaps laying where they fell with yellow plastic tarps over them, while the officers gently and competently interviewed the potential witnesses.

No one was going to be of much use to the police, I knew. What security cameras I could spot were out in front of the mall, and there were no windows into the alley. The only people who'd seen anything had been Mary and me...and our sniper, which I was presuming to be Maria Chernenkov.

"We were in the alley," Mary said quietly. "Building to the north of us, concrete security wall to the south. Shooter didn't have a lot of options for location. Either east-west or up high."

We were across the street from the mall, and I kept a careful eye on the officers as Mary rotated, studying the angles.

"You were facing me down the alley and had him," she continued. "Shot didn't pass me, so not from the east. If she'd fired from the west, you wouldn't have had nearly as much blood on you and she wouldn't have clipped your clothes."

She...was better at this than I was. I would have just been checking every high spot within a kilometer or so, but Mary was listing off the details and turning.

"There." She pointed. There was a small apartment building, about six stories tall, a block to the north. "She fired over the strip mall, probably from the roof of that building. Could have broken through the locks or climbed the outside, but that explains why she didn't take the shot immediately."

"She likely didn't head up until her redcaps had cornered you," Barry concluded. He shook his head with a chuckle. "She didn't think they were going to take you down either, I think."

"I don't particularly feel like trying to run up walls myself," I told them dryly. "Walk with me?"

Mary shivered but nodded.

"Okay."

Barry looked confused. "Brother?"

"Take my arm, Barry. We're walking Between It'll be cold, but it's safe. I promise."

The two shifters each took one of my arms, Barry looking confused and uncertain as he did so, and I stepped forward with them into the Between.

The werewolf inhaled sharply as the crisp chill washed over us, and started to jerk away. I pinned his hand with my arm instantly, using Inga's training in reinforcing my strength with telekinesis to hold him in place.

"Do *not* let go," I told him. "You can only breathe here because I will it, and I don't know if I can extend that to someone who isn't touching me."

"Fuck me," he breathed. "This is Between?"

"Yeah," I confirmed. "And from here, we can just walk up to the roof of that building. Hang on."

The "ground" was what I willed it to be, but we could see a shadow of the real world around us. We moved forward, and I adjusted our path to lift us off the ground and bring us up six stories and over a block of intervening space in less than a dozen steps.

"You *can* breathe, Barry," I pointed out to him. "It's safe. Hell, in a lot of circumstances, you're safer breathing here with me than anywhere else."

"Like if someone blows up a few tanks of chlorine?" he said in a tone of "huh, that makes sense."

"Exactly." I stopped, checking around to be sure we were actually on top of the building. "This is our stop. Hang on and...*step*."

———

THE ROOF of the apartment building was covered in gravel to help with drainage. There was a small hut-like structure to allow for regular access, which was closed and locked. For a moment, I thought we'd misjudged—but the smell of cordite caught my nose a moment later.

Our shooter had fired six times and hadn't bothered to collect her brass. Discarded shell casings were scattered across the gravel. Leaving them would probably make the human police feel better, but...yeah.

"Once we're done, we'll want to clean those up for our Unseelie friend," I said quietly. "The last thing we need is the mortal authorities actually tracing *any* of our supply chains for weaponry."

"Fair," Barry allowed. The werewolf was squatting where the shooter had to have been standing, and his nostrils flared in pain as he winced. "Silver. Not Bane, but silver…"

"And cold iron," I agreed. "I'd guess distilled garlic, too. Triple-kill rounds. Ruin *everybody*'s day."

"Yeah, missed the garlic with the silver," he admitted. "It's her scent, too. In case anyone wasn't sure it was our horsey bitch of an Unseelie."

"I didn't have much doubt," I told him, "but confirmation is good." I grimaced. "Though, to be fair, sending redcaps after Mary and shooting cold iron rounds at me is enough for me to be willing to put them down, whoever they are."

"No shit." Barry shook his head. "Came from the west. Left north."

He followed the scent to the edge of the building and looked over the side, down at the parking lot.

"She climbed up. Jumped down." He shook his head, then pointed. "You can see where she landed."

I'd missed it, mostly because I hadn't figured there'd be a visible mark. Chernenkov had landed in the grassy lawn, tearing up sod and dirt.

"I suggest we take a more…sedate approach in our own return to the ground," I said. "Between is cold, but I'm more comfortable with it than jumping."

Barry snorted, but he took my arm nonetheless. A moment later, the three of us stepped out onto the ground floor, in the shelter of the building's brick stairwell. No witnesses to our arrival—and I hoped no one had seen Chernenkov jump.

"All right, she'll be easier to track as a wolf, and you'll attract less attention as a couple walking their dog," Barry told me. "Time to fur up. Let's see if we can catch her this time."

The big man shimmered and was gone, replaced by a large wolf. An unfamiliar observer would probably think he was a husky or something similar, if only because his body language was *much* friendlier than any wild animal's would ever be.

He waited a moment for Mary to produce a leash and collar to disguise him, and then took off towards Chernenkov's landing spot, with Mary and I falling in behind.

———————

As BARRY HAD FIGURED, even the police barely gave us a glance-over as we left the parking lot, following Chernenkov's scent. A young couple with an oversized dog, out for the walk the animal definitely needed. Too far away to have heard anything out of the chaos that had swept over the area.

If they identified the building as the sniper's perch, they might have changed their mind—but the only reliable way to do that would have been to examine the Pouka's leftover brass, which was now jingling in my pocket.

Barry was doing a spectacular impression of a big, happy, well-trained floofball of a dog, bouncing forward and sideways to the "limits" of the easily-broken leash but always returning to "heel" at the sight of another animal or person. Despite the seeming joyful randomness in his movements, however, he was definitely leading us on a specific path.

Chernenkov had fled north, moving deeper into the suburb and weaving a twisted course around and through about ten blocks of houses before she exited into a massive park area. There were more dogs and people around at the entrance, but Barry led us through them with practiced ease.

Once we were out of sight of the crowd, the werewolf growled and took off in a straight line. Fast as Mary and I were, we were hard pressed to keep up with Barry's run. We'd be very obvious if we were seen, but Barry was clearly relying on our superior senses to avoid interception.

I appreciated his rush. The trail had to be growing cold now. Chernenkov would go only so far before acquiring a vehicle, which would dead-end the trail. We were probably already too late, a thought that was reinforced when we came down a hill into an almost-empty parking lot.

Barry sniffed forward into the lot, beelining to an empty spot between two large SUVs and circling it quickly as he poked around. Finally, using the two SUVs for cover, he shimmered and transformed back into a massive dark-haired young man.

"I *love* hunting old supes sometimes," he told me cheerfully.

"What do you mean?" I asked. "I'm guessing she had a car here and is gone?"

"You get *half* a dog treat, Jason my brother," he told me. "She's gone, but she didn't have a car here. She *stole* a car. And she's, what, two hundred? Hundred fifty?"

"Younger than that," I said bluntly. "But yeah, old by human standards. Your point?"

"She stole a *Flexfuel* car." He grinned at my blank face. "That means it can use a bunch of fuels, usually mixes of gas and ethanol. Smart engine, adjusts the mixture, but *super-distinctive scent*."

"Oh."

"Especially if the sensor is off calibration and the owner's been adding ethanol manually," Barry concluded. "She thinks she's cut off the trail, but I can track that vehicle till she runs it out of gas."

He paused, then sighed.

"On foot, sadly, but I can follow her. I suggest I do just that...and you two go get my truck." His grin widened.

"If nothing else, my shotgun is in there and we may need a quick getaway."

18

Mary went for her cousin's truck. I went back Between to pick up my own Escalade from the suburban office parking lot I'd left it in. I even had an email from Masters letting me know when she'd scheduled the next meeting for.

It said a lot about how much the accountant knew about our world that she didn't even question the fact that I'd unexpectedly teleported out of her meeting room due to a crisis. People like Meine Masters and Jiang Kuang—and Shelly Fairchild, for that matter—were a critical part of our ability to interface with and stay hidden from the mortal world.

They were also our greatest vulnerability to exposure, a risk mostly mitigated with threats of terrible retribution and deliveries of fat stacks of cash. My experience suggested that the latter, combined with the "health plan" of having access to supernatural healers, was the best course.

Somehow, I doubted that whoever was handling Maria Chernenkov's accounts had particularly fond feelings for the Pouka Noble.

With the potential consequences of my abrupt departure apparently smoothed over, at least for now, I drove back to the north of the city, following a continually updating GPS waypoint being fed to my phone by Barry's.

He stopped moving about five minutes before I caught up with him, and I found him smoking a cigarette and sitting on the hood of his pickup truck parked on a hill overlooking a warehouse district in the Northwest.

"Well?" I asked as I stepped out of my own SUV and stepped up to him. His automatic shotgun was sitting beside him on the hood of the truck, and I could feel the cold iron radiating from the weapon's magazine.

He pointed the cigarette at the closest warehouse.

"She parked the stolen car there," he told me. "It's *possible* she's left in a different vehicle, but no one has gone in or come out in the last ten minutes. I figured I shouldn't go barging in on my own, since you're so sure she'd kick my ass and all."

"He's right," Mary told the werewolf as she dropped out of the truck. She'd discarded the blazer of her business suit for a black Kevlar vest over her blouse. Instead of her little machine pistol, she was carrying a matching automatic shotgun to Barry's portable cannon.

"We may have big guns and cold iron pellets and our claws and teeth, but she's got all of the above too," my lover continued. "Now, she knows there's shifters coming after her, so she's probably loaded with triple-kill again—or, given the connections this bitch seems to have, even Bane."

That was a terrifying possibility.

"No one goes in alone," I told them firmly. I grabbed the long coat the Queen had given me from the truck as I spoke. It didn't look it was going to rain—but the rubberized fabric coat had been a convenient size to conceal a *lot* of enchanted armor. It also did a good job of covering the leather pouch of cold iron spikes...and the cold-iron-loaded MP5 I pulled out of the back of the Escalade.

Eric was still working on finding more toys for me to fight Chernenkov with, but it wasn't like my Queen hadn't already upgraded the equipment I brought to the party.

"I'll go first," I continued. "If she's expecting shifters, she may have loaded with Bane—and she may as well shoot *me* with plain lead. And we can hope she doesn't have many rounds of it!"

"Sure, let's use my Clan-sister's boyfriend and the local rep of a

Power as a human shield," Barry replied. "That sounds like a *great* plan."

"Fall in, joker," I ordered lightly. "I don't plan on burying you—and sending you in first might require that. You get me, Barry?"

"I get you."

———

IT WAS STILL MIDAFTERNOON, but the warehouse district was quiet. We were in that interim time between when all of the last shipments of the day have come in and gone out, but the workers were still busy offloading and prepping for the next day.

Anyone in the area was hard at work. They didn't want trouble and, well, I didn't want to bring trouble into their lives.

Unfortunately for everyone, somewhere in that district was a murderer who'd decided I was her next primary target. That was going to be a problem for everyone.

We moved quietly down the hill, leaving the cars parked well away from the district as we sneaked up on the fenced compound Barry had tracked the stolen car to. It was about as solid as security got in Calgary: a ten-foot-tall fence surrounding the entire property, with two vehicle gates, both with security booths.

The booths were the first sign of a real problem. I studied them from a distance and they were empty.

"Were there guards here when you swung by?" I asked Barry quietly.

"No," he admitted. "Thought we were just lucky. Guessing the place is shut down?"

"Maybe," I said slowly, studying further. There was no one visible in the grounds around the warehouse, but there were more cars parked there than just the stolen one. An eighteen-wheeler was backed up to the dock.

"No, it's still active. Cars, trucks, the works. They're just not bothering to run security. That's...never a good sign."

Even if you had nothing to protect, someone had to open the

powered gates for anyone coming in. Why would the gates be abandoned?

Unless, I guessed, everyone who was coming and going already had a remote control for the gates and the eighteen-wheeler was mostly for show. A situation that would never be the case for an actual warehouse...

"It's not a fucking warehouse," I said quietly. "It's a safehouse. The question is...crime, ours, or hers?"

"Whoever it belongs to, she's in there," Barry pointed out. "That means it's hers, right?"

"Yeah...but if it's a syndicate safehouse, we have to go in very differently than if it's just Chernenkov and her mercs...or if it's Clan or Court territory."

"It isn't Clan," Mary said quietly. "I know every Clan secondary property in the city—and even if there's one they haven't reported to Enli..."

"There's signs and signifiers," Barry agreed. "But if it's fae..."

"There'll be signs," I admitted. "Let's get closer."

I knew it didn't belong to Oberis. I didn't know every location his Court controlled, but I was pretty sure I knew all of the safehouses of this size. It wasn't like it was an operating business that was owned by a fae or the Court, either.

As we got closer, the sinking feeling in my chest got stronger, until I was close enough to get a good look at the guardhouse and could finally read the fae-sign.

"It's ours," I said flatly. "Well, fae."

"So, Chernenkov's fae, isn't she?" Mary asked.

"Yeah. But that fae-sign declares this a safehouse of Lord Andrell's Unseelie Court," I told them. I studied the sign for several long seconds.

"But you have the sanction to go in anyway, don't you?" Mary asked.

I swallowed.

"There is my *authority* and there is my actual power," I admitted in a small voice. "Technically, yes, I have the authority and the sanction to force them to admit me and show me around and prove Chernenkov isn't there.... In practice, however, any Unseelie Noble can and *will* tell me to go take a hike."

Barry exhaled, studying the facility.

"That's not even politics," he noted. "That's just your kin being melodramatic assholes."

"Well, they *are* fae."

"On the flip side, though, I may not have *sanction*," the werewolf said in a slow, thoughtful tone, "but they also can't argue that I could read the sign before I wandered in, can they?"

———

THAT WAS A TERRIBLE IDEA, and I told him so.

Instead of agreeing with me, however, Barry squared his shoulders and met my gaze.

"If you charge in there all holier-than-thou-I-serve-our-Queen, what are you going to get?" he asked bluntly.

I sighed.

"Kicked out, unless I'm willing to pick a fight that could start a war," I admitted.

"They can't do worse to me," Barry pointed out. "The last thing Andrell needs is a war with the Clan—and we *need* to know if she's in there, yes?"

"Yes," I ground out. "I'm not sure how you sneaking in there helps us, Barry."

"He can smell her," Mary reminded me. "You can't."

That...was true enough.

"And they'll be looking for you," she continued. "If she's in there, she has to be at least half-expecting you to find her. A werewolf stalking the grounds? That's probably not on their radar yet."

"It *will* be once she processes just what went wrong when she came after you," I pointed out.

"All the reason to go in now," Barry replied. "If she's there, someone has to go in after her. Would you rather risk that war knowing she at least was there...or potentially for nothing?"

Given that the currently available forces for a war between

Andrell's Court and the Queen's Vassals was, well, me...I could see his point.

"I don't like it," I admitted. "This is my fight."

"And I owe you about six lives so far, and you are my Clan-sister's heart," Barry replied. "Plus, this bitch has killed far too many people *and* came at Mary. This is the Clan's fight, whether you like it or not."

"You can argue till you're blue in the face, Jason, but Barry's right," Mary told me. "It's the second-best chance we've got."

She smiled wickedly.

"Of course, the truth is that the *best* chance we have is to send in an actual stealth predator like, say, a cat."

Barry and I traded a long look. Yeah. We'd already lost that fight.

––––––––

MARY WENT in as a cat while we provided overwatch. She was definitely stealthier than either of us, and I lost track of her around when she went under the fence.

"I feel like we should have argued harder," Barry noted.

"Do you really think we'd have won?" I replied. "I'm not with her because she's a pushover. Quite the opposite!"

"What happens if they do decide to start shooting?" he asked.

"Then hell follows me in," I told him. "Because if they shoot at one of Enli's top people, it becomes *my* job to stop it turning into a war. That job will neatly dovetail with saving my girlfriend, which is handy."

The werewolf chuckled and produced a pair of binoculars.

"Okay, she's right up to the building," he reported. "So far, so good."

I hated waiting. I hated watching someone else go into danger for me, and I hated *Mary* being in danger.

"She's in."

I exhaled sharply, stretching out with my hearing as we waited and I studied the building. We knew the Unseelie Court had picked up a portfolio of property in the city, and it wasn't like they *had* to report all of it to the Keeper.

It was generally considered polite to report major facilities to the Keepers, though, and Eric had told me about all of the ones they'd told him about. This wasn't on the list, which raised all kinds of interesting questions.

It was possible, of course, that this was a rogue group under Chernenkov's control, outsiders moved into the city entirely separate from Andrell's Court.

I wasn't sure I *believed* that, but it was possible.

"No sign of commotion yet," I murmured. "That's a good start, I suppose."

My companion nodded, his own attention focused on the building through the binoculars.

"Wait, I see someone," he said, offering me the binoculars. "Do you know them?"

Looking through the binoculars, I spotted the person he was pointing out. I'd have seen them without the aid, but I wouldn't have been able to make out their face.

"Fuck me," I hissed.

Standing outside the main entrance to the warehouse, smoking a cigarette, was Bryan Milligan, the same Unseelie Gentry who'd fought Chernenkov with me and been playing guard at Andrell's introduction. That scotched this being a rogue site...but begged the question of what *Milligan* thought was going on if the Pouka was there.

"You know him?" Barry asked.

"Yeah. He's Gentry, used to work with Robert before Andrell showed up," I replied. "He helped us put Chernenkov *down*; he can't be working with her."

"So, he may not know," the werewolf pointed out. He paused. "Um, from what you told me about Chernenkov...I'm guessing that hanging out near her might not be super-healthy for your Gentry friend."

"Probably not," I agreed, considering the situation. "On the other hand, I don't think we're supposed to know this place exists, which limits what I can do. He chose his Court and his path; I can only do so much." I grimaced. I at least had Milligan's phone number, but warning him would put the whole point of sneaking into this place at risk.

"This is not going to end well."

———

MILLIGAN HAD ALMOST FINISHED his cigarette before the commotion I'd expected finally erupted. He dropped the smoke and charged back into the warehouse with his hand inside his jacket. I tensed, considering.

"Let's move closer," I told Barry. If things started going sideways, I wanted to be close enough to hear gunfire and feel Power.

We crept closer, straining our ears for the sound of trouble. I began to make out shouting, but none of it was coherent through the walls of the building, even to me. There was no gunfire or magic yet, just shouting.

That was promising, at least.

Finally, the door to the warehouse swung open and Bryan Milligan appeared again. This time, the Gentry was guiding Mary out with a hand on her shoulder and a storm cloud on his face.

"If she's telling the truth, I want *answers*," he shouted back into the building. The response wasn't coherent from where we stood, but then Gráinne stalked out of the building after him.

"I don't give a *shit* why you think you can violate Court territory, shifter," she spat at Mary. "Covenant says I have to warn you, so consider yourself warned. If we find you on Court territory without permission again, your Speaker is getting a cat-skin *rug*. We clear?"

We were still almost a hundred meters away, but I could hear Milligan's growl.

"Control yourself, *Gentry*," Gráinne told him. "Escort the shifter off the property, then return to your duties."

The Noble returned to the warehouse, letting the door slam behind her, and Milligan continued to walk Mary out toward the gate. He tapped a sequence into a keypad, opening the gate without a word, then paused.

"Kilkenny's following her too, isn't he?" he murmured to Mary.

She nodded silently.

"Have him call me," the Gentry told her. "I don't like the questions you raised, Miss Tenerim, but this is a fae affair even at the worst. Now, go." He released her, gesturing for her to head out into the fading evening.

She obeyed, the gate sliding shut behind her as Milligan watched her leave. Less than twenty feet from the fence, Mary transformed back into a wildcat and took off at full speed.

"Well, I guess we circle around and meet up with her," I told Barry. "That went...better than I expected, from the looks of things."

WE MET BACK at the cars, Mary managing to actually beat us back to the street at the top of the hill. She was waiting for Barry and me when we arrived, a self-satisfied smirk on her face.

"I take it there was a canary in there for the cat to eat?" I asked her as I gave her a tight hug.

"Something like that," she agreed. "Gráinne is one *pissed* woman."

"That...was roughly my impression when I met her, yeah," I said. "You okay?"

"I'm fine," Mary said quickly. A bit too quickly, I thought, but I wasn't going to push her. "Chernenkov was there. Not entirely sure if she still was, but it's possible. More...Gráinne had to know. The Pouka's scent was all over her."

That was bad. Gráinne appeared to be Andrell's right-hand woman. If she knew where the Pouka was and Andrell wasn't talking...the best-case scenario was that the Unseelie Lord's house was far from in order.

The worst-case scenario was that the Unseelie Court was actively hiding someone marked for death by the Fae High Court.

"What did you find?" I finally asked, realizing I'd gone quiet and both of the shifters were staring at me.

"It's, well, a safehouse," Mary replied. "They've got pretty tight security inside—I managed to get into the building, but there's at least three or four separate areas in there, with sealed doors and security scanners."

She shrugged.

"I set off a thermal scanner I'd missed when I tried to follow Chernenkov's scent into what looked like a motel moved indoors. That, well, went sideways from there, and I decided that Shifting was a better idea than getting shot by the guards," she concluded.

"Started arguing with the guards, Gráinne showed up and so did the Gentry who escorted me out. I've met him before, somewhere, and he was local enough to argue Covenant with Gráinne, so I got out unscathed...but I was worried for a minute there that Gráinne was going to take the risk of war," she admitted, leaning into me.

"If Milligan was local...the rest weren't?" I asked.

"I don't know," she admitted. "They didn't talk like locals, but it's not like Calgary isn't known for immigrants of all stripes—but they also didn't know anything about the Covenants or the fact that they *do* cover a hot-pursuit situation like this."

Mary, as a senior—if not overly powerful—member of Clan Tenerim, was authorized under the Covenants to enter the jurisdictions of other supernatural communities if actively in pursuit of a criminal. The Unseelie Court should have *helped* her search for Chernenkov, not threatened to kill her.

At the very least, two senior members of the Unseelie Court had been there and the fae-sign declared it property of Andrell's Court.

"This is a mess," I said. "I need to check in. I'm going to have to break in there, I think, but that's a fight I don't want to start without warning Eric and the Queen."

"I know," Mary agreed. "But there was more in there than just safe-house rooms. Most of the place is still a warehouse, and I got a good look at what they're storing: guns. Lots of guns. Ammunition, explosives... I would have thought you'd know where their armory was."

"I thought I did," I agreed. Eric had, in fact, spent some time helping magically secure the armory the Unseelie had buried under the new Court. Why would the Unseelie have an entire second armory we didn't know about?

Unless... Inga had said the Masked Lords had been running a private military, a counter-force to the Hunt and the High Court. If *they* were setting up in Calgary, they could use Andrell's Court as cover for bringing in new people and gear. While one supernatural group was setting up shop openly, we'd write off any oddities as belonging to them, especially if Gráinne was working with the Masked Lords.

I sighed.

"I need to talk to the Queen," I repeated. "I think we're in deeper than I was expecting. Thank you, both of you," I told the Tenerim shifters.

Somehow, though, I was unsurprised when my phone started ringing before we said anything more.

"Kilkenny," I said as I answered it, barely registering who the call was from.

"Jason, it's Eric," the Keeper's gruff voice said in my ear. "You need to get to the Manor *now*. Andrell is here…and he is *pissed*."

After the day I'd had…I wasn't even sure just what the Unseelie Lord was angry about.

There were so many options.

"I'm on my way."

Shaking my head, I turned to Barry.

"I need another favor," I told him. "Can you make sure this place is watched? *Without* being caught?"

"Jason…we're shifters. We don't get caught unless we actually try and sneak *into* the building," he told me. "I'll talk to the boys and girls, and we can run it up to Grandfather if we need more than just Tenerim on it.

"If she leaves, we'll let you know."

19

I LEFT Mary with her cousin to get back home while I drove to the Manor. A big sign outside now declared that the bar was closed for "a private function," and it looked like Andrell had acquired several large black SUVs of his own.

Four of them filled one corner of the parking lot. Oberis's brilliantly white sedan arrived moments before I did, and there were other vehicles I recognized. Talus was already there, and Robert emerged from Oberis's car behind the Fae Lord.

"My lord," I greeted him as he intercepted me short of the bar entrance.

"What the *hell* happened?" he demanded.

"Four redcaps and our Pouka friend tried to kill Mary this afternoon," I told him flatly. "The Tenerims then traced the Pouka back to what appears to be a secret Unseelie Court safehouse, where they got thrown out by Gráinne. That's the only things *I* know about that could be pissing Andrell off today, at least."

"'Today,'" Oberis echoed dryly. "I'd say you're supposed to be *reducing* my problems, but, honestly, this doesn't appear to be your fault. Let's go see what he wants, but if you can, Jason...do me a favor?"

"I should probably remind you here that I'm supposed to be neutral," I told him.

"Yeah, well, don't tell him about anything he doesn't yell at you about, okay?" the Seelie Lord snapped. "He's looking for a fight and it's with you, not me. So, don't give him ammunition, all right?"

I sighed.

"If it were up to me, my lord, there wouldn't be any ammunition *to* give him," I replied. "I don't know what he's angry about, but whatever it is…it ties back to Chernenkov. Which means he's got a lot less ammo than he may think he has."

Oberis sighed.

"Can we at least avoid a fucking war?"

"*That*, my lord Oberis, I think we all agree on being the objective."

———

THE PRIVATE-EVENT SIGN was an indication that there would be no mortals in the Manor tonight, and a quick glance around the room as I walked in, a safe minute or two after Oberis, confirmed that. There were a good thirty-odd people in the bar, but all of them were fae.

After six months in Calgary with the joint Court, it was odd to me now to watch fae groups split neatly and instinctively into Seelie and Unseelie camps. That was a normal event in most cities, but Calgary had always managed to avoid that divide before.

Even now, it wasn't a clean divide. Gráinne stood against one wall, apparently having beaten me there from the warehouse without even knowing it was a race, and a collection of new and old Unseelie were gathered around her.

Talus was leaning against the exact opposite wall, managing to look utterly bored by the whole affair. Half a dozen Seelie Gentry and Greater Fae were sitting with him.

Despite those two groupings, however, easily half of the fae in the room had ignored the split. The main crowd in the middle of the bar definitely tended more Unseelie on one side and Seelie on the other, but it wasn't split into two camps.

Yet.

The split between Talus and Gráinne's groups was a warning of things to come if we didn't head off any potential conflict between the Courts *quickly*. Many of the cities I'd passed through before my wandering had brought me to Calgary had hard-forged divides between Courts, with Seelie and Unseelie as separate from each other as they were from shifters or Kami.

Keeping that from happening was my job. Well, my job and Eric's job.

The gnome saw me coming and was gesturing for people to let me through to where he was standing on the bar. Even with the bar beneath his feet, Andrell almost met his height, the Unseelie Lord towering over even my own lanky height.

"Jason, I'm glad you could—"

"Kilkenny, I claim blood right to speak for my dead!" Andrell snapped. "Four of my kin are dead, and you were the one to call it in. Why are my people dead? Why did you kill them?!"

He was leaping to conclusions, though it was hardly an unreasonable one—beyond the fact that four prepared redcaps should probably have been able to take me.

"Do you claim them, then, Lord Andrell?" I asked as I reached him and Eric. "Were they of your Court, bound by Fealty, that you are responsible for their actions? For their *crimes*?"

"What crimes?" he demanded. "That they ended up dead in the streets?"

"If they were yours, Lord Andrell, are you prepared for the war they tried to start?" I asked quietly, lowering my voice and forcing the entire Manor to silence themselves to hear me. "Will you bear the blood-gild for the mortal they killed? The consequences of launching an attack on the Clan Speaker's people?

"Are you prepared to go to war with Calgary's Shifter Clans, Lord Andrell?" I demanded. "Because I see no grounds to summon Lord Oberis to aid you if you do. If you brought feeders into this city without reporting them, *you* are in violation of the Covenants you swore to uphold."

I smiled thinly, hoping that I could at least force him to realize the thin ice he stood on.

"So, I ask again, Lord Andrell, do you claim them as yours? Do you admit to breaking Oath and Covenant within *days* of assuming your Court? Or should, perhaps, we compare notes and see just what happened to bring four redcaps into this city and loose them upon a friend of our Courts?"

Andrell flicked a dark glance over at Gráinne, and I wondered what layers were moving within layers in Calgary's new Court.

"We have no grounds to assume they were feeders merely because they were redcaps," he pointed out carefully. "Allowances are made and promises kept by many of their kin."

"I do not generally give much credence to the promises of men who introduce themselves by killing mortals and attacking shifters," I said. "I do not know who they were, beyond redcaps. I do know that they attacked Mary Tenerim, a friend of these Courts and this Manor, without provocation or warning, killed a mortal taxi driver, and started a gunfight in the middle of the street.

"I do not know how things work in Ireland, Lord Andrell, for I am a child of this continent—but here, we prefer to *avoid* open battles in the middle of the day!"

There was a long silence and then Andrell sighed.

"I see your point, Vassal Kilkenny," he allowed with forced politeness. "Perhaps you can tell me what occurred before either of us leaps to unnecessary conclusions, yes?"

"Of course," I allowed, pulling one of the barstools up and taking a seat. The immediate situation apparently defused, Eric dropped down behind the bar and poured us both beer. I was guessing that Andrell's didn't come with the warning look, though.

"Mary Tenerim is one of the armorers and administrators for Clan Tenerim, and she works closely with Speaker Enli," I explained quickly. "For...various reasons, I have a receiver on my phone for an emergency alert built into *her* phone."

If there was anyone in Calgary's Court who didn't know I was dating a shifter, that would be news to *me*.

"When I received the alert, I walked Between to her location, where I found that the redcaps had rammed her taxi with a truck and killed the driver. Ms. Tenerim had managed to fight them off and escape, but they chased her and trapped her behind a strip mall...at which point I arrived."

I shrugged.

"They'd underestimated their prey, and Ms. Tenerim actually had the situation in hand," I noted. "My intervention helped resolve the situation quickly, but the redcaps refused to surrender and forced us to kill them.

"Taking such an action to protect a friend of the Courts, Lord Andrell, is entirely within my authority—as is neutralizing such a blatant threat to the Covenants of Silence. My understanding was also that there were no redcaps in Calgary—the four I encountered appeared to be imported freelancers."

I shook my head.

"Which begs the question, my lord, of why exactly freelance fae hitmen were in our city."

"It does, doesn't it?" Andrell said slowly. "I apologize for my rash initial response, Master Kilkenny."

His *publicly* rash initial response. That wasn't going to come back to bite any of us at *all*, I was sure.

"You are correct that I am not aware of any redcaps in the city," he continued. "And given your story, I most specifically do *not* claim them as mine, protected by Court and Fealty. I will investigate their presence; I promise you this."

We shared a long look. There was something about the man that was starting to worry me, and not just that he was Unseelie. He was swinging too quickly between friend and foe—it was starting to give me whiplash!

Glancing around the room, I found myself meeting Gráinne's gaze as well. She seemed *much* less willing to accept my story, if the hard edge to her eyes was any sign.

"We are all tasked with keeping the peace and the Covenants, my lord," I told Andrell. "Any assistance I can provide in finding how these rogue Unseelie came into the city, I will, of course, provide."

"We shall find them," he replied grimly. "I will speak to those responsible for covering this up and make certain that proper measures are taken for the dead mortal's family as well. I will not claim these men as mine, but they were Unseelie. I will see their victims taken care of."

That wasn't required...but someone had to step in to see that the mess was covered up and the victim's family covered. We tried to be better about our obligations to the mortals in this day and age, a task that usually fell to the Keeper.

"You will also want to speak to Enli," I warned him. "Grandfather will not lightly let this attack on his people go."

Andrell sighed.

"You are, of course, correct, Master Kilkenny," he agreed. "May I impose on you to arrange a meeting?"

...Yeah, okay, I'd walked into that one.

"I can do that," I promised. "Let me know when you're available, and I will reach out to the Speaker."

―――――

WITH THE FLOOR show that everyone had been anticipating short-circuited by the measure of people actually being adults and talking out their problems, the crowd in the bar slowly began to disperse. Andrell wasn't the first to leave—that would be a sign of weakness, something no Fae Lord could afford—but he left quickly enough for it to be obvious.

Oberis didn't hang around for long afterward either, and the Nobles followed the Lords out.

Within an hour of my arrival, the bar was down to under half a dozen guests, which Zach and Tarva were easily able to take care of. At that point, Eric gestured for me to follow him with a sharp nod and led the way into his apartment under the bar.

The bare concrete floor of the apartment was covered in artful rugs, and the walls were smothered in heavy drapes. Other than the lack of windows, the room seemed well lit and cheerful, and Eric gestured me to a familiar overstuffed purple couch.

"Not bad," he finally allowed. "Someone had wound Andrell up and set him to ticking. He was about ready to explode and demand blood for blood when you showed up and neatly cut him off at the knees."

The gnome sighed.

"Which, of course, is going to have problems all of its own," he continued. "Enough people here guessed that he was planning on demanding your head to make you undercutting him like that at least a little humiliating."

"And no fae *ever*, let alone a Fae Lord, likes being humiliated." I sighed. "What else, exactly, was I going to do?"

Eric snorted.

"Short of challenging him to trial by combat in the middle of the Manor? You did the best you could. I'd make sure you set that meeting up, though."

"I'll add it to my to-do list," I snarked.

The gnome threw me a bushy-eyebrowed warning look.

"And what *else* is on your to-do list, if I may ask, my friend?" he said quietly.

"Chernenkov was involved in the attempted hit on Mary," I told him. "We took one of the redcaps alive—and the Pouka put a cold iron round through his head."

"Shit."

"It gets worse. The Tenerims followed her home—to a safehouse you and I don't know about, owned by the Unseelie Court, guarded by no other than Bryan Milligan and our friend Gráinne. A safehouse packed full of guns and Unseelie newcomers."

"Andrell is bringing more Unseelie into the city," Eric said carefully. "But not many. Including his Nobles, he's brought maybe a dozen people with him. He was sent to split the Unseelie from an existing Court, not to build a new one from scratch."

"There were at least two dozen Unseelie in that building, Eric," I told the Keeper. "I don't think we're talking Gentry or Greater Fae, even, but...Mary says Chernenkov was definitely there. Somewhere inside the layers of security in that safehouse."

"And *Milligan* was guarding it?" Eric asked.

"And clearly didn't know about the Pouka being there," I agreed. "I'm going to have to touch base with him, off the record, tomorrow.

But that safehouse stinks to high heaven, Eric, and if the Pouka retreated there, then…"

He sighed.

"Then you have sanction. It's still a damn stupid idea to charge in there, Jason."

"I'm planning on *sneaking* in there, thank you," I told him. "And I'm talking to the Queen first. There's more games afoot here than I think we know about."

For a moment, I was tempted to ask him about the Masked Lords, but from what Inga had said, he likely wouldn't know…and the Queen would prefer that story stayed at least quiet, if not secret.

"There's only so much sanction you can actually level against Andrell on your own," Eric pointed out. "Just from a practical perspective."

"And if he's sneaking in Unseelie freelancers, ordering hits on shifters, and hiding a Pouka the High Court has marked for execution, what do we do?" I finally asked.

"What do you think?" Eric replied, his voice harsh. "If you and I can't handle it and it's High Court business, there's only one more level above us.

"If you end up finding full sanction against Andrell, we'll have no choice but to summon the Wild Hunt."

20

By the time I finally made it home, Mary had passed out from adrenaline overload and exhaustion. I checked in on her, making sure not to wake her, and tucked the blanket up over her sleeping form with a content smile.

Then I carefully closed the door behind me and went back into the main room to boot up my computer. Logging into Fae-Net, I dropped a request to the Queen's phone, hoping she was available. It was early morning in Ireland, after all.

It took a few more minutes than it had after the whole mess with Chernenkov, but the videoconference software blipped up with an incoming call. I was surprised on accepting it, however, to get only a piece of iconography, a complex Celtic knotwork image that was clearly intended to be Mabona herself.

"My Queen?"

"It's me," she snapped. "I just got out of the shower, but this seemed urgent."

Translation: my Queen was probably naked or similarly underdressed, hence the iconography. That was fair enough in an age where even the fae found it easier to use voice-over-internet calls via virtual private networks than to teleport around.

"What's going on?"

"Our Pouka friend has allies," I said simply. "She used redcap mercenaries to try and kill my girlfriend and is hiding out in a safe-house being run by either Andrell himself or his right-hand woman."

The call was silent for several seconds.

"Fuck."

"MacDonald also warned me that the Masked Lords may have a hand in affairs."

"*Fuck,*" the Queen repeated, with more emphasis. "Damn it, Kenneth. I'm guessing Inga briefed you on the Masks?"

"Yes," I confirmed. "I'm sure I'm missing details, but they killed a number of the High Court Powers before I was born."

"Yeah. Calebrant stopped them, at the cost of his life," she said bitterly. "We never found the fuckers, but every so often, a handful of fae in the damn iron masks show up and cause trouble. There's an agenda behind it, but I haven't worked out what it is yet."

"Recruitment?" I suggested. "As I understand, they need twenty-one Lords or powerful Nobles to implement their ritual."

"Likely," she agreed. "If they're trying to set up a conflict in Calgary…they're trying to recruit Andrell. Possibly Talus or Oberis, too, though I wish them luck with *that* attempt."

"I don't know if the Masks and Chernenkov are related," I admitted. "But she hid—she may be still be hiding—in a safehouse Andrell's people didn't report to us. Guns, outsiders, high-security quarters. It all looks like something the Masked Lords might be using as a local base."

Mabona was silent again.

"Jason." She paused, as if uncertain how to continue the sentence. "If the Masked Lords are in Calgary, they will come for you. They'll come for you as my Vassal and they'll come for you for your bloodline."

"What, *they* know who my father is?" I demanded bitterly.

"They shouldn't," she said flatly. "But understand that *they* are the reason I conceal your lineage. If they learn…if they even *suspect*, they will come for you with everything they have. Listen to Inga, Jason. You must learn all she has to teach.

"Before it's too late."

———

INGA TOOK the Queen's instructions as an obligation to wring me dry. By the time she was done with me, she'd thrown me across the room half a dozen times and forced me to duel her blade to blade…with neither of us actually holding the swords in our hands.

The difference between what I was capable of after a couple of weeks of her training and where'd I'd been when I'd first arrived in Calgary was stunning. I'd arrived in Calgary before my father's blood had woken up in me—I suspected, in fact, that it was being claimed as the Queen's Vassal that had awoken the power of that blood.

Until then, I'd wielded the powers available to a changeling who was the grandson of one of the more powerful Seelie will-o'-the-wisps known in the last couple of centuries. Now…now I wasn't entirely sure what my father had been, but my best guess was a Noble of the Wild Hunt.

That certainly explained how Inga had clearly known him, even if it didn't necessarily answer any of the questions I had about him.

The one thing I'd realized, though, was that whoever my father was, he was dead. Most likely, adding up the pieces I'd been given, he'd died when the Hunt had ridden against the Masked Lords.

From what Inga had said about that fight, that didn't narrow the options down much.

Half-collapsing onto the steps outside her dojo, I dug up Bryan Milligan's phone number and called him.

"This is Milligan."

"Bryan, it's Kilkenny," I told him in my slow Southern drawl. "How's things?"

He chuckled.

"Messier than I thought, I'm starting to realize," he replied.

"Can we meet up? I could really use lunch."

And some answers, though without being sure who was listening in on his side, I couldn't say that.

"Yeah, I can do that," he said slowly. "I'm at home, but there's a neighborhood pub around the corner. Quiet place, the type no one knows about."

Meaning the type of place no other fae were going to be hanging out at. The Gentry seemed to understand just how much trouble we were digging for here.

"Text me the address," I told him. "I'll meet you there."

"Can do. Looking forward to it, Jason. I think you can answer some of the questions that are getting under my skin of late."

———

THE PUB WAS in a small corner unit of a strip mall tucked away in a quiet northwestern suburb. Well away from all of the major roads and malls; I hadn't even been aware there was a commercial strip buried in the community.

Though, admittedly, the city kept throwing up surprises for me. For all of the responsibility and attention I seemed to be gathering, I was still a newcomer there.

I parked the Escalade at the far side of the parking lot and entered the pub. It was very much a seat-yourself type of place, with only two waitresses running around at what would have been the lunch rush in a restaurant closer to places people worked.

Milligan waved to me as I entered. He'd found a booth tucked away at the side of the restaurant, well away from the kitchen or the bathrooms. It was awkwardly positioned next to the speakers, an additional aggravation for our enhanced senses, but a cover for a conversation we probably didn't want any mortals listening in on.

"How's the new boss?" I asked as I took a seat. "Same as the old one?"

He snorted.

"That's both more and less true than you think," he pointed out. "Andrell and Oberis have a pretty similar management style. At first brush, he really is a good guy."

I nodded my agreement as I spotted the waitress approaching, and checked the menu. I ordered a burger and a beer and waited for her to move away with our orders before turning back to Milligan.

"And at second brush?" I asked.

"I don't know," Milligan admitted. "Secret safehouses? Sure, whatever, Oberis trusted Eric completely, and he *still* has a bunker tucked away that the Keeper doesn't know about—and I'm guessing at least one more I don't know about, either."

"But that safehouse is full of outsiders, isn't it?" I asked. That was a Covenant violation all on its own. New arrivals were required to present themselves at the Manor. The High Court was supposed to know where all of our kind were.

It helped us cover up the inevitable incidents and maintain the Covenants of Silence.

"Yeah," he agreed. "Not least, a certain foursome of redcap freelancers stayed there for two nights before they went and turned themselves into a political hot potato."

I exhaled sharply.

"They were there too?"

"Yeah. I met them, though no one told me the Pouka was there," he concluded. "You're sure about that?"

"We followed her from the street fight," I told him. "Mary and Barry helped me track her after the murders at the stable. They know her scent and they followed her to that safehouse—and Mary smelled her inside.

"And all over Gráinne."

"Fuck me," Milligan whispered. "I know enough Poukas to know I don't want to be anywhere near that crazy bitch. She'll knife me while I take a piss."

"Quite possibly," I agreed. "You're in danger in that safehouse… and that safehouse is a Covenant violation all on its own. Plus, if Andrell is protecting a Pouka marked for termination by the High Court…"

"That's a clusterfuck that's over my paygrade," the Gentry told me. "Look, I'm not going to pick a fight with an Unseelie Lord. Having a separate Court isn't doing me any huge favors, but I don't write the rules and the Covenants, eh?"

"I know," I said. "But I need to find Chernenkov and bring her down. If she's there and it's Andrell's safehouse, this becomes a Wild Hunt problem—but I need to *know*.

"Can you get me in?"

Milligan was quiet as our food arrived, using his meal as an excuse to avoid answering my question. Finally, halfway through his burger, he put it down and met my gaze.

"I can get you in," he told me. "But I can't protect you once you're inside. I can't fight a Pouka—or Gráinne, for that matter. And I won't even try."

"Worst-case scenario, I can escape Between," I reminded him. "Let's make it happen."

"I'm there tonight. Come by after dark; text me when you arrive," he told me. He shook his head. "I don't *think* Andrell is all the way into this, but…"

"Even if it's just Gráinne, we still can't go to him without proof," I agreed. "I'll cover for you, I promise. I just need you to let me in the doors."

21

I WASN'T PLANNING on starting a war tonight, but if I had a shot at taking down Maria Chernenkov, I wasn't going to pass it up. The heavy oak wardrobe in our bedroom had been a gift from Eric and had a false back that was far larger on the inside than the outside, and I opened it up as I prepared for the evening's festivities.

First came the dark gray undershirt the Queen had given me shortly after claiming my Fealty. The fabric concealed layers of impact-resistant gel capsules and Kevlar, all of it inlaid with orichalcum defensive runes on the inside.

Fortunately, those runes also regulated my body temperature. As I checked the weight of my equally armored and enchanted long raincoat, I knew that was going to be important. Multiple layers in tonight's promised stifling heat would be a problem otherwise.

The leather pouch with its cold iron spikes went into the raincoat's inside pocket. A shoulder holster with my revolver—loaded with triple-kill rounds of garlic, silver and cold iron tonight—went over my torso, and the harness for my MP5 went over that in turn.

The submachine gun was loaded with cold iron rounds. No fae, not even a changeling, liked carrying true hand-forged cold iron in any form, but cold iron bullets were the most nerve-wracking. A triple-kill round would impede fae, shifters or vampires alike.

A cold iron bullet had only one intended target: other fae.

The raincoat covered both weapons and I dropped magazines for the MP5 and speed loaders for the .38 Detective Special into the other inside pockets. Studying the closet, I decided that grenades would probably be overkill and there was no way I could hide the South African–built AK-47 clone or the Russian automatic shotgun.

Having access to both the fae *and* shifter channels for illegal weapons definitely opened up options for Mary and me. For a sneak-and-peek, however, bringing heavy firepower was probably unnecessary.

It was damned tempting, though. If things went sideways, I could easily find myself facing a furious Pouka, an Unseelie Noble and an entire safehouse worth of fae mercenaries.

Of course, in that case, I was better off running away Between. Somewhat regretfully, I closed the secret compartment on the long arms and adjusted the harness to make sure I could move quietly with the MP5.

It was time to get to work.

———

ON THE OTHER side of the hill that loomed over the warehouse was one of Canada's ever-present Tim Horton's coffee shops. I grabbed two coffees and an iced cappuccino in the drive-through, and then parked the Escalade in the back corner of the parking lot as I walked over to the chunk of green space looking down over the industrial district.

I sat on the grass and drank the iced cap as the sun set, watching the compound and waiting for the shifters to find me. When I spotted the coyote drifting, mostly stealthily, around the top of the hill, I met the animal's gaze and gestured toward the coffee cups.

For a moment, I thought I'd just offered coffee to an actual wild animal, but then the animal loped up to me and *shifted* into a broad-shouldered squat man with messy blond hair.

"O'Malley," he introduced himself. "Pat O'Malley, Clan Fontaine."

O'Malley was familiar, though I intentionally didn't try and place him. A lot of my encounters with Clan Fontaine when I'd first arrived had involved either fists or bullets. If I had met O'Malley, it probably hadn't been polite.

"And you are a *saint*, Mr. Kilkenny," he continued gratefully as he took a swallow of the coffee. "We've been cycling on and off, but it's been a long day."

"Anything interesting going on?"

He snorted.

"They're trying to be quiet, but there's a few folks coming and going. Muckety-muck types, at least one of your Nobles," he told me. "I got a description and a scent image of your prey, though, and if she was in there, she hasn't left."

"Good," I said grimly. "Any idea how many are in there?"

He shrugged.

"No one is leaving, just a handful of specific people going in and coming back out. I don't think they want anyone else to know they've got people in there. *Especially* not us, and I think they know they're being watched."

That would be a logical conclusion after they'd caught Mary the previous night, but...

"What gives you that impression?" I asked.

"There are three guys, all Unseelie I've met around town, keeping a *damn* close eye on the place," O'Malley told me. "They cycled off teams once, about an hour ago, but they've kept three of your heavy hitters outside the whole time.

"They're watching for trouble and they're ready for hell to come crashing down on 'em."

He bared his teeth.

"From what I hear, if that bitch is in there, Grandfather is definitely considering introducing them to something of that kind."

Which was a headache I didn't need.

"This isn't shifter business yet," I told him. "I appreciate your help —a lot—but this is still fae business and we will deal with the bitch ourselves."

Grandfather would be...unhappy if we brought the Wild Hunt in.

But then, no one would be happy if we brought in the Hunt. That was why we needed to be *certain* before I summoned the High Court's pet army.

Plus, well, anything a Hunter could do, I could do.

"I'm guessing you're not alone?" I asked.

"One of Clan Mackin's gals is watching the east side," he confirmed. "I can bring her the coffee while I'm keeping my eyes open."

"Good. Everything *should* stay quiet," I told him. "If it doesn't…" I shook my head.

"If it doesn't stay quiet, I will be teleporting the hell out of there, so do *not* come in after me," I instructed. "You'd be taking a risk for no purpose at all…and you need to report back to Grandfather."

"That doesn't feel right," O'Malley complained, but he nodded. "It's your op and your call. We'll be out here if you need us."

———

I TEXTED Milligan as I reached the fenced compound, carefully staying in shadows that should conceal me even against fae senses. From the way the Gentry came out through the gate in the fence and looked around, I hadn't done too badly.

I joined him by the gate, moving as quietly as I could, and he nodded calmly as I approached.

"Three of us from Calgary on exterior patrol," he murmured. "Myself, Jane Connelly and Chris Armstrong. They don't know what's going on, but we've split the outside into thirds tonight, so they shouldn't pass through between here and the door."

He passed me a key card.

"I said I'd left my card at home when I got here, so Lyle lent me his," he continued. "He's one of Andrell's Nobles and he's an *ass*, so if it falls back on him, I don't care much. Plus, it probably has better access than mine, too."

I chuckled.

"That was clever. Well done."

"If I'm guarding the Pouka I helped you ash, I'm pretty sure my life expectancy is missing a few centuries it's supposed to have," he said bluntly. "Plus, if my Court is shielding a Pouka Noble who is eating people...then fuck my Court."

He walked me back through the gate in the fence, watching for his compatriots.

"There's no security cameras," he told me quietly. "I guess they didn't want *any* record of who's here. You're clear to the door. After that...it's all on you."

"I'll be fine," I assured him. "And believe me, Bryan, I'm not planning on leaving by the door I came in by."

He chuckled softly.

"Good luck, Kilkenny," he told me.

———

THE KEY CARD Milligan gave me opened the exterior door without even blinking at me, and I found myself inside a building that had been a large open box originally. There was a two-floor segment that looked like it had been offices, but the rest of it had just been a wide-open space. Presumably, it had originally had shelving and storage racks to fill it.

Some sections still had that, sealed off with key card–locked fences, but most of the space was now taken up by structures that looked like a cross between small apartment buildings and motels. There were two of the sections inside the warehouse, each looking like it had around twenty small suites in it. A third building looked like it had started as secure storage and been turned into a cafeteria.

The shelving and storage racks only made up about a quarter of the space now, and I'd entered next to one of the security gates blocking access into the storage section. My stolen key card easily slipped me inside, out of view of the handful of people—all fae—wandering the interior of the warehouse.

As I slipped past the shelving, the feeling of cold iron stopped me in my tracks, and I paused to examine the contents of the shelf next to me.

Most of the crates were somewhat familiar from my time up in the

States, neat stacks of US Army–issue crates stamped with their contents on the exterior.

Guns. Mines. Ammunition. Rocket launchers. The one small storage area I was standing in held enough firepower to fight a small war—and the crates where I'd stopped radiated cold iron. The stencils proclaimed that each contained sixteen hundred 7.62mm cartridges.

From what I was picking up off them, the stencil was probably accurate—and some well-paid armorer had replaced the original bullets with cold iron rounds. They'd have basically reloaded the rounds from scratch, but they'd done it on a massive scale.

Not *every* crate of bullets appeared to be cold iron...but enough. Thousands of bullets designed to killed fae. Tens of thousands.

Possibly more.

The boxes from the custom-blade fabricators were almost scarier. The top box was open, allowing me to see that the blades were silver —*heartstone-infused* silver. Shifter's Bane. That meant someone had used part of the supply to make weapons that were supposed to be insanely restricted.

Thankfully, it didn't look like there were that many of those, but someone had set up an armory for murdering fae and shifters in mass quantities.

To be fair, it wasn't like Oberis didn't have an armory with stacks of weapons and munitions just like these. He had, so far as I was aware, at least three. But none of them were to this scale—even Andrell had armories that he'd reported to Eric.

This was someone preparing to fight a war...and worse, this whole structure wasn't new. They were using Andrell's Court to provide security for it, but those interior motels hadn't been built in the last six months.

Mary hadn't had time to see just what was hidden back there. She'd been looking for Chernenkov—who was probably in one of those motels, and it looked like you need a key card just to get to the stairs and doors. I'd bet money that getting onto the second-floor balcony took another key card.

Tiered security by people who didn't trust anyone. My key card was probably good enough to get to where I needed to go, I hoped. There was more going on there than just one rogue Pouka Noble. If I was lucky, there was data in the office.

It was time to be sneaky.

22

IN MY FAVOR were the facts that I had senses far superior to those of a regular human, had the dexterity to be extremely quiet, and was sneaking around the portion of the warehouse well away from the apartments where most of the Unseelie were hanging out.

Against me were the facts that those Unseelie had roughly the same level of perception and were expecting any potential intruder to be equally supernatural. Fortunately, they didn't seem to expect that anyone *would* make it in past their exterior guards.

As I circled around the apartments, I saw that my guess that the upper balconies were behind another layer of security was correct. Not only was there another set of security doors barring the stairs, there was actually a guard at each of the four stairs going up.

More redcaps, in fact. At least half of the Unseelie I could see were redcaps, which was more of that particular breed of fae than I'd seen in my entire life. They did *not* have a particularly good reputation, though I suspect that, like most stereotypes, it didn't apply to all or even most of them.

In here, away from public eyes, the redcaps weren't covering their natural caps. The odd structure of hair and flesh and cloth that topped their heads gleamed with fresh blood, and the men—all of them were men, though I understood that there *were* redcap women—all wore black Kevlar armor vests and carried slung M4s.

The uniformity of their gear and clothing suggested what I'd judged the first set to be: mercenaries. A group of freelancers, working as a team and apparently completely without morals or loyalty to the Courts.

Not that I could blame them much. The official Courts were not gentle on feeders. Allowances were made, as we didn't want to commit genocide, but we weren't going to let the redcaps kill someone every week or so to soak their cap in blood.

Even these ones were almost certainly using animal blood, or we'd have noticed a new pattern of disappearances. After the vampires had managed to sneak into the city, Calgary's supernatural community had kept a *very* close eye on missing-person reports.

Dangerous and hideous as the redcaps were, however, they clearly regarded the safehouse as, well, safe. Their job was to stop the rest of the Unseelie wandering around from going upstairs and bothering the people living on the second floor—probably whatever Greater Fae or Nobles they'd sneaked into the city.

As I sneaked up to the office structure, I realized that someone had also set up a catwalk from the second floor of the office to the upper balcony of the apartments. A fifth redcap was standing guard at the balcony end of that catwalk, a layer of paranoia that made the back of my neck itch.

Assuming that I was seeing one shift of two, there were at least ten redcap mercenaries in the warehouse. Probably at least that again in other regular fae, and at least a dozen fae important enough to be behind the redcap guards, almost certainly including Chernenkov.

Forty or more Unseelie. The entirety of Oberis's Court had totalled about two hundred fae of both stripes. What the *hell* was this?

I hoped there were answers in the office as I used the key card to open a side door and slip in. I just hoped that the answer wasn't going to take the form of a Fae Lord in a cold iron mask.

That would be a very short answer, after all.

———

THE BOTTOM FLOOR of the office had been gutted at some point in the past. There were no desks, no cubicles, no internal walls, even. The entire area had been turned into a single open space, and one wall was lined with practice swords and dummies.

This was apparently the training area for the Unseelie staying there, and from the burnt and wrecked status of some of the dummies, they were training with more than blades. Or, potentially, had had quite a bit of frustration to work out.

Certainly, there was nothing of immediate value for me in there, and I made my way over to the stairs quietly and carefully.

The second floor was still clearly in use as an office. There was a row of separate offices along one side, probably with windows to the outside, and a set of cubicles with computers. All of the machines were on, humming away with the monitors in standby mode.

I checked a couple of the cubicles, but I was unsurprised to find them all locked. It was too much to hope that what appeared to be a secret cohort of Unseelie rebels had worse data security than a general warehousing corporation.

What they also had, however, was paper. Clearly, most of it was going through a scanner and into a shredder—a desire for absolute confidentiality serving to help create the mythical "paperless office"—but the invoices and documents in the middle of being processed were still on people's desks.

I took photos of the invoices, recording company names and numbers to find something to track down later. I tried not to touch anything—even as I wondered just who staffed the dozen cubicles and six side offices. With what the shifters had seen of movement in and out of the building, it was almost certainly not a human staff.

The mercenaries probably made for poor data entry clerks, but the skill wasn't beyond most fae. Just, well, beneath them.

A lot of the paperwork was clearly issued to American numbered companies. Some of it was issued to an Irish police force, others to several US sheriffs' departments. One set of paperwork was a stack of legitimate-seeming equipment transfer orders from the US and Canadian Armies.

Guns and munitions and reloading gear had been sold to what

appeared to be legitimate purchasers, but both the gear and the paperwork had ended up here. A fictitious NATO formation, front companies and real cops had been used to place the orders, and an entire arsenal had been assembled.

Hopefully, the names and numbers would be useful for Shelly and others to track it down. The side offices weren't key card–locked, and I wasn't up to picking a lock with telekinesis. I made an abortive attempt to unlock one of the offices through the window and discovered that the doors had old-fashioned locks that required the key from both sides.

That wasn't an accident. Someone had done that as security against infiltrators with the Gift of Force. I had enough data now to confirm that something very strange was going on there...but not enough data, I had to admit, to even prove that this wasn't a perfectly legitimate facility operating under Andrell's authority.

Large chunks of what was going on there were Covenant violations...but they were "apologize and promise to never do it again" violations, not "sanction a Court and Lord" violations. The scale was unusual, but unannounced "visitors" and secret facilities were hardly a new problem.

I needed something more. I needed, if nothing else, to be one hundred percent certain that Maria Chernenkov was there.

Stepping over to the door leading out onto the catwalk over to the apartments, I carefully looked out the tiny smudged-up window. The redcap guarding the other end of the catwalk might have looked bored and inattentive, but there was no way I was going to be able to cross that narrow pathway without being spotted and intercepted.

I could take one redcap. With Inga's training, I could probably take two or three. But if there were a dozen of them around here, plus friends...even if I had grounds to start this fight, which was iffy, I couldn't finish it.

Fortunately for me, however, I was a *Hunter*, which meant I had options another infiltrator wouldn't. I took a deep breath and studied the distance between where I stood and the roof of the apartments, looking for a spot where I could emerge unseen.

And once I was ready, I stepped Between.

I EMERGED on the roof of the apartment structure, crouched down behind what little cover there was up there. No one seemed to notice me, but I remained still and quiet for a minute or more as I waited to see if that stayed the case.

The office had been abandoned for the night and was easy to stay hidden in. People were living in these apartments, and they were under active guard by the redcap freelancers. Staying hidden was going to be hard, but I needed to make sure I knew if Chernenkov was there.

Just as I was about to move, however, there was a commotion beneath me. More of the redcaps emerged from the lower-level apartments, looking like they'd been roused unpleasantly by alarms or something.

Brushing sleep from their eyes, the four mercenaries formed up in the center of the courtyard like an honor guard and waited. A few moments later, an attractive-looking young woman appeared out of one of the storage sections, carrying a long narrow box.

It took me a moment to realize why she looked familiar, and then a cold sinking sensation took over my chest. The woman carrying the case was a hag. More, I was pretty sure she was related to Laurie, the hag whose involvement in the plot against MacDonald had earned her a death sentence.

The hag reached the guard of redcaps, who fell in around her with practiced ease, and then a sixth person emerged from the staircases, forcing a sharp inhalation from me.

There was no way to tell if the fae was male or female. A shimmering glamor covered them head to toe, obscuring height, build, skin...everything except the iron mask they wore over their face.

I had suspected that the reason there was an arsenal there was that the Masked Lords were using it as a base. It was still a shock to the system to actually *see* one and understand just what Inga had meant when she said the Masks concealed them completely.

The hag presented the case to the Masked Lord, who took it and gestured for the guards to follow them. Whatever was going on, it didn't seem to be about me, thankfully. They were heading for the office, the training area I'd seen on the ground floor.

If nothing else, I supposed, that was a Greater Fae and a Masked Lord who definitely weren't up on the second floor with me. Knowing there was a Masked Lord there changed the equation, but not entirely.

I needed to know if Chernenkov was there—assuming that the Pouka Noble *wasn't* the Masked Lord in question, anyway. I slowly crept up to the edge of the roof, peering over at the other set of apartments to see if anyone was visible through the windows.

I wasn't surprised that didn't work, however. Fae weren't exactly known for their exhibitionism, quite the opposite, and every window was covered with curtains. I could see some motion behind them, but it looked like I was going to have to get closer to see who was home.

Each step closer was another risk of being found. I could leave right now. The presence of a Masked Lord was *probably* enough to bring in the Wild Hunt and end this whole affair...but I wasn't here for the Fae High Court's political enemies.

I was here for the monster who'd eaten five young women simply because it was *convenient* for her.

Feeling like an idiot and wishing I had some kind of magical cloak of invisibility, I clambered up and over the edge of the roof, dropping myself down onto the balcony beneath while checking to make sure none of the guards could see me.

Only the one guarding the catwalk to the office was on this level, and that was now around the corner of the apartments from me. The balcony I crouched on was empty, which gave me a moment's breather.

I now found myself trying to work out how to peek in through the windows without being obvious. The Gift of Force, thankfully, provided a solution. I twitched the curtains of the apartment I was crouching outside of, hopefully keeping the movement natural-looking, as I peeked through.

The room on the other side was a pretty typical bachelor apartment. Tiny kitchenette, bed, couch and some chairs. Nothing out of the ordinary except that it was in a motel-style structure *inside* a warehouse.

It was also empty. As was the next one. The third left me feeling more than a little dirty, as the occupants were in the middle of having sex—and I had to look closely enough to be sure neither was Chernenkov, once I knew they were distracted.

The fourth apartment left me feeling dirty in a different way, as the occupant was a nightmare, currently doing kata in a sports bra…and nothing else.

That was probably part of my distraction as I checked the next apartment. Either that, or I underestimated the senses of a Pouka Noble. I flicked the curtains aside and found myself meeting Maria Chernenkov's gaze.

For an eternal few seconds, we just looked at each other—and then she was moving, charging toward the door.

Stealth was now officially history and I grabbed the MP5 under my coat and opened fire, hoping to take Chernenkov down. Cold iron bullets smashed the glass and hammered the apartment around Chernenkov, A handful of hits flung her backward, but she was already transforming into the terrifying black horse I'd seen at the Stampede.

Suppressed or not, I'd just emptied an SMG clip inside the warehouse, and the entire area was starting to explode. I was backpedaling, trying to buy time to think and potentially reload the MP5, and then the Pouka unleashed her fear aura.

Unthinkingly, I stepped Between to escape…and then discovered what had been in the case the hag had handed the Masked Lord as I was painfully yanked back into reality.

23

I LANDED on the hardwood floor of the safehouse training room like a sack of bricks. Stuck in the middle of them, I could now *feel* the three golden poles they'd taken from the case—a trap that would drag anyone walking Between to this exact spot.

"Really," a distorted but *probably* female voice said cheerfully. "Did you think we had no defenses against the Hunt, Mr. Kilkenny? Did you think we would not be ready when we *knew* Her Vassal here had the Gift of Between?"

The glamor-wrapped figure of the Masked Lord yanked me to my feet, sending me stumbling away from her to the laughter of the redcaps and hag in the room.

"We were not so foolish as you believed, it seems," she told me. "And you, it appears, are more foolish than we believed possible. Have you learned what you sought, child? Has what you saw been worth your life?"

The chorus of laughing redcaps had an eerie resemblance to a hyena pack, I reflected as I pulled away from her. The MP5 had landed well away from me, but I was still armed.

Even as the thought crossed my mind, the Lord gestured, and a sword ripped itself from the storage racks along the wall and flipped to her hand. I'd missed it among the practice weapons, but the edge to the blade was clear.

This was no practice weapon, and the way she wielded it with Force and hand alike told me that I was utterly outmatched if I were to try and fight her with a blade.

"Maria may complain, I suppose," the Lord said thoughtfully, "but this is my sanctum you've invaded. The Masks decree your death, Sir Kilkenny. Your mistress and precious High Court will join you soon enough."

She might have been mocking me for *my* foolishness, but she'd clearly assumed that the submachine gun one of the redcaps was currently kicking to the wall was the only gun I had on me. As she charged me, I drew the revolver and fired.

I'd never before considered just how terrifying a Jedi deflecting blaster bolts had to be to the poor stormtroopers until that moment as I opened fire on a Fae Lord in all her fury. Six times the revolver's report echoed in the training room.

Six times it was followed by a crashing noise as the Masked Lord parried the bullets with inhuman speed. I was fast, faster than any but the absolute peak of humanity…but I couldn't do that.

I tossed the gun aside and dodged away, Inga's training channeling my telekinesis to move me faster than my apparently weak limbs could. Steel flashed through where I'd been standing, and the Lord laughed.

"Is that the best you've got, little Vassal?" she asked mockingly. "A gun and a dodge? This is going to be even less challenging than I expected."

Inga's training had left me feeling like I could take on anything. Now I was getting a rude awakening in just how limited I actually was.

I conjured a whip of flame laced with Force, twisting it through the air to catch the sword as the Masked Lord struck again. I didn't have the speed to actually parry or deflect her blow…so I destroyed the sword, scattering molten metal across the hard floor of the training room.

"Damn," she said mildly. "I *liked* that sword." She shrugged. "Oh, well."

A new blade, this one forged of glamor and Force instead of steel, flashed into existence in her hand. To drive the point home, so did five clones of the Masked woman, all *also* carrying glamor blades.

"Honor requires I fight you," she noted. "A Vassal of the Queen herself? You deserve our best. But you don't deserve my time and I will not toy with you."

The only good news I could think of was that I'd emailed the pictures I'd taken in the office to Shelly. Even if I didn't make it through this, *some* good had come of it.

I also wasn't going to give up, outnumbered six to one by a single opponent or not. Green fire and invisible Force flared around me as my whip extended, turning into a spinning sequence of Power as I forged both attack and defense from the same spell.

She laughed and attacked—and I met her with everything I had. After the first few seconds, I'd lost track of which of the glamor-wrapped Masks facing me was actually a person, but all of their attacks would be deadly.

Her glamors were strong, but not strong enough to survive being hammered with the Fire and Force of my whip. Glamor-blades shattered and re-forged all around me as I danced around them, somehow managing to evade the strikes I couldn't destroy.

My whip flashed through one of the mirror images, shattering the illusion as I cut it in half in what would have been a lethal blow if I'd hit the Lord herself.

I took advantage of the moment of weakness, launching myself into a telekinetically-augmented dive through the gap in the circle of death she'd woven around me.

I didn't make it.

A glamor-blade hammered into my leg, catching me in midair and slamming me to the ground. She *left* the blade there, pinning me to the ground as she hammered a second blade into my other leg. I tried to conjure Fire again, only for her to break both of my arms with a single blow.

"I thought you weren't toying with me," I spat back at her. This whole fight had already lasted longer than I'd expected, and I could *hear* the Lord breathing heavily as she dropped the illusions to leave only the glamor-blades pinning me to the ground.

"I wasn't," she said in a soft, intrigued, tone. "How interesting. Shame, then, that this is the end of it. Good night, Mr. Kilkenny."

I sensed the cold iron knife before I saw it...and then she slammed into my chest, finishing the job of pinning me to the hardwood ground. Agony flared away from my people's ancient bane...and then darkness took me.

24

I woke up to the sound of voices, which was something of a surprise. I also woke up to searing agony throughout my head and neck...and a disturbing *nothing* from below my neck. Focusing through the pain, I came to a very distinctly uncomfortable conclusion:

At some point after I'd been stabbed, someone had broken my neck. *Probably* not intentionally, I realized as I opened my eyes.

I'd been tossed roughly against the wall, out of the way, and a sheet haphazardly thrown over me. I could see shapes through the sheet, but that was it.

And I was alive. The Masked Lord had assumed a cold iron knife would instantly kill me and yanked it out relatively quickly. Except...I was still one-quarter human. I had the healing abilities of a fae and only *part* of their vulnerability to cold iron.

"I want to eat his heart," a familiar voice snarled. Chernenkov was apparently in the room with me.

"I hate to deprive you, sister, but eventually his body *will* be found," a different female voice replied. Wait. That was *Gráinne*. Calling Chernenkov "sister"...though that was probably metaphorical, not literal.

"You already stuck a cold iron blade through it anyway," the Pouka grumped. "Ruins the flavor, even if the fear would have been *delicious*."

That descriptor made Gráinne our Masked Lord. Useful information, if I somehow managed to live through this disaster.

"And him?" Gráinne asked quietly.

"He's on his way. He wants to check in on me," Chernenkov replied. "I told him he needed to keep away until things were resolved, but having the Vassal show up here was just too much for him."

Gráinne chuckled.

"You two are sickening," she told them. "We can't let it interfere with the plan; you know that."

"I know," Chernenkov agreed. "So does he. Soon, I won't have to hide here anymore."

That didn't sound like a good thing to me, but I guessed the Pouka had a different opinion on that.

"I'll have the redcaps deal with the body. They'll dump it in the river."

"He wants to see it, to be certain," Chernenkov replied. "Leave it here, sister. The smell of blood is relaxing."

The Unseelie Noble chuckled again, then paused.

"He's here," she said calmly. "I'll give you two some privacy, though I'll note the floor in here isn't all that comfortable."

"What, tried it yourself, have you?" Chernenkov asked.

"I've landed on it, training," Gráinne told her. "Haven't had sex on it. Let me know how it goes?"

"I'm not *that* desperate, sister," the Pouka said. "Yet, anyway."

Even through the sheet, I saw them embrace and one of the two shadowy figures—presumably Gráinne—left the room. Staying still to remain hidden was easy. Nothing below my neck was responding, anyway.

I couldn't see the door the unnamed man entered through, but I saw his shadow cross the sheet and wrap Chernenkov in his arms, a fierce embrace and kiss that radiated affection even through the shadow-puppet show I was watching.

"My love, you shouldn't have come here," she told him. "Until Oberis and his Court are destroyed, we remain vulnerable."

"I know," he replied, and I was glad that my crippled body kept me from reacting. The man was Andrell.

"The Masks' plan continues," he noted. "I know my part in it, and I will play it. So will you. But I will be *damned* if I let a Hunter's changeling sniffing around keep me from you."

They kissed again, and the full depth of how fucked we were began to descend on me.

It was at that moment, of course, that Andrell crossed over to me and yanked the sheet off. I was still broken, unable to move. There wasn't a lot of work to be done in faking being dead.

"Shame, really," the Fae Lord said as he studied my "corpse." "I kind of liked him. Oh, well."

He twitched the sheet back over me and turned back to Chernenkov.

"Make sure the body isn't found," he ordered. "A missing Vassal is bad enough. A *dead* Vassal will bring down the Hunt, and that will be one hell of a delay."

"His allies have to know about this safehouse," she told him. "We'll need to relocate."

"Yeah," Andrell agreed. "I'll organize resources. I'll have somewhere for you all to stay by tomorrow night."

"That's your part in this," Chernenkov agreed, kissing him again.

He chuckled.

"Among other things, yes." Andrell sighed. "I have to go. I can only be away so long without drawing attention."

"Gráinne and I will take care of everything," she promised.

"I know. You two are amazing. Thank you."

I tried to stay conscious to follow the rest of the conversation but the pain was too much. Blackness slipped over my vision and I was gone again.

———

I woke up the second time to the sound of water and a strange bobbing sensation. It took me a moment to realize I was on a boat…which was probably a bad sign.

However, I realized I also had some, if not much, feeling back in my lower body—and someone had locked a neck brace onto me to keep my broken neck in position while it healed. That was a good sign.

"'e's awake," a guttural lower-class British accent growled. "How you doing, guv'nor?"

I slowly opened my eyes, finding myself face to face with a broad-shouldered man wearing a bright red MAKE AMERICA GREAT AGAIN trucker cap and a wide grin.

Redcap. I was on a boat with a redcap who'd been ordered to dispose of my body. And I was still alive?

"I feel like I broke every bone in my body from my neck down *and* somebody stabbed me," I noted carefully. Talking hurt less than I expected.

"That would be about right," he said cheerfully. "When I saw you *lived* through being stabbed in the chest with a cold iron knife, I went, 'That's one lucky fucker, Percival.' And he's the Queen's Vassal. Deserves hisself a second chance and can pay for it, right guv'nor?"

"There's a USB key in your pocket," another voice added, this one definitely Bryan Milligan. I shifted my head, carefully, to see the boat. "It contains the details of several Swiss bank accounts Percival here has access to, right?"

"'Xactly," the redcap confirmed cheerfully. "Now, fuck the Masks, six ways to Sunday. Boss knew when we hired on, di'n't tell the *rest* o' us till it was too late. I'm out. Next plane to Dublin.

"Now, if it so happens there's a million or two euros in those Swiss accounts by the times I lands in Dublin, the Masked Bitch ain't going to be any wiser about you still being in the land of the breathing, if you follow my drift. If those accounts are still lookin' sparse and lonely, well, even secure and encrypted disposable email addresses are cheap these days."

"We figured you'd be good for it," Milligan noted. "Or if not you, the Queen. Now, we're out here to dump your body in the river, which all three of us know isn't happening. The Mask's people wrecked your phone, and I'm guessing you should probably let them continue thinking you're dead for a while yet.

"That said, where do you want us to dump your 'corpse' and who should I call?"

I sighed.

"Anywhere, I suspect, and call Talus," I told them. "He'll know the best plan." I trembled as a wave of exhaustion swept over me. "I… think I'm going to just sleep here, though. That sounds gre—"

———

I woke up with a warm damp cloth over my eyes, a lack of neck brace, and feeling restored throughout my body.

Not that said feeling was pleasant or anything. My legs still felt like someone had stabbed swords through them, my arms still felt like they'd been broken, and my chest still felt like I'd been stabbed.

It had been a rough day. I was, at least, actually on a bed this time. After a couple of moments, I even registered that someone was holding my hand, and squeezed gently.

"You're awake," Mary said softly. "You, my love, need to stop terrifying me. How do you feel?"

"He feels like he's been beaten into unconsciousness and almost killed," her brother said in his best clipped doctor's tones. "You're lucky to be alive, Jason."

"I worked that out, thanks, Clem," I said to the shifter doctor. "I got stabbed in the heart with a cold iron blade. *How*? One-quarter human, but…"

"Your armor," Clementine Tenerim told me flatly. "You were stabbed in the heart, yes. But while the knife broke your skin and pierced your heart, the cold iron didn't actually touch your flesh and, most importantly, didn't leave anything *behind*."

He sighed.

"I'm going to remove the cloth over your eyes," he told me. "Let me know if it's too much."

The warm cloth slid aside and I looked through a dimly lit room to see the two shifters. Considering what my sight was like, there were no lights on in the room at all.

I squeezed Mary's hand again and turned to face Clem.

"I'm okay," I told him. "Or, well, as okay as I can be. And I *will* be okay."

"Any of my usual patients would already be healed," he reminded me. "But yes, I agree with your assessment. The armor vest didn't break under the blade, but whoever stabbed you was strong enough that it was dragged into the wound with the knife.

"I'm…not entirely familiar with the type of wounds you have in your legs, but I can guess," he concluded. "And the arm breaks are mostly healed already. You'll want to stay in bed for at least a day to make sure everything is in order, but after that, you'll be fine for… whatever you need to do."

I exhaled, closing my eyes.

"Where am I?"

"The goblin colony," Clem replied. "Talus called me after someone —he wouldn't tell me who—called him. He said to tell you he couldn't be seen to be involved, not yet."

Which was…fair, if frustrating.

"He also told me to let everyone think you were dead. I decided that didn't apply to Mary," my girlfriend's brother noted dryly. "The colony will protect you, but…seriously, Jason, what *happened*? You were stabbed through the legs with a fucking *battle glamor*."

"I noticed," I replied. "Fae politics, Clem. The kind where people who get dragged into them end up dead. I should never have involved the Clans."

"Yeah, well, someone *fucked* with a Clan-friend *and* my boyfriend," Mary told me. "The Clans are involved now."

"They *can't* be," I said harshly. "Seriously, Mary, I know how you guys take oaths and loyalty, but you can't get involved in this. This is part of a Powers-cursed fae civil war that's being going on since before I was before born.

"Regardless of how deep Andrell has dug himself, I can't pull shifters into this. I need to reach out to the Queen." I winced, remembering the USB key. "And I need to make sure someone gets paid."

"Talus had me pull the USB stick from your pocket and send him the contents," Clem told me. "Whoever needed money got paid. He swore on his life."

I sighed and nodded in relief. Talus was a better friend than I deserved…and richer than I tended to remember.

I'd still make sure the Queen paid him back. But if that was handled, I had time.

"And *you*, Sir Vassal, Sir Kilkenny…my brother, you need to rest."

Clem might be a weakling as shifters went, but he was more than strong enough to pin my exhausted self to the bed with one hand. "Sleep, Jason. You can call the Queen in the morning.

"Everything *will* get sorted."

25

By the time Clementine was willing to let me get out of bed, I was about ready to go crazy. I didn't heal as fast as, say, Gentry or shifters —or goblins, for that matter—but I healed most injuries in a few days. With proper medical care, and Clementine was very good at his job, I could recover from being nearly stabbed to death in a day or so.

Not that that recovery made me any happier about the situation. The goblins cheerfully put me up in one of the spare units in the condo townhome complex Talus had bought for them in the seventies when he'd brought them to Canada. There were a hundred or so units in the complex, and the colony had a total of maybe forty families and two hundred-ish goblins.

Honestly, if goblins were more able to go out in human society and less insular in general, they really should have been a bigger player in the city's supernatural politics. They were almost a quarter of the supernaturals in the city, but most of us didn't even know they were around.

Fortunately, they felt they owed a debt to Talus and seemed to like me. Theino showed me into the plainly furnished apartment and checked in on me carefully.

"We will conceal your presence here until you are ready to reveal your location," he told me. "I do not know what the best choices for you are. Despite our oaths to Talus, we have little involvement with your people."

I sighed and massaged my still-aching chest.

"Believe me, Theino, you're better off that way," I replied. "The more I learn about my own people, the more I think that no one should get involved with us."

He smiled, baring his tusks.

"If we had not been involved with your people, we would have died," he pointed out. "Talus rescued my grandfather and our families from the war. Without our involvement with the fae, this colony would not exist.

"You do your people a disservice."

"Perhaps," I allowed. "On the other hand, one of 'my people' just stabbed me in the heart. I think I'm allowed a few disservices."

Theino laughed and pointed me to the fridge.

"There's food in the fridge, and pop," he said. "None of it is particularly amazing, but you should be able to sustain yourself."

"Thank you," I told him. "I owe you."

The basic thanks was no longer as much of a promise of a debt from a fae as it had once been—we were hardly *that* separate from humanity —but I *owed* a debt to Theino and his people. Someday, I hoped to repay it.

"Is there a way for me to make contact with my Queen?" I asked quietly. I knew the goblins didn't have anything connected to Fae-Net, but I needed to call home.

"Talus made arrangements," the Speaker to Outsiders told me. "There is a laptop on the table with the appropriate connections." He bowed to Mary and me. "I leave you now. If you need anything, do not hesitate to ask."

He bowed himself out and I turned my gaze to my lover.

"I'm fine," I assured her.

"I know," she admitted. "But you're going to call your Queen and charge right back into it, aren't you?"

"That's the job I took, the oath I swore," I admitted. "And..." I sighed. "They were saying something about destroying Oberis's Court. I can't let that happen. I *won't.*"

"I know," she repeated, and kissed me. "I need to go check in with Grandfather. May I tell him you're alive?"

I closed my eyes and sighed.

"I think we must keep that secret for now," I admitted. "If you must tell him to prevent the Clans challenging Andrell or something similarly terrifying, do so."

"That may be necessary," she said.

"The Covenants forbid the Clans' getting involved in this kind of mess," I reminded her. "Remind Enli of that if you must. This is my fight. I should never have dragged you all into it."

"We would have dragged ourselves into it," she told me. "I can restrain Grandfather for a time, but understand this, Jason Kilkenny: we *know* Oberis. We trust Oberis. If Andrell moves against him, the Covenants can be damned.

"The Shifter Clans will *not* watch the Seelie Court burn."

———

"Somehow, Jason, I'm unsurprised to find that you have nearly managed to get yourself killed. Again," Mabona said as the screen resolved into a videoconference. "You are all right?"

"Thanks to some friends and a mercenary-feeling redcap, yes," I confirmed. "Speaking of which, we'll need to find out just how much Talus paid said redcap. I don't think that's a debt we want to have outstanding."

"Agreed," she said instantly. "I'll have my people reach out to him. That's secondary, however. What did you learn?"

I leaned against the plain kitchen table and considered how to organize everything I'd seen in the safehouse.

"Andrell's Court is concealing Maria Chernenkov," I told her. "I wasn't sure, initially, if Andrell knew himself—the safehouse was being run by Gráinne, one of his Nobles. After I arrived, they used what I think was a gnome-forged device to trap me when I tried to escape Between.

"At which point I was attacked by one of the Masked Lords."

Mabona was silent for several long seconds.

"You are certain."

It wasn't a question.

"I've never seen one before," I admitted. "But...cold iron mask with orichalcum runes powering one of the strongest concealment glamors I've ever encountered? I'm guessing that only belongs to one group of people."

There was an edge to Mabon's expression I'd never seen before. Was it...fear? Was the Queen of the Fae *afraid*?

The Masked Lords had almost killed her once. *Had* killed three Powers of the High Court. Fear was...reasonable, even on her part.

"The description fits," she finally said. "Do you know who was behind the Mask?"

"I do," I admitted. "Gráinne, the mistress of that safehouse and servant of Lord Andrell. She believed I was dead, thanks to a redcap who was less than impressed with his new employer. She spoke with Chernenkov afterwards, speaking of being the one to fight me."

"You don't understand how grievous this accusation is," Mabona told me. "If Andrell conceals a condemned woman *and* a Masked Lord, the fallout in the High Court will not be minor. The Lord of the Unseelie backed Andrell's play for this new Court himself."

I sighed.

"It's worse than that," I replied. "Up to that point, I believed Gráinne was doing this herself...but then Andrell arrived. We knew Chernenkov had a fae lover in the city.

"We didn't know it was Andrell himself."

"He knows she is condemned *and* her crimes," my Queen said levelly. "What is he thinking?"

"They are planning to destroy Oberis's Court," I said. "Some plan of the Masked Lords. Andrell serves them, if he isn't one of them."

She was silent. Someone else might have cursed by whatever gods they served, but it was hard to blaspheme when you *were* the closest available equivalent to a god.

"My Queen, I see no choice but to summon the Wild Hunt."

My words hung like anvils in the apartment the goblins had lent me, and they struck her like a blow.

"We...cannot," she finally told me. "I do not command the Hunt on my own. I must take this all to the High Court...and if I do, Andrell *will* be warned. I can trust the High Court, but they have assistants, friends, staff...and at least of one those will betray us."

Now it was my turn to be silent. I'd assumed all along that if I could prove Andrell had betrayed his oaths, the High Court would deal with him. My job had been to find the evidence to summon the Wild Hunt, not to stop him myself.

"My Queen...what do I do?" I finally asked.

"You must capture either Chernenkov or Gráinne," she told me. "Both are now condemned by *my* word and *my* authority. You must capture them, and you must bring them to me. I will take them to Ankaris and they will tell *him* the truth.

"Then...and *only* then, can we unleash the Wild Hunt upon Andrell without going to the entire High Court."

I swallowed. Gráinne had just obliterated me. Chernenkov had nearly killed me, two Gentry and a Noble when we'd fought. And my Queen wanted me to *capture* them?

"How?" I asked.

"Strand will fight with you," she told me. "The Valkyrie may have retired, but she knows her enemy. You have friends in the city, ones the Covenants say should not get involved.... Use them as best you can.

"But understand that this is a fae battle. The shifters and others can help you lure them out, but you and Inga must capture the Masked Lords' servants yourselves.

"If you have need of arms or armor, speak to Eric. Use your supposed death to deceive them. You are my Vassal, Jason Kilkenny. I know you will not fail me."

I SPENT THE DAY THINKING, trying to see a way through the task laid before me. I hadn't yet reached out to anyone, but I was still completely unsurprised when someone knocked on my door. It was a relief to see Shelly Fairchild…and a surprise to see Lan Tu.

"May we come in?" Shelly asked. "We didn't arrive together, if that's what you're wondering, but since we're both here, I figure we may as well all chat."

I chuckled and waved them in.

"I'd say my house is yours, but this is more Lan Tu's house than mine," I told them. "What can I do for you ladies?"

"My *trùm* sent me with a package for you," Lan Tu told me, the young goblin woman taking a seat at the kitchen table and laying a long, narrow box on the laminate in front of her. "He said to be clear that it was…" She paused, clearly trying to remember MacDonald's exact words. "He said it was 'a gift, not a boon.' And that you would understand what he meant."

I nodded slowly. Whatever was in the box, the Wizard did not regard it as payment of the boon he owed me for saving his life. It was a gift, offered without strings—a rare thing in the supernatural world.

I opened the box, completely unsure what I was going to find. Whatever I'd expected, however, it wasn't a sixteen-inch-long rod of black wood, laced with orichalcum runes along its entire length.

A baton?

"Why would the Wizard send me a baton?" I wondered aloud.

"He said you would ask exactly that question," Lan Tu told me with a small smile. Even with her tusks, the young goblin woman managed to be utterly adorable. From what I knew of the goblins in Calgary, assuming that *adorable* meant *harmless* would be unwise.

"He said to tell you to remember that he has seen you fight."

I'd fought the Wizard's traitorous minions in his own home. Plus, the Wizard's Sight meant that he could have watched almost any of my various fights over the months I'd been in Calgary. But what…

I finally caught up. I picked up the rod and flexed it experimentally. Despite its dark exterior, it moved easily. It was no hardwood, but exactly the kind of flexible wood that would have once served for a bow…or for a handle.

With a *snap*, I cracked the whip handle through the air, conjuring Fire and Force through it with carefully measured strength. My usual green faerie fire burned with an intensity I'd never commanded before, a new core of deadly white power.

"Is that...as terrifying a thing as I think it is?" Shelly asked carefully.

"Few are those men like my *trùm* forge arms for," Lan Tu said quietly. "Fewer still are those who receive those arms as gifts."

"I didn't think that the heirs of Merlin *gave* gifts," I told the goblin woman. "Not without strings, not without duties. Powers do not give gifts without price, Lan Tu. What does your master desire?"

"He said you would know," she replied. "He said you would say something of the sort—and that 'what would be done regardless cannot be regarded as a price.' He asks that only that you fulfill the oath you already swore and bring the monsters in his city to justice again."

I snorted. If MacDonald's price was that I dealt with Chernenkov and the Masked Lords, I would pay it gladly.

If his price was that I broke an Unseelie Court, defied a Power of the High Court, and challenged an order that had brought civil war to the fae for my entire life...well, MacDonald was right.

I was going to fulfill my oath.

———

ONCE LAN TU HAD LEFT, Shelly produced a bottle of wine and a pair of glasses from a bag. She filled the glasses and handed me one.

"I don't pretend to follow half of what goes on with you lot, but I'm right in that that's a spectacular gift, right?" she asked.

"MacDonald is a Power," I said quietly. "Basically, a little-g god. If he chose to, he could destroy Andrell's Court with a snap of fingers. But the Covenants and his own oath say he can't. But...he won't stand by and let Andrell cover for a murderer."

"So, he gives you that?" she gestured to the whip handle.

"Yeah. Lan Tu is right when she says there are few Wizard-forged weapons in the world, and the vast majority are in the hands of the Wizards' Augments, men and women like the Enforcers MacDonald used to have," I told her. "This is beyond spectacular, Shelly. But...the task I've been set is beyond impossible."

"So, the Wizard is giving you a chance?" she said.

"Maybe. It might be enough." I shook my head. "Might not be, either. I don't fucking know. I can't fight a Noble, Shelly, and my Queen wants me to defeat two—and take at least one prisoner."

The human sighed.

"And that's assuming Andrell doesn't try and stop you himself, I take it?" she asked.

"If Andrell tries to stop me, it's done," I admitted. "It's over. I can't fight a Fae Lord, Wizard-forged weapon or not."

I studied the black handle on the table, with its fitted shoulder holster. It was no real surprise that the holster fit my body as perfectly as the whip itself fit my hand. A Wizard's power was nothing to be trifled with.

MacDonald was an ally, possibly even a friend...and he *terrified* me.

"I'm guessing you had your own reasons to be here," I noted. "What have you got for me?"

"I went over the receipts and invoices you sent me. The ordering companies were fronts, lies and forgeries. I'm sure that's a surprise."

"I don't suppose you found anything useful?"

"I lost the trail in Cuba again, which I find fascinating," she replied. "Not a lot of people have the connections to run an ownership trail through Cuba. Panama? Sure. Monte Carlo? Definitely. Switzerland? Harder than it used to be, but still doable."

"*Cuba?* That's an odd one."

"Does that help us at all?" I asked.

"Interestingly...yes," Shelly told me with a chuckle. "Because so few could do that, they relied on that cover more than they should. And while *I* have no connections in Cuba, it happens that I go for lunch every couple of weeks with a lawyer who works for a company helping Cuba exploit their local oil reserves."

I blinked.

"So?"

"So, she managed to get someone in Cuba to trace the records for us," Shelly told me. "We didn't get all of them. There were more traces out of Cuba than I expected, and some of *those* disappeared in Panama and other places. A bunch went to Delaware, though, which is a pretty good shield."

"Delaware?"

"Lot of odd rules around ownership. It all traces back to about six law firms, to be honest, and I can't do much from there without asking questions that will draw attention," she admitted.

"Which means we know more but not anything useful," I noted.

She chuckled.

"I don't know who owns the end of the chain, no," she agreed. "What I did manage to do, however, was find some other things in Calgary they own...including a certain warehouse."

Now she had my attention.

"And what else?" I asked slowly.

"Nothing else as large," Shelly told me. "Another two dozen or so rental properties like the one Chernenkov was staying at. A handful of restaurants, a bar...and a motel on Sixteenth Ave."

"Give me the list," I said. "I need to go looking again."

She passed me a USB key.

"Be careful, Jason," she told me. "I don't think these are owned by the Unseelie Court. If these 'Masked Lords' are in play...these are their Calgary assets."

"I know," I confirmed. "But...I have a job to do."

Shelly shook her head.

"I don't envy you. Good luck."

26

INGA AND MARY showed up in the morning. Somehow, I was unsurprised that both women came equipped for war—and my lover showed up with a massive rolling suitcase that turned out to contain the two long arms I'd left in the wardrobe's hidden compartment.

"I don't have any spare MP5s," she noted, "but Talus said you'd know how to use this."

Not only was the Israeli-built .45 caliber Jericho automatic familiar, unless I was severely mistaken, it was the exact same gun I'd been given by Queen Mabona...and abandoned in a vampire den under the city.

Apparently, Talus's people had retrieved the weapon and hung onto it for the last six months.

"Yeah, I know this one," I admitted. I took the gun, double-checked its action and holster. "What about ammo?"

"We have a few magazines that should fit," Theino told me as the goblin stepped through the door. "And a stockpile of cold iron rounds." He shrugged with a degree of minor embarrassment. "We owe our lives to Talus, Master Kilkenny. That does not mean we weren't prepared for some of the fae to betray us."

"Thank you," I told him. I then caught up with the fact that the goblin was wearing a sleeveless tactical vest and had a .45 automatic of his own at his belt. "You look loaded for bear."

"Of course," he agreed, pulling a black bandana out and tying it across his face. "I will be coming with you. My people may hide from even the supernatural world, but we have our debts and we will not stand by while Talus's family and Court are threatened."

Inga snorted, the Valkyrie carrying none of the modern weaponry the rest of us were packing. She wore the silver blade of her old affiliation along with a pair of cold iron-bladed knives.

"Guns break and run out of ammunition," she told us. "Blades and spells are more reliable. Or claws, I suppose, in Ms. Tenerim's case."

Mary chuckled.

"Claws and teeth are all well and good, but when I shoot someone, I don't have to wash my mouth out with whisky afterwards," she noted. "And I don't have the speed or strength to want to tangle with any serious supernatural in hand-to-hand. As the saying goes: 'God made men and women, and Sam Colt made them equal.'"

"I'd rather you were nowhere *near* any fighting at all," I told Mary. "Of course, I lost that argument before I ever *met* you, so I don't even try anymore. Come on, then, all of you. I've got info from Shelly that gives us a place to start."

I'd borrowed a projector from the goblins and spent the night going over the data Shelly had given me. When I laid it over an online map, it gave us a set of red pins on the map I was showing on the living room wall.

"This was the safehouse." I tapped the pin in the northwest. "Has anyone checked that out since my...visit?"

"O'Malley went looking for you when he hadn't heard anything in a few hours," Mary told me. "He called it in; he was worried." She shrugged. "By morning, we saw them moving out. We tried to follow them, but there were a lot of vehicles and we only had three people on hand when they moved."

"I could hope, but I'm not surprised," I admitted. "I'm surprised O'Malley went looking for me. I told him not to."

She laughed.

"When O'Malley first met you, one of his friends was introducing your face to the pavement," she pointed out. "I think he feels he owes you something for that. And he wasn't dumb enough to try and rescue you; that's for sure."

"Was there anything left?" I asked.

"If there was, no one will ever know," Theino said grimly. "They set fire to the place and burned it all down. Fire department is still buzzing over just why there was so much gasoline in the place. Was supposed to be an industrial distribution center, after all."

"Damn." I wished I was surprised, but if there was anything the Masked Lords had to be good at to survive twenty-odd years of conflict against the Fae High Court, it was covering their tracks.

"We don't know any other locations of theirs for certain," I told my companions, then gestured at the map. "We have some possibilities, though. Blue pins are locations *I* know, official locales of the Unseelie Court in Calgary. Purple dots are locations where we can trace ownership into the same cluster of front companies and bullshit that owned the safehouse and the house Chernenkov was originally staying at, and were buying the guns and ammo that filled the safehouse.

"We can safely assume all of *that* has moved," I noted grimly. "Which means that our enemy has serious military-grade hardware at play."

"Love, there's a South African army battle rifle and a Russian assault shotgun leaning against the wall behind you," Mary reminded me. "Military-grade hardware is hardly a monopoly of our enemy."

"We have a handful of military small arms," I told her. "*They* have enough small and heavy arms to equip a special forces company. Guns, rocket launchers, grenade launchers, explosives." I shook my head. "Yeah, we have a lot of that, but not to this scale and quantity. The Masks are preparing for a war...and the target is the Calgary Seelie Court.

"If that strike gets launched, we've failed," I said flatly. "Open war in the fae community isn't something we can come back from. We can call the Hunt in at that point...but a lot of people will die."

"The Hunt is no more of a precise tool than any other military force," Inga agreed. "If Ankaris comes here to end a war between

Courts, dozens will die. He is…more of a blunt instrument than Cale-brant was."

"We know that Gráinne will probably be where Andrell is," I noted. "That's not a fight I want to pick. If we can lure her to a spot away from the Lord, we can go after her. Our easier target, in many ways, is the one we've been after from the beginning: Chernenkov."

"You are officially dead," Mary reminded me. "What's the plan?"

"Our most likely places for Chernenkov are these."

I tapped three locations on the map. I'd spent a lot of time thinking about it, and now I laid it out for my allies.

"The fourth most likely place is Andrell's Court itself, but I think he'll want to keep things separated for now," I noted. "The next up is a motel owned by the Masked Lords. It's still open, popular with mortal travelers, but they could tuck a few redcap mercs and Chernenkov in there.

"Second is an old-style pub in the northeast. It's not officially a hotel or boarding house, but they've got a couple of rooms upstairs.

"Third is one of the new hotels at the airport, which the Unseelie Court owns in its entirety through various fronts and funds," I concluded. "We need to check out all three."

"I can tell if she's at any of them," Mary told the others. "I know her scent."

"That might open up a solid option, then," Inga noted. "Mary and I go have lunch at the bar and the hotel, and Theino goes and sneaks around the motel."

"No one will see me," the goblin promised. "Few see a goblin unless we want them to—or a Viet Cong."

"I hate to ask this of—"

"Everyone in this damn room is a volunteer, *including* you, last I checked," Mary cut me off. "We'll find the bitch, Jason. And then, well, I bet you we can think of a way to use that to lure Gráinne out into the open, too.

"And if you give me a clean shot at the bitch that stuffed a cold iron dagger in my boyfriend's chest, believe me, she is *not* going to be running to Andrell to complain about Covenant violations."

IT WAS NOT my inclination to let others go into the field for me...but that our enemies believed me to be dead was one of our few advantages there. I kissed Mary goodbye and let my friends go out to see what they could find while I returned to the computer map and tried, desperately, to work out just what the Masked Lords' plan was.

I could see the logic behind their objective if I'd guessed it right. If Oberis's Court was destroyed, preferably in a way that couldn't be pinned on Andrell, then Andrell would find himself in the position Oberis had been in: the only Court in Calgary.

That Court would then be responsible for heartstone distribution, which would allow them to siphon off heartstone for the Masked Lords. Mixed with gold, it would provide them with the orichalcum for powerful magical weapons.

Mixed with mercury, it would provide them with quicksilver, the terrifyingly addictive but powerful substance that dramatically enhanced fae abilities. Armed with quicksilver in my blood, I'd been able to break through the barriers against teleportation and stepping Between that MacDonald had woven over his Tower.

Without it, well, the "merely" gnome-forged barriers the Masked Lords had used against me had stolen my strongest defense and tool when I fought Gráinne. If I could avoid being trapped like that again, the Wizard's gift might even the odds between me and the Fae Noble.

Might. We were talking about a *Noble*, after all. Who was I to think I even stood a chance?

I sighed and studied the map.

A single Court that they controlled would be an unending supply of advantages for the Masked Lords. It would give them somewhere to store weapons without fear of discovery. A place for safehouses no one would be hunting. A strong home base that they could strike from with impunity.

In fact, it was almost a surprise that they hadn't had one before. I didn't know enough fae history to be sure of that, though. All I knew about the Masked Lords had come from Inga.

That they'd killed three Powers was terrifying, but they'd then disappeared for my entire life. A few conflicts here and there, and now this. Was this an example of what they'd been doing in those previous incidents? Laying groundwork for takeovers, burying resources, making allies?

It was...all too likely. Control of Calgary and the heartstone supply would be a powerful tool in their arsenal.

On the other hand, to pull that off, they needed to make sure that the attack wasn't blamed on Andrell. Which, I supposed, was what Chernenkov was there for. A rogue actor with her own grudge against Calgary's Nobles and Vassal...

Fuck.

She'd never meant to detonate the chlorine bomb. There were reasons for a Pouka to do so—fear seasoned the meat for them, as I understood—but they really didn't justify an atrocity of that scale.

And she'd never meant to carry it out. That was how *we'd* known she was there. She hadn't been betrayed. The whole fight at the Stampede had been a setup.

Which meant there was one more factor in play, one more potential thread to pull that we hadn't even though of.

The laptop I'd been given didn't have much in terms of software, but Talus had seen it loaded with an encrypted and anonymous Fae-Net email, with at least his address in its memory.

The email I sent was short and to the point:

Who told us Chernenkov was coming?!

IT TURNED out that Talus had left video-call software on the laptop as well, which promptly started ringing about ten minutes later. I accepted the call to find myself looking at the older fae's office. I'd never actually *been* to Talus's office—my understanding was that even Oberis didn't know where his right-hand man hung his hat in Calgary —but from the view, it was somewhere in downtown.

Somewhere *very high* in downtown.

A moment after the call started, Talus himself stepped back into the view of the camera and dropped into an expensive-looking black leather executive chair.

"Sorry, I was adjusting the camera to, well, hide my office," he told me with a mischievous grin. "We need to talk, but I'm not giving away *all* of my secrets."

"We do need to talk," I agreed. "Chernenkov was never going to blow the Stampede, Talus. That whole thing was a setup—to get *us* to give her a reason to go after Oberis's Court with mercs and firepower."

Talus's amusement dissolved.

"Fuck. You're sure?"

"They didn't exactly hand me their business plan," I said drily. "But it adds up. The Masked Lords need a base, and they needed a 'rogue operator' to clean out Oberis's Court without landing the blame on Andrell. Which brings me back to my question, Talus. Who told us Chernenkov was coming?"

"We have a lot of information channels," Talus said slowly, his fingers flying over a keyboard I can barely see. "I think...yeah, that one originally came through one of our *mortal* information channels; someone flagged some odd combinations of names and supplies.

"Secondary validation was...from the Unseelie themselves, a Noble in the Lord of the Unseelie's staff named...*fuck.*"

"Talus?" I demanded.

"It was Gráinne," he told me. "Gráinne Coghlan. Now, of course, the right-hand woman of Lord Andrell."

"And the one person in this city I *know* to be a damned Masked Lord," I replied. "That doesn't really help us. Who was the mortal source?"

"Kuang runs our mortal intelligence network," he said slowly. "Jiang Kuang, at Masters and Co. One of the interface firms."

"I know them," I said grimly. "I even know him. I think I need to pay a visit."

"Jason, you're supposed to be *dead*," he pointed out. "That has advantages still."

"Yes, and if I show up in supernatural spaces, that's a problem. But Kuang works in an office where we quite specifically have no other supernatural presence. And even if he knows enough to know I'm supposed to be dead, I think I can convince him to stay quiet."

Talus sighed.

"I can't take care of it myself," he admitted. "Be careful."

"Aren't I always?"

"No," he said flatly. "No, you aren't. Don't get yourself killed for real, Kilkenny."

27

I'D MEMORIZED the layout of the building Masters' firm was in when I'd needed to go back to pick up the Escalade after the attack on Mary. There were several quiet corners and utility sections where people rarely went, and I stepped out of Between into one of those.

If I'd been ten seconds later, I'd have caused some unfortunate problems. Instead, when the building maintenance worker came around the corner, she found me shaking off the fuzz of teleporting into a building and looking dazed.

"Hey," she barked. "You're not supposed to be back here."

I was over the daze by now, but I let it infuse my voice anyway as I turned to her.

"Sorry, miss. I was looking for the bathroom?" Between the daze and the drawl, I probably sounded like a complete moron, but that served my purposes at this exact moment.

She shook her head exasperatedly.

"Getting back here looking for the bathroom takes some doing," she noted. "I'm going to have to talk to my guys; there shouldn't even have been an unlocked door!"

I blinked at her in faked confusion.

"I thought the door was for a bathroom and kept going," I told her. "Am I close?"

"Are you close?" she echoed with a laugh, her exasperation still present but muted at the apparently harmless idiot in front of her. "No. Wrong side of the building entirely. Look." She stepped over to me and pointed down the utility corridor. "You go down that hallway, grab the door on the left. That'll let you into the *public* section of the building. Go left, follow that hall to the end, turn right, and the bathrooms are on the left.

"You got that?"

"I got it," I told her. "Thanks, miss."

I gave her my best "Southern idiot" grin and followed her directions out into the hallway. From there, I grabbed the elevator instead of the bathroom and went up to the top floor.

I entered Masters and Co's offices with a firm stride, barely slowing as I came through the door, and then came to a rest at the front desk.

"I need to speak to Mr. Kuang about my employer's accounts," I told the receptionist crisply. The young man looked almost as confused as I had pretended earlier—and then I reeled off the name of one of Talus's larger holding companies.

"Of course, sir!" he said instantly. "Let me see if he's free."

For an account of the size I was claiming to represent, I'd be stunned if Kuang didn't manage to find himself suddenly available.

———

IT TOOK LESS than five minutes before the receptionist escorted me back to Kuang's office. Only the two managers at the firm were familiar with me, which helped cover my tracks, but I needed to be careful regardless.

As soon as I entered Jiang Kuang's office, however, he recognized me. He also, clearly, recognized that something unusual was going on.

"That will be all, Wesley," he told the receptionist. "Thank you. Close the door on the way out please."

The young man stepped outside, closing the door behind him, and Kuang regarded me levelly.

"Lying to get into my office is rarely to anyone's benefit," he told me. "On the other hand, that you even *had* that name to conjure with tells me Talus sent you, even if you don't represent that company in question. What do you want, Kilkenny? The follow-up meeting Masters scheduled is in a few days."

"Didn't anyone tell you?" I asked as I took the chair he specifically hadn't offered me. "I'm dead. Your meeting will have to get rearranged with Eric."

"Dead," he echoed. "I'm…unfamiliar with fae corpses, but you look rather alive to me. Politics, I presume?"

"Politics," I confirmed. "I will need you to keep that you ever saw me very, very quiet."

"Mr. Kilkenny, this company's *purpose* is to allow your people to interface with the mortal world without anyone even learning you exist. Discretion is quite literally our stock in trade."

"I need you to keep my current status from *all* of your contacts," I told him flatly. "Seelie. Unseelie. Humans with…interesting contacts. I believe you even do work for the shifters in the city."

"Not much, not yet," he told me. "That section is pretty heavily firewalled for privacy, but it's growing. What do you need, Mr. Kilkenny? My discretion can be assumed."

"Can it?" I murmured. "I'm not sure I believe that, but then, I have evidence you're working for at least one employer we don't know about."

The hesitant pause as he reached for his coffee cup would probably have been invisible to a human. Kuang was *very* well controlled.

"I… We have many contracts and deals," he finally said. "We keep their nature secret. If you knew all of our clients, Mr. Kilkenny, we wouldn't be doing our jobs."

"And if you betrayed us for money, you definitely weren't," I told him. "Who paid you to tell us the Pouka was coming?"

He took a sip of his coffee and laid it down on the desk.

"Talus pays me to maintain a network of contacts that is far from legal under mortal law," he pointed out calmly. "The information came through that network and I passed it on to him. I understand that he validated it separately."

"He did. But that validation was from someone I now suspect is an enemy," I said calmly. "Which leaves me with every reason to suspect the initial source of the information. And you, Mr. Kuang, are *lying to me.*"

It was more than a guess but less than a certainty. He was *too* controlled in his motions, too sure in his words. He'd gone into full legal-defense mode, a state that would have fooled any human. But habits and skills learned to deceive humans didn't work on fae.

He went for a panic button. My hand was out without thinking, telekinetic force wrapping around his wrist to freeze him in place. He tried to go for it with his other arm, and I sent him spinning across the room in the swivel chair as I vaulted the desk.

Kuang landed flat on his back on the floor and I knelt next to him.

"I have no desire for this to get ugly," I told him, "though I find myself wondering just who that panic button calls that you thought it was worth pressing on *me.*"

He coughed.

"The Unseelie," he admitted. "It's supposed to go to one of their Nobles' cellphones. Not sure how fast they'd get here."

"Not fast enough," I told him. "Listen to me, Jiang. You've stepped into the middle of a war you know nothing about and have betrayed not merely Oberis but the Fae High Court. You're a mortal, in the know, and in the service of a Fae Court...and you betrayed the High Court.

"Your life is *mine.*"

I suspected he was quite sure that I wouldn't kill him in cold blood. He was even right. That didn't mean this was a conversation he wanted to have.

"Chernenkov and Andrell's Court weren't here yet," I concluded. "You had a contact. Someone who gave you information and paid you to make sure Talus knew about it. Didn't you?"

He looked up at me from the floor and I watched the fight go out of him.

"Until Andrell showed up, I didn't know there even *was* another faction at play," he told me. "I thought someone was paying me to *help* you guys.

"And then, once the Unseelie showed up, this scary-tall Irish lady showed up, told me I'd betrayed Oberis in taking the money and was utterly fucked. If I helped them out, they'd protect me and see me paid."

"And if you didn't, they'd make sure Oberis learned you were on the take," I said. "How many other sweetheart deals did you have?"

From his terrified expression, more than we would have preferred. Most of them had almost certainly involved breaking the very confidentiality his business relied on, but only to other supernaturals.

"Who was your contact?" I demanded.

"Anonymous email originally," he said desperately. "Had the right tags to hit my inbox without going to spam, but no sender. Just a promise of money and information.

"Met someone at a bar at the new airport hotel. They gave me a flash drive with the information and a draft on a numbered company for fifty grand. Like I said...I thought I was being paid to help out."

I sighed.

That was useful background, but it didn't really tell me anything useful. Except...

"They asked you for more data," I said sharply. "What did you give them?"

He cringed away from me, but my sympathy suddenly evaporated.

"What did you give them, Jiang?"

"I told them where Talus's office is," he said quietly. "She asked this morning. I don't know..."

"Do you have any idea how badly you've betrayed the Courts?" I asked him, then shook my head. "It doesn't matter. I'm glad you came clean. We may still be able to salvage something from this. But I need you to tell me *exactly* what you told her."

I didn't know where Talus operated from, but if I was going to save his life...I needed to know.

Now.

———

OF COURSE, Talus's office was in one of the most expensive, most prestigious buildings in downtown...which made it one of the busiest, most crowded and most *public* buildings. I didn't know the layout well enough to step Between directly to a quiet spot in his offices, either.

Fortunately, the Court maintained several facilities downtown that I was more familiar with. Knowing those spaces would, if nothing else, be clear of mortals allowed me to cut an hour or so off my rush to get to Talus's office.

The handful of people inside the print shop I materialized in stared at me in shock. Just because they were all fae didn't mean they were used to watching people appear out of thin air, after all.

None of them were people I knew well, which meant that, today at least, I didn't know I could trust them. I gave them a calm nod and strode out into the front half of the print shop—a facility we maintained because, well, even supernaturals needed business cards and pamphlets, and some of those shouldn't be printed by mortal hands.

The young woman managing the front desk was a changeling I had met before, but she missed me emerging behind her because she was utterly focused on the customer in front of her.

Which was fair. Robert was a Fae Noble, after all, and there was a lot about him that could be distracting if you were attracted to men. For myself, my main priority was that he was *here* and powerful enough to make a difference if I was about to go toe-to-toe with Chernenkov and her friends.

"Robert, we have a problem," I told him, cutting into his flirtation with the changeling. He blinked in confusion for a moment, then caught up.

"What kind of problem?" he asked, snapping into readiness mode before he even processed that I was supposed to be dead. "Kelly, to me!"

His Gentry escort seemed to materialize out of nowhere, the young-looking woman nodding to me politely as she joined her ward-slash-boss.

"Unless I'm severely mistaken, Maria Chernenkov is about to storm your father's office with a posse of redcap mercenaries," I told him. "We need to get there *now*."

"I..." Robert swallowed. "That's a hell of a status report, Jason. Plus...aren't you *dead*?"

"Rumors exaggerate, et cetera, et cetera," I told him. "Chernenkov is coming for the Court and I don't care *what* tricks are up her sleeve; she isn't going after Oberis while Talus or you are alive."

Fighting a Fae Lord was suicide. Fighting a Fae Lord with his Nobles at his side? I wasn't sure what the term for that was. *Already dead* probably covered it.

So, Chernenkov would go for the Nobles—Talus and Robert. One at a time.

Robert coughed delicately.

"I'm with you, Jason," he told me. "But...truth is, even *I* don't know where Talus has his office."

Robert might be Talus's son, but he'd been unacknowledged until very recently. The two were still working out their relationship, and Talus was apparently truly paranoid about his home base.

"Fortunately, the same *idiot* who told Chernenkov where it is told me," I replied. "It's only a couple of blocks from here, but..."

"We'll need to clear the building," Kelly suggested instantly, the blonde Gentry in the process of tying her hair back. "I suggest calling in a bomb threat to 911?"

"If you've got to move, you've got to move," the changeling at the cash desk told us. "I barely followed your conversation, but I can bloody well call in that I overhead a bomb threat if you give me the address, eh?"

28

Timing was everything.

In this case, timing was…not quite fast enough

We could only move so quickly through the crowded streets of downtown. All three of us were armed, and this was *not* a city where we wanted to draw attention to that. Shoulder holsters were only so stealthy in weather where a suit jacket made you look overdressed and on your way to melting.

It didn't bother *me* as much as it clearly bothered the locals—what the southern US states regarded as "hot" would have turned this entire city into a pool of sweat—but Kelly and Robert looked clearly uncomfortable in the blazers they wore to cover their guns.

We were halfway there when a helicopter buzzed overhead. The green-painted Canadian Forces vehicle had no business in downtown Calgary—a suspicion only aggravated when it flew into a landing on the roof of the tower we were headed to.

Robert and I shared a look.

"They had a pile of military gear," I noted.

"Fuck us all," he replied. "Let's move!"

Police sirens began to echo as we moved, the city's mortal guardians moving to protect the innocent from the threat we'd arranged to call in. We needed them to make sure the innocents were removed from the building—but *we* needed to get into the building before the cops arrived.

We picked up the pace, moving toward the building even as the first crowds began to exit it. Whatever alarms were ringing weren't audible from the outside, and we made it all the way to the entrance before we saw anyone directing people outside.

"Keep moving, people," a uniformed security guard was telling everyone. "There's a developing situation; we need you to evacuate. We'll let you know when it's safe to come back in."

I led my companions in, ducking through a door that didn't have any guards next to it and over to the elevator.

"They're locked down," Kelly said after poking at the buttons. "Probably waiting on police or fire keys; they're evacuating everyone through the stairs."

"That rules out us going up the stairs," I replied quietly. I studied the elevator doors for a moment. "Robert, you up to picking locks?"

The young Noble stepped up to the elevator call panel and waved a hand over it. There was a crunching sound, hopefully inaudible at a distance, and the Down button flashed live.

"Picking, no," he said cheerfully. "Forcing? Yeah, sure."

The elevator doors slid open and we were inside before anyone could question us. I slammed the button to close the doors and repeated Robert's trick with the outside lock to unlock the panel.

"Top floor," I said aloud as I hit the button. "Of course he's on the top floor."

"I'm guessing the helicopter wasn't friendlies," Kelly replied. "I suppose they knew about the top floor too?"

"Yeah," I confirmed. "I got the address from the same people they did."

The elevator started moving and I shook my head.

"I just hope that this elevator gets us up there while Talus is still holding out."

THE ELEVATOR OPENED to the sound of gunfire.

It wasn't directed at us, which was a momentary relief. It was, however, directed at the dozen or so staff running for the door to the stairwell. A mix of changelings, fae, and regular humans, none of whom really had any business in a fight without at least being armed.

Four redcaps with automatic weapons turned the lobby of the building's top floor into a slaughterhouse. Cold iron bullets were overkill, but they were what the bastards had—and they made sure that even the Lesser Fae and changelings in that crowd weren't getting back up.

Robert was moving before I could even think to react. I was faster than a human, but the Fae Noble with me was faster still. Glamor-forged armor flashed into existence around him, glittering silver plate that clung to every line of his body like a second skin.

He didn't even bother with his gun this time, just conjuring the same glamor-blades Gráinne had used against me as he waded into the redcaps.

They had enough time to realize what the hell was going on and then he was in the middle of them. One redcap went down in pieces— and then Kelly and I opened fire.

We each took down one of them and Robert tore the last one in half.

"Some of these people may live," Kelly said as she dropped to her knees among the wounded. "What do we do?"

I traded looks with Robert. Three of us...and Robert was the most powerful, but *also* the only one with any Healing gift.

"We owe them," I said quietly. "Your *family* owes them."

"And you?" he asked. "Against Chernenkov?"

I smiled thinly, holstered my gun and drew the Wizard's gift. The whip handle was warm in my hand, its power flickering against my skin.

"I beat her once," I replied. "I can fight her. I can't heal these people."

"Kelly, go with Jason," he ordered. The silver plate dissolved from his skin as he knelt down next to her amongst the wounded, summoning the white glow of his Healing Gift around his hands. "Save my father. Do what you must."

"I will," she promised. "Kilkenny?"

Fire flickered around the tip of the whip handle and I smiled grimly.

"I swore an oath," I told her. "Let's go."

———

I DIDN'T KNOW where we would find Talus on the top floor office, but there was an easy solution to that: following the screaming and the sound of gunfire. Unfortunately for us, a second fire team of redcaps was using the same logic and checking in on their missing friends.

We came around a corner and found ourselves face to face. Kelly fired first and I *stepped* as the assault rifles opened up.

Bullets flashed through where I'd been standing as I emerged behind the redcaps, a whip of green-white faerie fire slashing across the hallway at neck height. A redcap went down to gunfire, a second to my flame, and the survivors tried to focus on both me and Kelly at the same time.

It didn't end well for them.

Kelly charged over their bodies to join me, then stumbled backward as a new player entered the fight. The nightmare I'd run into in the safehouse was *here*, the ash-skinned woman blurring into Kelly in a full-body blow that probably would have thrown *me* out the side of the building.

The Gentry merely stumbled, then returned the blow. The two women swerved around each other, bullets and fire flashing at a pace even I could barely follow.

"I've got her," Kelly barked. "*Go.*"

The nightmare took advantage of her distraction to break her arm, a sickening cracking sound that echoed in the hallway. For a moment, I hesitated.

Then Kelly snapped her arm back into place, healing it in time to smash her fist into the other fae's face. The nightmare went flying into the plaster wall and crashed into the office next to us.

"Go!" the Gentry repeated.

I went. Gentry versus Greater Fae like the nightmare was a roughly even fight, one that Kelly would probably win—but one my involvement might not change the tide of. Or at least, not fast enough to be worth the effort.

Not when Talus's life was still at stake.

Through the corridor the nightmare had emerged from was what *had* been a solid steel security shutter. It had slammed shut, probably as soon as the first wave of mercenaries had entered the building. Since then, someone had half-melted, half-torn it from its hinges.

I charged over the wreckage of the shutter into what had clearly been Talus's inner sanctum. There appeared to be a couple of offices inside the reinforced security shell, but mostly it was a wide-open area that looked like it belonged in a museum.

There was everything from golden artifacts that looked like they predated the Pyramids to a carefully maintained but half-burnt-out multi-barreled rocket launcher from the Second World War. Some of the artifacts in the room radiated Power, but most were just…historical. Or gold. Or otherwise valuable.

It was a trophy chamber that was probably worth more than the building it was inside…and half of the display cases were wrecked. A business-suited woman—not, I was glad to realize, Shelly—was sprawled against one of the office doors, her throat torn out.

Another half dozen redcaps were in the room, setting up a drill of some kind against the security shutters that had dropped down around the main office. That office was up against the wall of the building, almost certainly the one Talus had called me from.

Presumably, he was inside. Behind the redcaps, the familiar form of a black, pony-sized horse with vicious fangs stalked. A pair of black-dressed Gentry, one man and one woman, stood next to her.

Both Gentry paused and turned to face me as I entered. So did the Pouka.

"You're *dead*," she hissed. "I *saw* your corpse. Gráinne killed you!"

"Like you, it seems I take more killing than that," I told her—and snapped my faerie-flame whip out to its full extension. "I'll be sure to try harder this time."

UNFORTUNATELY FOR ME, Chernenkov apparently didn't care about little me that much.

"*Deal with him,*" she hissed to her Gentry minions. "The rest of you —crack this damn shell!"

Both of the black-clad Gentry promptly produced long-bladed knives. Silver-handled knives with cold iron blades.

The damn things were almost a stereotype...but they were a stereotype for a reason, and the Gentry *blurred* toward me with a speed I could never match.

I wasn't there when they arrived, stepping Between across the room to emerge behind them as they came to a confused halt. I slashed out with the whip, trying to disarm the woman. She felt the whip coming, however, and dodged, twisting out of the way of the blow as her lover charged me again.

He caught air as I stepped Between again, curses filling the air as I emerged next to the woman.

This time, she didn't quite dodge the whip. She managed to twist so I missed the knife...and I managed to twist so I caught her wrist.

My flame on its own was hot enough to burn. I could hurt supernaturals with it, damage them, distract them...but on its own, I could never sever flesh and bone. Especially not *Gentry* flesh and bone, known for standing up to everything up to anti-tank rounds.

With the Wizard's gift, however, my whip of flame burned white-hot, and even flesh that would have punched through steel gave way. My whip wrapped around the Gentry's wrist and seared clean through her. The cold iron knife fell to the ground with her hand still attached, and a scream of agony echoed through the museum-like trophy room.

The boyfriend came for me with his knife—and the now one-handed woman pulled a gun. Gunfire echoed again in the exposed space, but I had already stepped Between. She'd chosen her angle poorly and her bullets slammed into one of the redcaps, sending him careening away from the drill as cold iron rounds tore through flesh and magic alike.

"You. Will. Burn. For. That."

Yeah. She was angry.

Gunfire echoed again and again as she tracked the pistol after me. I flickered in and out of reality she could see, trying to taunt her into wasting ammunition, into spending her bullets on me.

Unfortunately, the other Gentry caught what I was doing, and I missed him changing course. I stepped out of Between into a clothes-lining arm. I'd at least had him enough off balance to avoid getting knifed, but I stumbled backward as his arm hammered into my throat.

Bullets barely missed me…and then the woman finally ran out, the automatic clicking on empty as she howled at me and charged.

She didn't reach me.

The metal shell around Talus's office exploded perfectly. The debris blasted outward in a pattern that was clearly controlled, clearly guided by the will of the powerful supernatural being these idiots had *dared* attack.

Gentry flesh could withstand tank rounds—but tank rounds didn't move as fast as those chunks of steel. Talus's attack ripped the charging Unseelie into a dozen pieces.

The boyfriend got off lighter, thrown backward as several chunks of steel hammered into him. Unfortunately for him, I was right there— and my whip of faerie flame sliced as easily through his neck as it had through the woman's wrist.

The redcaps didn't even have time to realize how severe their mistake had been before the scything debris cut them down.

Chernenkov, however, flickered into shadow before the steel hit her. Debris smashed display cases and walls, revealing the heavy metal of the outer security walls, but it missed her.

And me. It all missed me. If I hadn't guessed the nature of the explosion by how perfectly it had shredded my opponents, the complete lack of even a scratch on myself would have given it away.

The figure emerging from the wreckage was the final clue, however. Silver plate of glamor wrapped itself around Talus as one of the swords in the trophy cases flipped across the room to him.

This was the grown-up version of the knives the Gentry had come at me with. A massive bastard sword with a silver hilt gnome-forged onto a cold-hammered iron blade, with orichalcum runes inlaid onto both handle and blade.

"You wanted me out of my shell," he told Chernenkov as the sword lit up with the power forged into its runes. "Here I am."

He smiled thinly as the Pouka Noble re-formed from the shadows she'd hidden in.

"Bitch."

———

IF THERE WAS one thing Chernenkov didn't lack, it was courage. The clawed horse snarled and charged at him. She was fast, too. Faster than I remembered her being—which tied into the logic of the Stampede attack being a setup.

While she probably hadn't planned on being blown up as part of it, she'd been holding back, *intending* to lose. Now...now she wasn't, and even Talus was hard pressed to get his sword in place to parry as she was on top of him, claws and teeth and flaming breath *everywhere*.

All I could do was watch for a few seconds, unable to follow the fight well enough to risk interjecting my own abilities. Then, finally, there was a pulse of telekinetic energy and Talus *flung* her backward.

Along with everything else within five or six feet of him. A display case shattered and a wall was stripped bare, exposing the armor beneath.

She snarled—and I hit her with my best shot, focusing all of my Power into a telekinetic blow that would have snapped a car in half. It picked her up and tossed her across the trophy room, but she skittered to a halt with her claws embedded in the floor.

Then Chernenkov shifted, moving from the black horse into the dark-haired woman I'd become frustratingly familiar with. She responded to my kinetic strike in kind, a wave of Force flashing across the room that picked me up and flung me backward.

To my surprise, I managed to slow my flight, controlling my motion with my own Gift and landing upright as she snarled at me. Fire flashed toward me, but I stepped Between to avoid it.

Her moment of distraction hadn't helped her. Talus was on her, the cold iron sword lashing out in a series of blows that would have overcome any defense *I* could muster.

The Pouka, however, was a shapeshifter. Her body flowed like a shadowy liquid, dodging around the sword and Talus's glamor-strikes as she closed with the Fae Noble again.

This time, though, I was certain enough of where she was to strike. A whip of Fire lashed out, wrapping around her torso and *yanking* her backward, away from my friend.

She snarled—and Talus struck, a lightning-fast decapitating blow that *should* have ended the fight then and there.

Something...happened instead. My whip collapsed, holding nothing as she turned to shadow, diving forward and *into* Talus. Claws of shadow tore through his glamored armor, ripping out chunks of his flesh, and the black horse took shape again.

Her long head snapped down into his chest, tearing at his chest as she tried to rip out his heart. The sword went flying as power flared around Talus, energy pulsing as he tried to throw her away again.

It didn't work. She was half-shadow and half-claws, tearing into his flesh, and for a moment, all I could do was watch as she killed my friend.

And then I did what I could. I charged across the room, flicking Between to cross the distance in a fraction of a second, and I was on Chernenkov with fists and feet and flaming whip. Force augmented my blows and the whip handle smashed into her face repeatedly, flinging her away from Talus.

The Fae Noble was collapsed on the floor, his wounds *steaming* with the Pouka's venom, and the black horse hissed at me.

I conjured a second kinetic blast...and this time, the window was behind her. Chernenkov smashed into and through the glass, the window of the fiftieth-story office shattering under her weight as she went flying into the air.

She didn't reach the ground. Somewhere between there and the ground I saw her turn into a shadow...but she was running.

She was running north.

She was running toward the airport, almost certainly to Gráinne's hotel safehouse.

Talus coughed up blood.

"Fuck," he gasped. "You aren't...supposed to be here."

"Nope. Complaining?" I asked.

"Hell, no. I owe you." He carefully shook his head. "I'll heal...but not quickly. Where'd she go?"

"There's a hotel they're using as a safehouse near the airport," I said. "I think Inga and Mary are there."

Talus closed his eyes.

"You can step Between," he told me. "I'll be fine. *Go.*"

"Robert and Kelly are here, taking care of your people."

"That's good to know." He gasped again as new steam vented from one of his wounds. "Go," he repeated.

He was the Noble. I was merely the Hunter's changeling.

I went.

29

ONE OF THE reasons the trap Gráinne had set for me had nailed me quite thoroughly was that I wasn't used to stepping Between being blocked anywhere. From the fiftieth story of a downtown office tower to the parking lot of an expensive airport traveler's hotel was a five-minute walk through the Between, and there were no barriers to slow me down.

I emerged in the shadow of the artificial hill shielding the hotels from the highway, somewhat visible from the road. I figured I could be reasonably confident no one zipping down the highway from the airport was paying close-enough attention to the hotels to see someone appear out of thin air.

And anyone who did see me would assume they'd just missed me earlier. We put a *lot* of effort into the Covenants of Silence, but humanity's own miraculous ability to self-delude was our greatest ally.

From where I appeared, it was a ten-second scrabble up the hill and I was in the parking lot of the hotel. I spotted the dark green car Theino's grandfather had once used to rescue me from vampires in one corner and sighed.

Everyone was here. This...could get really ugly, really fast, and there were mortals everywhere. There was no self-delusion in the world that would save us if an Aesir, a Noble, a Hunter's changeling and a goblin threw down in public.

There were three restaurants attached to the hotel, and I paused in the hotel lobby, considering which one was most likely to be where my friends had ended up.

"May I help you, sir?"

Of course. This was a *nice* hotel, which meant I couldn't rely on being ignored. Plus, well, I looked like I'd just been in a fight and scrabbled up a hillside. Dirt and ash were all over my coat, and I smiled brightly at the neatly dressed young man checking in on me like it didn't matter.

"I'm meeting some friends in one of the restaurants," I told him. "But I forgot to ask which one. Tall blonde woman and a redhead? Might have been accompanied by a man with a face-mask?" I shook my head jokingly. "He's OCD about germs, the silly man."

"Ah, yes..." The staffer was still taken aback by my appearance, but he clearly knew who I meant. He pointed to the attached steakhouse. "I believe they went for lunch there, sir."

"Thank you!"

I gave the man another cheerful smile and strode toward the restaurant. On the way across the lobby, I realized that there was probably visible blood on my coat on top of the ash and mud. No wonder the hotel staff were being taken aback.

"Um, sir, may I...help you?" the hostess asked as I entered the restaurant.

I'd already spotted Mary past her, so I just smiled and pointed.

"I see my friends over there; I'm good."

She looked tempted to try and argue over whether I should go into the restaurant in my dirty clothes, but I swept past her before she could try and dropped myself at the table.

"Isn't this a bit more public than you were planning on being?" Mary asked immediately. "Are you okay?"

"I'm fine. Talus is hurt. *She* is on her way here."

The table went dead silent.

"Then our conversation before you arrived will be most relevant," Theino finally told me, pitching his voice so only his supernatural table companions could hear him. "This hotel has done their best to appear to follow the superstition of having no thirteenth floor, but I wandered up a few floors and measured the heights.

"There may not be an elevator button for it, but there most definitely is a thirteenth floor—and it's not the one they've labeled the fourteenth," he concluded. "Which suggests, of course, that if there's a safehouse here beyond them simply booking rooms..."

"It's on that floor," Inga finished for him. "Are you ready to start a war, Kilkenny?"

"Hell, no," I told her. "But they already did. Are you ready to help me finish one, Ms. Strand?"

"Since before you were born, child. Since before you were born."

———

WE LEFT cash on the table to pay for our meal—with a generous tip, I suspected, though it wasn't like I'd seen the receipt—and headed for the stairwell. Several hotel staff half-tripped as I passed them, clearly taken aback at my rather...unusual appearance.

"Tell me: am I bleeding on the carpet?" I murmured to Mary.

She snorted.

"No, but somebody definitely bled on you. Not sure the staff are picking that up so much as just all of the mud, though."

I shrugged. There wasn't much I could do about it. Talus or Robert could have glamored themselves to look normal. I didn't have that option.

Once in the stairwell, however, there was no one to give me unusual looks, and I took a small moment of relief in that, even as we climbed up thirteen floors. The blank wall between the twelfth and fourteenth floors, however, mocked us.

"In a regular hotel, this might be a maintenance floor, only accessed by the utility elevator," Mary pointed out. "Or there's a secret entrance..."

"Or it doesn't matter," Inga replied. She gestured and I felt her Gift flare to life. One moment, it was a plain wall, with the almost-decorative false-stone pattern so common in modern buildings.

The next, it turned out that there *was* a secret door—as the Valkyrie tried to tear a hole through the wall and the entire panel came out under her strike. Plaster and brick shattered, the metal framework of the concealed door clattering to the floor like thunder.

"No one missed that," Theino said calmly, ditching his blazer to reveal the same Kevlar vest he'd been wearing earlier and a concealed harness for a machine pistol of the same ilk as the one Mary carried. "Not fae. Not mortal. They know we're here."

I wasn't sure just *where* Inga's sword appeared from, but it was in her hand as the goblin spoke. Mary's machine pistol was out, and her pupils thinned as she drew more of her bestial other nature into herself.

I slipped the black wooden stock out of its holster and let its runes warm my skin.

"Chernenkov probably hasn't made it here yet," I pointed out. "Let's go find out who she was running to."

30

THE THIRTEENTH FLOOR of the hotel wasn't laid out like a hotel. It looked like there might be some hotel rooms at one end of it, but the side we entered had a wide-open lobby that looked like it could be closed off into individual conference rooms.

The wreckage of the door lay in the middle of one side as we entered. Most of the space was empty, but a small cluster of fae had been having some kind of discussion at the other end of the lobby-slash-conference room—next to what looked like a vault entrance.

Knowing Unseelie—knowing supernaturals in general—it was probably an armory. The way half of the people in the room had rushed through the heavy metal door when we'd arrived suggested that guess was correct.

Somehow, I was unsurprised to see that the central figure in the group of half a dozen fae was Gráinne herself, her hag friend at her side. The Unseelie Noble stepped out to face the intruders, but whatever she'd been ready to say died on her lips as she saw me.

"*You*," she hissed. "That's not possible. *You're dead.*"

"And how would you be so sure of that?" I asked as my friends spread out around me. "As I recall, the person who shoved a dagger in my heart was a Masked Lord, someone so *very* confident in their ability to tell me that my Queen would follow me into death.

"Unless you were there, Gráinne, how would you know?" I gestured around us. "Though, so far as we can tell, this place is a safe-house for the Masked Lords, which means I must demand your surrenders until we can bring in investigators from the High Court's staff to go over the place with a fine-toothed comb."

"This is a secure facility of the Unseelie Court. You have no authority here, *Seelie*," she spat.

I sighed.

"Miss Gráinne, you forget yourself," I warned her. "I am a Vassal of the Queen of the Fae. My authority is the High Court's authority and I speak for them, not the local Seelie Court. You are all suspected of treason against the fae. Lay down your weapons."

The Unseelie Noble chuckled sadly.

"It seems you are harder to kill than I expected, but all you have achieved is the death of your friends," she told me. The cold iron mask materialized in her hand, teleporting from wherever it was stored by some inherent magic of the mask itself.

"We both know how this ends," she told me as she placed the mask on her face, the glamor sweeping over her to render her unrecogniz-able once more. "We both know the steps. But so be it. Let us dance."

I smiled.

"You forget one thing," I told her. "Here, you haven't trapped me in one world. Plus, well."

The whip stock in my hand warmed further as I channeled magic through it. Flame and Force flashed out, forming the green-white whip once again.

"Someone gave me a present since we last 'spoke'."

———

An Unseelie will-o'-the-wisp flung fire. Redcaps emerged from the armory with assault rifles and opened fire. Mary and Theino opened fire with machine pistols. Gunfire echoed in the confined space. Fire flared—and Inga and I charged.

Gráinne came to meet us—and her hag ally flung Power. Inga and I stepped Between, emerging on top of the Noble and the Greater Fae challenging us. More Power flared and Inga parried the hag's force strike with her sword, closing with her as the Noble lunged at me.

I caught the glamor-blades Gráinne had summoned with the Fire of my whip, shattering her spell as I closed. A shield of glamor appeared in midair, deflecting the whip as I struck at her, and a familiar cold iron knife stabbed at me from beneath.

I *stepped*, emerging from Between behind her and striking out with a bolt of flame from my free hand. She moved with blurring speed, parrying the firebolt with a newly conjured glamor-blade—and three mirror images of the Unseelie Noble flashed into existence.

One of them collapsed as a russet-furred lynx leapt through it to hit the will-o'-the-wisp behind it. There was a short and painful scream, and the amount of random fire flickering around the room dropped dramatically.

I was keeping enough track to be sure which images were illusions, and struck out with the whip again, wrapping flickering green fire around Gráinne's sword hand as she moved to strike at me.

For a moment, I thought I was about to end the fight there—Nobles weren't *that* much tougher than Gentry, and I'd cut a Gentry's hand off with the whip earlier. We struggled, and then her Power closed down over mine, severing the whip as she flung herself backward.

Her skin was smoking, burn marks visible on her wrist even through the glamor as she snarled at me.

"What *are* you?" she demanded. "A changeling can't fight me!"

She flung glamor-blades at me, a dozen knives of deadly-sharp solid illusions.

I stepped Between again, emerging farther away and to the side of the salvo of knives. The rest of the fight was going our way. The will-o'-the-wisp and the redcaps were down, and Mary was back in her normal form. Both she and Theino had stolen the assault rifles the redcaps had returned with and were starting to lay down fire on Gráinne and the hag.

The hag was dueling Inga and losing, hard. The hag had Force and Fire and Glamor. The Valkyrie met Force and Fire with Force and stepping Between—and illusion was irrelevant against a woman who could smash walls with her fists.

As I watched, Inga's cold iron knives flipped up over her shoulders and slammed into the hag's chest. The old-looking woman froze in mid-gesture, her Power flickering out as the cold iron poisoned her.

Then I turned to Gráinne.

"It's over. Yield."

"You know nothing," she spat—and charged. A flickering glamor of spiked armor and flashing blades formed around her as she came at me.

Inga met her halfway, steel meeting glamor as the Valkyrie charged the Noble. I could barely see them move, both of them faster than I was. Then Inga went flying, smashing into the wall with blood leaking from a dozen wounds.

Gráinne was limping as she faced me, though, and I could see blood pooling on the floor under her.

"The Covenant demands the Cold Death for treason," she snarled at me. "I will die standing first!"

Fire flickered out from the Wizard-forged whip handle again.

"I don't have it in me to send another to the Cold Death," I told her. To walk Between required a very specific Gift. Without it, anyone left Between froze and suffocated, dying slowly as a place utterly inimical to life sucked them dry.

That was the Cold Death. I'd taken one man to it to save the city. I wouldn't condemn another one to it if I had a choice.

Gráinne charged. I struck, Fire flashing across the room in a blow she didn't even *try* to dodge. The blast burnt through her chest and throat, flinging her backward as I burnt away her heart and ribcage.

She was dead before she hit the wall.

———

INGA LOOKED LIKE CRAP. Theino had taken a couple of solid hits and was poking delicately at his right tusk, which appeared to be about half-missing.

Mary, as usual, looked gorgeous. Maybe a bit sweaty. People, even fae, weren't very good at shooting someone whose size changed at random.

"Someone will have called the police," my girlfriend noted. "Even if the management knows who they work for, they can't keep the staff from calling the cops when they hear gunfire. This floor is not that well sealed for sound."

"Listen," Theino told her in response. Mary looked at him in surprise, and the goblin held his finger to his lips.

All I could hear was silence. Not even the mechanical noise of the hotel—or the elevator shaft less than twenty feet from us.

"They may not have been sealed with mortal means, but the place is silenced by magic and Power," he told us. "The door may be a bigger problem. We need someone with illusions."

"Shove it back up for now," I told him. "Then call Robert. He's with Talus; one or both of them should be in good enough shape to make their way here."

I turned back to Inga as the goblin went back over to the door.

"Are you going to be okay?" I asked.

"Oh, yeah," she said with a pained smile. "*Going to be* is the critical phrase, though, Jason. I'm going to need a few hours and a couple of *really* good steaks."

"Chernenkov is still on her way," I told her.

"You have to catch her," Inga told me. "Hell, you need to take her *alive*, from what the Queen told me. You've got those iron spikes?"

I tapped my coat.

"Yes."

"One will hurt her. Two will slow her down, a lot. Three will trap her in place, rob her of her ability to jump through shadows. Once you've pinned her, you can capture her as easily as kill her. Kill the shadow, the Pouka won't have much left."

I looked at Theino and Mary. One of the advantages of my ability to identify supernaturals was that I could tell when one of us was hurting. Theino was in far worse shape than he was pretending. At a guess, he'd taken at least one bullet he was trying to hide.

"Mary, stay with Theino and Inga," I told her. "There's got to be a first aid kit around here somewhere; see what you can do about their injuries."

"I'm not..."

"Were you or were you not shot?" I interrupted the goblin roughly. "I'm not blind, Speaker to Outsiders."

The formal title had the impact I hoped. He bowed his head and shifted slightly, revealing where blood was slowly oozing out through his vest.

"I will heal," he noted.

"But you're useless to me now," I told him. "I want the three of you *alive*, people. I'll deal with Chernenkov."

I wasn't sure I could.

But on the other hand, I'd just defeated an Unseelie Noble. I wasn't supposed to be able to do that, either, no matter what help I had.

31

FORTUNATELY FOR THE sensibilities of the hotel staff, the armory the Masked Lords had been maintaining also included several changes of clothes, one of which fit me.

Clad in fresh jeans and sleeveless vest, I cleaned my coat and threw my "battle ensemble" back together. I even found some extra magazines of cold iron that would fit my Jericho, reloading the pistol and tucking the spare mags in my coat.

By then, Theino had managed to call in help and Mary had bandaged up his and Inga's wounds. The safehouse looked more like the triage area of a war zone, with wounded being treated on the tables and the dead shoved in a corner, but my sympathy for the Masked Lords' minions was...limited.

Inga waved me over as I started to leave, coughing up a small amount of blood as she did.

"Are you sure you're going to be okay?" I asked.

"I've had worse," she told me. "Listen, Jason. You need to be careful. There's more going on here than I think either of us knows."

"Well, Chernenkov is Andrell's lover, and I'm pretty sure Andrell *is* a Masked Lord and they're trying to take Calgary as their new base," I replied. "I'm not sure what else could make things more complicated."

She laughed, then coughed up more blood.

"There are a few things," she admitted. "Secrets I was sworn not to betray. I have other oaths as well, though. Jason…if the Masked Lords realize what you are, they will move hell and earth to hunt you down. You have to stop Chernenkov…but you can't fight Andrell. You have to leave him to the Hunt."

"Not least because Andrell would eat me alive with one hand tied behind his back," I replied. But there was something else, something she wasn't telling me.

Inga winced.

"I…I can't say more," she replied. "But promise me, Jason. She'll run to him—and you can't fight him. You can't. The consequences…"

"I'm not planning on fighting a Fae Lord, Inga," I told her. "But I can't let Chernenkov get away. Too many have died. Too much blood, too much *bullshit*."

Inga winced, closing her eyes as Mary put iodine on one of her injuries.

"I know. Do…do what you must, my young friend," she told me, her eyes still closed. "Just know that…you can't come back from what comes next."

With those ominous words echoing in my ears, I left the safehouse. The elevator delivered me smoothly to the main floor, where the calm normality of the lobby confirmed our assessment of the soundproofing on the thirteenth floor.

No one here was aware there'd been a gunfight upstairs. I couldn't help but shake my head as I walked out into the parking let, shielding my eyes as I looked up at the setting sun.

Chernenkov had fled by shadow, but she couldn't go far or fast doing that. As I understood it, that was more draining for her than stepping Between was for a Hunter like myself. She hadn't grabbed the helicopter she'd arrived in, Talus's people would be dealing with that right now, but she'd almost certainly have a car somewhere.

I found a bench next to the parking lot entrance and began to study the cars coming in. The trickiest part to all of this would be to avoid public notice…but I had a plan for that, too.

I HATED to call someone's else's misfortune our good luck, but there had apparently been a major accident on Deerfoot Trail, the major arterial highway carrying traffic from the southeast of the city to the northeast.

That had bought us the time we needed to deal with the safehouse while Chernenkov was, quite literally, stuck in traffic. Of course, that had left my companions wounded and drained more of my own resources than I'd prefer, but what choice had we had?

Also, I felt significantly less drained than I would have expected. I'd gone toe-to-toe with an Unseelie Noble, conjured some of the most powerful combat magics I'd ever wielded...but I felt as fresh as if I hadn't fought her.

That was weird, to put it mildly. It was also helpful, as it meant that I actually might stand a chance against Chernenkov when she arrived.

I had no idea what she was driving, so I found myself checking each car as it pulled into the lot. The biggest potential problem would be if Chernenkov had somehow been warned that we'd assaulted the hotel safehouse.

If she had, this was going to be a long, pointless wait.

Fortunately, it appeared that either she'd lost her phone or no one had managed to send a warning. I'd been outside for about fifteen minutes when I spotted her. She was driving a black coupe, something on the cheaper end of sporty, and was slowing down to enter the parking lot when *she* spotted *me*.

I half-expected her to try and run me over. Or pull out a gun and go for a drive-by.

What I was *not* expecting was for her to slam on the handbrake, pull a perfect bootlegger's turn into the other lane, and floor it in the opposite direction.

There was a limit to what I could do in public, but I started running after her as I assessed my options. A blip Between while no one was looking—I hoped—helped me keep up as she twisted the car around the traffic heading toward Deerfoot.

Even with fae reflexes, she was going too fast to adjust for the stack of stopped vehicles when she flung the car toward the on-ramp. Deer-foot southbound was as clogged as the road she'd been stuck on coming north, and the on-ramp was a solid mass of cars.

She hit at least three before the coupe came to a complete halt, smashing vehicles into each other as she created one of the worst multi-car pileups I'd ever seen.

The shouting and honking had barely started before Chernenkov was out of the car and running. Another quick jump Between and I was after her as we pulled away from humans into a green space of scrub and dirt.

Apparently, Chernenkov was much less certain about how a fight between us would go a third time.

THE SAYING I'd heard before, with reference to ships more than anything else, was that a stern chase was a long chase. I could jump Between faster than Chernenkov could jump between shadows, but she was running and I was pursuing.

And there was only so much disappearing and reappearing either of us could do. There were humans around, even if we started in a green space. Even running after each other was almost guaranteed to get calls into the police.

Gunfire...was right out. Magic was even more so. Chernenkov cleared out of the greenspace next to Deerfoot Trail and into the community within a minute, dodging around pedestrians as I went after her.

I was pretty sure I saw at least one woman pull out a phone after she knocked them aside. I suppressed the urge to knock the phone from her hand as I passed—the police were getting called. We just needed to get out of sight before they arrived.

There was a gap as we cleared the strip mall where there were no humans around, and I tried to close with her, rapidly stepping in and out of Between.

She slipped into the shadows, dodging me as we crossed a quite stretch of road and then returning to normal space as we charged past a gas station.

This was *not* going as planned. Neither of us was running much faster than most humans, though few humans could have kept it up for as long as we did. We passed through several neighborhoods, another strip mall, and then we found ourselves charging into a familiar industrial district.

She was headed for the Unseelie Court.

Night was starting to fall around us, and the industrial district was deserted now. I risked a bolt of flame, a distraction as I closed the distance.

Chernenkov, however, had come to the same conclusion I had. I stepped out of Between into a dark alley, maybe a block from the warehouse that served as Unseelie Court, and directly into a clawed fist.

That *hurt*, sending me reeling backward as she snarled at me.

"Fine," she hissed. "You want to play, despite it all? Gráinne should have let me eat your heart!"

"She might agree with you now," I told her. "Except Gráinne's dead. The Covenants prescribe the Cold Death for her crimes, so I guess you can call that mercy."

She snarled, long sharp teeth appearing in a mouth that wasn't really designed for them.

"Damn you. You lie. You're *nothing*. A changeling. *How*?"

"I am a Hunter's changeling and a Vassal of the Queen of the Fae," I told her quietly as I drew the whip stock from its holster. "Maria Chernenkov, you are charged with murder and working with the enemies of the High Court, with treason of the first order.

"Surrender, and Her Majesty may show clemency. Fight me, and I will have no choice but to execute the penalties laid out by the High Court for your crimes."

———

WE HAD AN AUDIENCE. I wasn't sure where they had come from, but that was perhaps inevitable given that we were now very much in

Unseelie territory. A dozen fae now lined the end of the alley, which was probably part of why Chernenkov had finally turned at bay.

"Fuck your High Court and fuck your Queen," she hissed. "If I rip your throat out, that ends this."

"Not really," I told her. "You attacked a Fae Court, tried to start a war. There will be consequences no matter what happens now."

Flickering shadows surrounded her now, dark flames highlighting her limbs as she partially transformed, claws and teeth and spikes forming on her flesh. Shadow lashed out at me, darkness lunging toward me like an arrow.

Fear rippled off her as well as she tried to pin me in place for her attack. I'd felt the trick too many times before, though, and I shrugged it away this time as I dodged her arrow and responded in kind.

Fire and shadow flashed through the alleyway as we clashed, and then I flicked my whip out toward her. I almost managed to wrap the fiery tendril around her, but she flashed to shadow and flipped out of the strike, closing with me at a terrifying speed.

I didn't even think. The first of the cold iron spikes was in my left hand and went flashing out as the Pouka closed.

I missed her shadow but slammed a six-inch-long cold iron spike into her stomach. She hissed loudly, stumbling backward while a stream of curses spewed forth.

"You'll pay for that. I will tear your heart out and *eat* it."

She ripped the spike from her flesh, tossing it aside as her skin steamed against our kind's bane.

"I know how to kill you this time, Maria," I told her. "Surrender. There can still be mercy."

"What, if I betray everything?" she laughed. "I know Seelie *mercy*. Seelie *generosity*. I will die standing, not kneeling and whinging like a starving animal!"

That was the second time someone had said they'd die standing to me today, and I was starting to get sick of it.

"I'd really prefer it if no one died at all," I said conversationally. "Not least since my Queen *really* wants to talk to you. If you insist, however, I don't have to bring you in in one piece."

My whip lashed out and our deadly dance of Fire and shadow

resumed. She dodged around the flame and struck with her claws, closing with me inside the curve of the whip. Claws and teeth and shadow lunged for me…and then I wasn't there.

I stepped Between, emerging behind her, and this time, I did catch her with the whip. I yanked her back toward me and a second spike was in my hand. She broke free of the flame tendril…and for one necessary moment, she was still.

And so was her shadow.

The cold iron spike hammered through her shadow into the concrete, shattering the ground under my blow. I released the spike and it *moved* away, shifting with her shadow as it pinned her.

She wasn't pinned to any particular spot. Just to…reality, I guessed.

It apparently *hurt*. She'd been angry at me when I'd stabbed her flesh with an iron spike, but when I stabbed her *shadow*, she screamed.

No human could have made that noise. A bloodcurdling shriek echoed through the warehouse district, and Chernenkov recoiled from me.

She was slower now. The spike in her shadow was clearly impeding her somehow. I didn't pretend to understand how it worked. I only knew that she was vulnerable, and I pressed my attack.

Fire flickered down the alleyway as I tried to pin her in place, trapping her between the whip of green-white flame and bolts of Fire on the other side as I drew a third cold iron spike.

She hesitated and I charged. Fire slammed her into place, holding her shadow still for a precious moment and I swung the cold iron spike for the blow that would truly cripple her…

And a blast of force caught me in mid-strike, tossing the spike and me aside alike. Chernenkov skittered away and I controlled my descent with Force to land on my feet, facing Lord Andrell.

Fury marked his beautiful face. Power flickered around his hands and he snarled at his Court.

"Will you all just stand by and watch him murder one of ours?" he bellowed. "Fight, you mewling fools!"

32

THERE WERE over a dozen Unseelie around me now. No redcaps, which suggested this was the official Unseelie Court, but several Gentry. A hag. A nightmare. A couple of Svartálfar, black dwarves related to gnomes like Eric. One of the Nobles who'd arrived at the airport with Andrell.

There were others too, but the math ran through my head in moments as they hesitated. They might not want to fight me—they all knew who I represented—but they had sworn Fealty.

Their oaths bound them as much as mine bound me.

"Lord Andrell," I challenged him quietly. "You know my orders. You know what this Pouka has done. You swore to assist me in hunting her down. Why?"

"You cannot simply execute Unseelie in the streets!" he barked.

"The High Court disagrees, though I was actually tasked with capturing her," I told him. "To bring her before our Powers to face justice for her crimes. As we once spoke about the redcaps we now know served her, do you claim her, then? Is she of your Court, bound by Fealty, that you are responsible for her actions? For her *crimes*?"

"For her to feed and live is no crime except in the eyes of the Seelie," he snarled. "You have tried to break us, to turn us into dogs that beg at your heel for the scraps you allow us. I will *not* permit you to punish her for what she is!"

"That is not my command," I told him. "My command was to capture the mastermind behind the attack on the Seelie Court in this city, to interrogate her to learn of her ties to the Masked Lords, and to bring safety to this city.

"I swore an oath, Lord Andrell. So did you. To uphold Court and Covenant. You even promised me to bring this one to justice."

Chernenkov was out of the gap between us now, trying to blend into the background of Unseelie watching the standoff. At Andrell's word, they would all attack. So would she.

"So, I ask again, Lord Andrell. Do you claim her? Is she of your Court and bound by Fealty?"

"She is my *wife*," he snarled, the words echoing in a sudden still silence. "I am hers and she is mine, by whatever oaths or terms you demand. I refuse to allow you to judge her, destroy her. Let the High Court be *damned*."

"Ah," I said. "I'm guessing there's an iron mask floating around here somewhere, isn't there, Lord Andrell? Or was Gráinne your contact and your own treason merely by association?"

"We should never have bowed to the High Court," he told me. He was calmer now, which was somehow even more terrifying. With a now-familiar gesture, he snapped his hand out and the same cold iron mask Gráinne had worn flashed into existence.

"My sword, Vestri," he commanded. The Svartálfar he was speaking to hesitated. "You are bound by Fealty," he snapped. "My *sword*."

The black dwarf gestured, drawing a blade out of the shadow around us. I knew what it was before I even looked at it. Like Talus, Andrell had a gnomish warblade. In his case, probably forged by one of the Svartálfar around him.

A silver-hilted cold iron blade, with orichalcum runes along its length.

"You have broken oath and Fealty and Covenant, Lord Andrell," I said quietly. I couldn't fight a Fae Lord. But I also couldn't fight his entire Court...so I'd choose the fight against my actual enemy. "In the name of Our Queen, I challenge you. For the honor of our people and the will of the High Court, I demand that you face me."

He slammed the mask onto his face, its magic sweeping over him as the glamor concealed his form. It was a pointless gesture today, when everyone around him knew who he was and what was happening, but with his defiance in the air, I supposed there was no reason not to.

"So be it," he said harshly. "Are you prepared to die, Hunter's changeling?"

"I am a Vassal of the Queen of the Fae," I told him. "Whether I am prepared is irrelevant. I swore an oath."

DAMN, he was fast.

One moment, he'd been snarking at me about his wife and my willingness to die. The next, he'd crossed five meters of distance and was striking for my face.

I wasn't there. I stepped Between to buy myself breathing room, reappearing back into reality behind Lord Andrell with the whip in my hand. Green-white fire flicked toward his back, but he was turning almost before I emerged from Between.

The cold iron blade flashed through the tendril of flame, severing the spell and collapsing my whip out of existence. A dozen flashing swords of glamor snapped into existence around me, diving toward me at blistering speed.

Inga's training served me well. I leapt backward, driving my movement with telekinesis even as I threw shields of force in front of the path of the glamor-blades. Illusory—but all too deadly—swords shattered on my shields.

Instinct screamed and I dropped to the ground, landing on one knee as a series of blistering-hot bolts of Fire tore through where I'd been floating.

Andrell advanced behind his attack, the warblade held loosely in his hands as he approached me. Bolts of Fire, ice and glamored Force flickered down the alleyway, clearing a gap behind me as his Court got out of the way.

I met it all with a single shield of Force. Inga had taught me to use angles and skill to deflect attacks, and the barrier I flung up was an invisible mountain range of shifting planes that caught attack after attack and flung them to the sky or the ground.

For a moment, Andrell's attack hammered against my shield and I held.

Then the wave of strikes flickered out and I met the Unseelie Lord's gaze across the darkened alleyway. Part of me wanted to mock him, to demand if that was the best he had.

The problem was that I knew it wasn't.

"Impressive," he murmured quietly. "What *are* you? No changeling, no quarter-human, should be able to stand against a Fae Lord, even for a moment."

He shrugged. There was no lapse between his words, his shrug and his attack. Even as he was speaking, an inferno of Fire and ice erupted from thin air, hammering toward me with the fury of a Fae Lord.

I wasn't there. Cold flickered over my skin as I stepped Between and emerged behind his attack—and less than a meter from Andrell himself. The Wizard's gift flared with power as I struck, channeling every ounce of magic and strength I had into a blow that would have gutted a *building*.

Pure-white flame lashed out from the whip stock, heat that seared even me as it flashed out and wrapped around Andrell.

He caught the flame. His free hand flashed out and he parried the whip of heat and Force with his forearm, wrapping the tendril of white-hot flame around his flesh and using it to pull me to him.

I let him, gathering force in my other hand and punching him in the face with it.

I didn't actually expect that to *work*. His head snapped back as I hit with the force of a speeding truck and he went flying backward, my whip of flame tearing off flesh as he collapsed against a wall.

The smell of burnt pork filled the alleyway, and I could see ash and blood on the ground as he stumbled.

"They say to defeat God, all you have to do is show that he bleeds," Andrell said quietly, his thick Irish accent still beautiful despite it all. "Having *killed gods*, I disagree with that assessment."

There was something new in his voice as he drew himself up straight to face me. He was favoring his left arm now, though any injury *I'd* managed to inflict on a Fae Lord wouldn't last long.

"I know you now, boy," he hissed. "I should have known before we ever came. Of course, Mellie's child would be His. What lies have been told and blood has been shed to keep you secret? What hell did that bitch of a Queen bury your mother in to shield you from us?"

"Yield, Andrell," I told him. "There can still be clemency here, even for you."

He laughed. With the full physical power of a Fae Lord, his laughter echoed like gunshots in the silence of the alleyway.

"You don't get it, do you, boy?" he demanded. "I am what you named me, yes. I am a *Masked Lord*. When the High Court grew too full of themselves and showed weakness, I rode against *gods*. You have drawn blood, which even your Queen failed at, but there is no mercy here. No peace.

"Your Queen *neutered* the power and glory of the Sidhe! We will be reborn in fire and blood once again."

"You've already failed here," I pointed out. "This city will never be a sanctuary for you."

"There are other cities. Other wars." He laughed again. "Even being the only *known* Masked Lord has its advantages. Think of the traps we can lure fools like you into if you hunt me. You can't win this; you know th⁣t."

"I've already won," I told him softly. "You have no Court here, Andrell. No Fealty. No Covenants. You have betrayed all of them and are *nothing*."

He was silent, and I could tell that he was looking at the Unseelie who'd surrounded us in an ancient ritual that any back-alley scrapper would recognize the heart of.

He knew I was telling the truth. His Court would not follow him out of there. He could kill me, but I'd already won. Calgary would never be a sanctuary for the Masked Lords. The watchers would carry the story, and it was unlikely even the Unseelie Court here would survive.

Andrell could kill them all, I supposed, but he could no longer bind them with Fealty.

Oaths flow both ways, and he had broken them.

———

THE LONG MOMENT of silence was broken by his laughter again.

"So be it," he told me. "You are the first in a long time to draw blood on me, boy. I'll give you that. But we know how this ends."

New glamor wrapped around him and he *grew*, gaining height and bulk as he approached me. Fire and shadow wrapped around his newly giant form as he doubled in height.

"Kneel, boy, and I will make it quick."

"Oh, go fuck yourself."

Fire flashed in the alleyway again, and a gnomish warblade met wizard-augmented Fire. His Power flared against mine.

The Wizard's gift let me stand against him. For several eternal seconds, I met the strength and fury of a Fae Lord and withstood him.

It didn't last. It couldn't. The warblade *exploded* in Power, Fire and Force shattering my flame and throwing me away. I barely managed to slow my landing to something reasonable, but Andrell advanced on me with the fury of the lesser god he truly was.

"I know you now, boy," he repeated. "I killed your father. Now I'm going to kill you."

"The funniest part is that I have no fucking idea what you're talking about," I told him as I stepped Between to dodge a blast of fire. Giant or not, the Lord was terrifyingly fast, and despite a momentary feeling of power, I couldn't face his magic.

He laughed and lashed out at me in a single second. I barely deflected the Fire into a wall and danced backward.

We were making one *hell* of a mess of this alley, but the Unseelie continued to circle around us. It wasn't every day you saw a Fae Lord fight *anyone*. It was even rarer you saw anyone *survive* facing a Fae Lord for any extended period of time.

I mostly managed it by not being where he struck. Between was my salvation as I dodged in and out of reality to avoid his blows, far too overwhelmed to try and strike back or actually *fight* him at this point.

My day was starting to take a toll on me as well. I could *tell* that my reservoir of Power was fading fast. Even stepping Between was starting to drain me, to take longer...and Andrell could tell.

I stepped wrong and he was waiting for it.

A fraction of a second longer to enter Between was too long, and a man-sized icicle hammered into me. I managed to get enough Force in front of it to blunt the blow, but that was all.

I felt my ribcage shatter under the impact, and I was flung into the wall without any chance of saving myself. More bones broke with audible snaps as I landed.

My Power fled me. The Wizard's gift fell from nerveless fingers as I processed that my right arm was basically shattered. I couldn't move. The nerveless feeling in my legs was far too familiar.

I...I had broken my spine.

Again.

Lower down this time, I realized as I heard Andrell approach me. I still had feeling in my arms. My right arm was a useless wreck, but my left arm was still working, barely.

Andrell had scaled down to merely half again human-sized by the time his hand descended on my neck and he lifted me up to look me in the eyes.

"Your father would be proud," he told me quietly. "He was the bravest warrior I ever faced. It's over."

"It is," I agreed—and then rammed the Jericho into his chest and pulled the trigger as fast as I could.

Forty-five-caliber cold iron rounds hammered into the Fae Lord's ribcage. Defensive glamors shattered. Bone shattered. Flesh was torn and bullets ground home into bone that managed to withstand the force.

He dropped me as he suddenly shrank to normal, gasping in pain. I dropped the gun as I fell, my useless legs refusing to even try and stabilize me, but we met each other's gaze for an eternal second.

I swear I saw him nod approval.

And then Lord Karl Andrell, leader of the Masked Lords and Unseelie Lord of Calgary, died.

33

I THOUGHT that Maria Chernenkov had screamed with inhuman power when I'd rammed a cold iron spike into her shadow. That was only a pale imitation of the scream she unleashed when Andrell died.

I was barely upright enough to watch her emerge out of the circle of watching fae and charge me. There was no way I could stop her. There were no bullets left in the gun. I'd lost track of the whip stock, and even if I had the Wizard's gift to hand, I have no Power left to fuel it.

Fortunately for my exhausted indifference to whether I lived or died, the *rest* of the Unseelie weren't as lost to shock as I was. Bands of Force wrapped around the Pouka as she charged, yanking her to the ground as two Nobles emerged from the crowd.

I didn't know their names. They'd arrived with Gráinne and Andrell, and if you'd asked me, I would have assumed they were Masked Lords themselves. I would apparently have assumed wrong.

Their combined Power held Chernenkov down and one of them turned to the rest of the Unseelie.

"The show's over, people," she said harshly. "We can all guess the consequences of this, but they aren't ours to execute. Go home."

The Unseelie Court seemed...rebellious, but that was their core nature. After a moment, they started to drift away, leaving me alone with two Unseelie Nobles, a dead Lord, and a weeping and trapped Pouka Noble.

"Lord Vassal," the male Noble greeted me. "I don't think we were introduced. Ryan Shawnee. Can you stand?"

I laughed bitterly.

"Give me a day and a couple of cheeseburgers, sure," I told him. "Until then, not really."

"You were missing. Presumed dead," Shawnee told me.

"Presumed with a degree of certainty by our own Court that I found odd," the woman told me. "Brianna Shaughnessy," she introduced herself. "Ryan and I worked for Jon Andrews, the Lord of the Unseelie and Power of our people. He sent us into Andrell's service to see this Court set up efficiently and well."

"That went well," I told her.

She shook her head.

"Where's Gráinne?" Shaughnessy demanded.

"She would have been why your Court was so sure I was dead," I replied. "She shoved a cold iron dagger in my chest. It didn't work out as she planned, but...she was a Masked Lord, too."

"Was," the woman echoed. "And now?"

"She's dead. Her body is in a safehouse in a hotel by the airport, under guard of a Valkyrie of the Wild Hunt."

"Appropriate," Shawnee said. "We will need to speak to Andrews, but that is the next step from here. The Hunt must be summoned. This is no longer a matter of Court politics. A Vassal is wounded. A Noble and a Lord dead. This...creature"—he gestured at Chernenkov—"is our prisoner. We will see her delivered to the Hunt when they arrived."

"Thank you," I told the two Nobles.

"I'd worked with Lord Andrell for twelve years, Kilkenny," Shawnee said flatly. "I don't pretend I like where this ended, but I didn't know he was a Masked Lord."

"That was the purpose of the Masks," I noted. "Can you...take care of him?"

"We will," Shaughnessy promised. "And you?"

"Call Eric," I said. "He'll…he'll know what to do."

That was the last thing I remembered saying before darkness overcame me.

I WAS at least inside when I woke up. It was dark and I wasn't entirely sure where I was, but at least I wasn't lying on the dirty concrete ground of an industrial alley. Instead, I appeared to be lying on a cheap mattress that wasn't quite long enough for my height. Someone had wrapped a splint around my shattered arm, and I could tell that I'd been positioned carefully to allow my spine to heal.

It had even started doing so. I had some sensation in my legs. No control yet, but some feeling. From that alone I judged I'd been out for at least an hour.

"He's awake," Inga said aloud. "Eric, get over here."

A ball of light flickered into existence above me, and I realized where I was. I was lying in the middle of the main floor of the building Andrell had taken over as the Unseelie Court. Lifting my head ever so slightly, I saw that I was the lucky one.

The row of tarp-wrapped bodies lying in front of the stage told me how much worse it could have gone for me. I didn't even want to think about how many of them were my fault. A *lot* of fae were dead now.

Eric crossed into my line of view, the stocky gnome looking…terrified. Not tired. *Terrified.*

"You found one hell of a beehive to smash up, Jason," he told me gently.

"How bad?" I asked.

"Between the attack on Talus's office, the hotel safehouse and your semi-accidental assault on the Unseelie Court…" The Keeper shook his head. "We're at thirty-one dead and eleven seriously wounded, counting you *and* Talus. Another dozen mortals who worked for Talus are dead, which would have been a *lot* worse without your intervention."

Over forty dead and wounded fae. Half or more of those were the freelancers Chernenkov had brought into the city, but they'd clearly taken their own toll before they'd gone down.

"And, of course, the biggest headache of all." He sighed and pointed. At the center of the row of corpses were two that I recognized more due to the glamor still shifting around them. The masks were still on the bodies of Gráinne and Andrell, and the two Unseelie Nobles who'd captured Chernenkov stood guard over the dead Lord.

"A Fae Lord has died," Eric half-hissed. "That *never* goes without question. Worse, a Fae Lord was killed—and that never goes without consequence."

"He didn't leave me much choice," I said.

"So I understand," he confirmed. "As a Vassal acting on the Queen's orders, you are shielded, to a point. But this..." He shook his head. "I'm guessing this wasn't the plan."

I half-laughed, half-coughed as I looked up at him.

"Plan was to bring Chernenkov or Gráinne in front of the Lord of the Wild Hunt and put all of the information and events in his hands," I told Eric. "But Chernenkov ran to Andrell and he..." I sighed.

"And he was her husband, so he wasn't willing to let me capture her. Which ended, well..."

I gestured to the row of corpses.

"How much trouble am I in?" I asked carefully.

"I don't know," he admitted. "The only time I know of when a Fae Lord died in battle was when Calebrant rode against these same bastards. No one was questioning what Calebrant had done—not least because he was dead by the time questions were asked."

"I didn't even know the Masked Lords existed until a week or so ago," I said. "This all came at me fast. Too fast."

Eric sighed.

"And now we get to see the consequences of that," he told me. "The Queen is on her way. The Wild Hunt are on their way—Ankaris is bringing two full troops of the Hunt. But..." He hesitated, then sighed and continued.

"Lord Jon Andrews is also on his way," he warned me. "The Lord of the Unseelie backed Andrell and the creation of this Court specifically, and he is coming here. Vassal or no, if he demands you be punished for killing Andrell, there isn't much even Mabona can do."

"Peace in the High Court is worth more than I am, huh?" I said, closing my eyes again. "I hate my job. Can you get me something to eat?"

A warm paper bag was shoved into my still-functioning hand.

"Takeout from the Manor," Eric told me. "Cheeseburger should still be warm, though the fries are probably a write-off by now."

"You are a god among fae, my friend."

"No, I'm not," he said quietly. "Three of those will be here within a couple of hours. You'll be better off if you can stand at that point."

34

It was for the best, from what Eric had said, that Mabona was the first to arrive. The Queen of Light and Darkness, Mistress of all Fae and my own personal overlord stepped out of Between in a flurry of shadows that felt, for a moment, like an entire flock of birds had been released into the open space of the Court.

I was propped up at this point so I could eat, but I was still broken. There was no way I could stand on my own two feet, but I gave her as solid of a bow as I could. I may not have enjoyed everything my Queen had laid upon me, but she *had* earned my respect.

"This won't do," she said crisply as she surveyed me. It felt like she could see clean through me, assessing injuries with a glance. She probably could, actually. "I know you can't stand, but you're a mess."

"I've had better days and weeks," I agreed. Before I could say more, shadows and wind swept over me. The whip handle MacDonald had given me had been nearby, though I hadn't seen it. Now it was back in its holster, as was my Jericho. The mostly fitting clothes I'd taken from the safehouse disappeared, vanishing in a burst of her Power as new clothes replaced them.

With a thought and a gesture, my Queen had transformed me from an unarmed cripple in tattered clothing to an armed servant of the Queen of the Fae dressed in a perfectly fitted business suit.

Of course, I was still crippled. I knew it was within her capacity to heal my injuries, but I could guess her point in leaving me broken for now.

"I did not plan for this, my Queen," I told her.

"Somehow, I suspected that," she agreed genially. "I didn't think that even my Hunter's changeling was going to pick a fight with a Fae Lord. Where is Gráinne? And Chernenkov?"

"Gráinne's over there." I gestured at the row of bodies. "One of the ones in masks. Chernenkov should be held captive around here somewhere, waiting for Andrews's judgment."

"Her presence alone will help him reach the correct conclusions," she agreed. She turned to the two Irish Nobles guarding Andrell's body. "Shawnee, Shaughnessy, where is the Pouka?"

"In the cells Andrell built into the Court," Shawnee replied. "Under guard by three Gentry and bound by iron and magic."

Mabona sighed.

"Eric?"

"My Queen," the gnome replied, seeming to reappear out of nowhere.

"Check on the Pouka," she ordered. "I doubt that Chernenkov is done giving us headaches."

Eric nodded and marched out of the room while Mabona surveyed the space.

"Lot of work," she noted. "Shame, really."

"My Queen?" Shawnee asked.

"Do you really think any other Unseelie Lord is going to want to *touch* this city now?" Mabona asked conversationally. "After the clusterfuck Andrell has created?"

The Unseelie Noble sighed.

"Can I get a plane ticket back to Ireland, at least?" he asked plaintively.

The thundercrack of a new arrival from Between, as flashy as Mabona's but much, much louder, interrupted the further conversation, and a tall black man, towering even for a Fae Lord, stalked out of Between, followed by four Noble guards.

Shawnee and Shaughnessy were kneeling in an instant.

"Lord Andrews," the two Nobles greeted him in chorus.

"I sent you to keep Andrell safe," Jon Andrews noted, his voice the grinding of granite in a thunderstorm.

Time and exposure had inured me somewhat to the sheer presence of the Queen. I had no such immunity to the Lord of the Unseelie. Power coiled around him, both physical and magical. Like MacDonald and Mabona, Jon Andrews was a Power, a sliver of divinity given flesh and form.

"Show me him," he ordered.

"Wait," Mabona snapped. "This is not a matter for merely our eyes. Ankaris is coming. Let him stand witness, as neither of us are neutral here."

"Your Vassal killed a Lord of the Unseelie," Andrews replied. "This cannot pass without punishment."

"Your Lord was one of the Masked bastards who killed Calebrant, Alisha, Brigette and Connor," Mabona told him without heat. "I'd say that if someone deserved punishment here...that punishment was delivered by my Vassal."

The air in the Court tore again. And again. Wider and wider until the air itself fogged up with the chill of Between in a way I'd never felt in the normal world.

Sixteen Hunters led the way, nine women and seven men. They were unmounted today, but there was no question of who and what they were. Eight were true Hunters, able to open the paths Between. The other eight were "merely" regular Gentry who'd joined the Hunt.

All were armed, the silver swords of the Wild Hunt and sleek black automatic rifles I'd never seen before. Silently, they moved out to surround the room as the second troop followed them through.

These were equally armed, also only half true Hunters. Of their non-Hunters, however, four were Noble and four were Gentry.

The entire building shivered with the presence of the last one out of Between, who closed the path with a gentle snap of his fingers. Lord

Ankaris was of merely average height for the fae, matching my own not-quite six feet, with long dark hair and sharp features.

Hauntingly familiar sharp features, in fact. There was something about the man that made me swear I knew him, that I'd met him before.

Which was impossible. Ankaris might not be a full Power, but he was a member of the High Court, the Lord of the Wild Hunt. He was as far beyond a regular Fae Lord as a Fae Lord was beyond me, the status and power of a lesser member of the High Court still unique in our people.

"So," he greeted the hall with a softly lilting Irish accent that reminded me of Andrell. "My Queen. My dear cousin. We are here. My people will guarantee the security of this Court while we discuss affairs."

He strode down the center of the room, approaching the two masked bodies without hesitation.

"Let us begin."

———

It was funny. There was no question in anyone's mind that Lord Ankaris was the junior member of the High Court, the only one of the Nine not a full Power in his own right. At that moment, though, both Mabona and Andrews fell in behind him like obedient children.

The thirty-odd armed Greater Fae and Gentry now guarding the exterior of the room probably didn't hurt, though I think the key point was simple: out of the three of them, Ankaris was the only one who would have had the authority to execute Andrell on his own.

The High Court as an entity could proscribe any fae, order any execution or punishment they wished and the Fae Lords were not exempt from that power. The Wild Hunt's master, however, was charged to enforce the Covenants on the Lords.

He was the judge and executioner for men like Andrell. That was why we'd intended to bring Chernenkov to him—he could have proscribed the Unseelie Court under his own authority.

Instead, well, Chernenkov had brought me to Andrell and that had ended...messily.

"I see two Masks," Ankaris concluded as he studied the bodies. "I know who I am *told* is under them, but I think some certainty is required. You two." He pointed at the two Nobles who'd guarded Andrell's body. "Have these bodies left your sight?"

"This one has not," Shawnee confirmed, pointing at the one I guessed was Andrell. He then pointed at the other glamored corpse. "This one was delivered to us by the Valkyrie Inga Strand."

"Ah. Hunter Strand, attend!"

My bed had been turned so I could watch, though this show wasn't for me. And it was a show. Melodrama runs in our blood...but I suspected that everyone had already decided how this was going to end.

Inga stepped from where she'd been adjusting my bed and crossed over to her former employer.

"Lord Ankaris," she greeted him.

"You're supposed to be retired," he noted. "What brought you here?"

"Our Queen asked me to train the Hunter's changeling in our skills and Gifts," Inga told him. "The evidence suggests I did quite well."

From the way Andrews coughed, the Lord of the Unseelie had just swallowed a laugh he couldn't show tonight.

"So it would seem," Ankaris said calmly. "And why, Hunter Strand, was I not informed of a Hunter's changeling?"

That...was a shock to me. What did he mean, he hadn't known I'd existed?

"Her Majesty asked me not to," Inga told him. "I am no longer bound by Fealty, so the decision to honor her request was mine."

The Lord of the Wild Hunt didn't look pleased, but he nodded and turned back to the bodies.

"Lord Andrews, I suggest we have your people remove the masks," he told the Lord of the Unseelie. "I would prefer this be without question or hesitation, wouldn't you?"

"So be it," Andrews replied. "Shaughnessy, do it."

The woman stepped up to Andrell's body and removed the iron

mask from his face. She carefully laid it aside, the cold iron almost certainly painful in her hands. As the glamor collapsed to reveal Andrell's body, even *I* winced.

It was going to be a closed-casket funeral. I'd put ten bullets through his torso and made a complete wreck of his chest, and the entirety of one of his forearms was nothing but charred ash and blood where there should have been skin.

Shaughnessy, however, seemed unbothered as he stepped over to the second corpse and removed the mask from Gráinne. She'd basically pulled a suicide-by-cop, and the flame strike I'd killed her with had left a surprisingly neat hole through her torso and neck.

"The same power," Ankaris observed softly. "I smell the magic on them both; they both fell to the same warrior. And..." He trailed off and shook his head.

"Lord Andrews," he said formally, "I do not think there is much question before us. Andrell was a Masked Lord, a member of the rebels that rode against us. Guilty of treason and betrayal, the fate he suffered was what I would have brought down on him."

Ankaris sighed.

"More merciful, even. You know what the Covenants require for their crimes."

The room was silent.

"Shawnee, Shaughnessy," Andrews said sharply. "You watched the duel." It wasn't a question.

"What happened?"

"Kilkenny came to arrest the Pouka Noble Chernenkov, as per the High Court's proscription," Shaughnessy told her master. "He fought her, pinned her shadow with cold iron. Before he could capture her, however, Lord Andrell interfered.

"When Kilkenny challenged him with Gráinne's allegiances, he revealed his own Mask and attacked the Vassal. His death was self-defense."

"Self-defense," Andrews half-whispered. He turned to study me for the first time. He didn't approach, but I felt him measure me with his gaze.

"And you, Kilkenny, what have you to say?"

I couldn't even rise.

"Andrell fought me for love," I told him. "I do not know what he has done in the past or how involved he was in Chernenkov and Gráinne's plan to destroy Oberis's Court. He fought me when Chernenkov was in danger.

"She was his wife."

The Lord of the Unseelie snorted.

"Shawnee? Shaughnessy?"

"That is what Andrell said, yes," Shaughnessy said carefully. "He *also* claimed to have been in the battle at Tír na nÓg and to have struck down gods with his own hands. My Lord...by his own words he was condemned.

"Master Kilkenny merely saved the High Court time...and his own life."

"Very well." Andrews straightened. "I want Chernenkov," he told Mabona. "I'll spare your Vassal, I'll even accept he did what must be done, and let this Court return to Oberis—but I want Chernenkov.

"She *will* tell me how deep this rot goes."

"Done," the Queen confirmed. "I trust you, Jon, to see this through. We both know that there are Seelie among the Masked Lords as well as Unseelie. Yank the string and see what unravels."

"I swear it shall be done."

"That may be harder than I think any of us would wish," Eric interjected. I couldn't see him, but from Andrews' expression as he turned to face the Keeper, I doubted it was a pleasant view.

"One of Chernenkov's guards is dead," Eric continued. "Milligan here will live if someone can heal him shortly, and Kenner is just unconscious. The Pouka's gone. Long gone."

Shaughnessy winced.

"Three Gentry should have..."

"She was a *Noble of the Pouka*," Eric snapped. "Even spiked by iron, no mere Gentry could hold her. She didn't even *need* to harm them. She did that because she *could*."

"She'll be far and away by now," Andrews said grimly. "But she is not beyond *our* reach." He turned to Ankaris.

"Lord Ankaris, may I borrow your Hunters? It seems I have work to do tonight."

"Oisin," Ankaris snapped, and a tall Hunter I'd seen before stepped forward. "Take your troop with Lord Andrews. I would see this affair done tonight—and if the Wild Hunt can't bring Chernenkov down, well..."

"We shall see it done," the Hunter replied. "Hunters of the Blackened Shield! To me!"

Sixteen of the Hunters coalesced around Andrews as he stalked from the Court.

Ankaris watched them go and then turned his gaze on me. He met my eyes, but his words were for Mabona.

"And now that business is done, I believe you and I must speak about this child, my Queen."

35

"Dɪᴅ you think I could be in the same room as him and not realize who he was?" Ankaris demanded. "Did you think I could look at his *face* and not know who he was? Not understand at last what you'd done?"

"I did what I swore I would do," Mabona snapped. "What gives you the right to judge me?"

"The Covenants of the Hunt," Ankaris said. "I have too damned few Hunters as it is. I don't care if they're changelings; if they can walk Between, I *need* them. And the Covenants say that they are to be at least reported to me."

"He is my Vassal and *I* am your Queen," she retorted. "This conversation is *over*."

"Would someone care to explain just what is going on?" I asked carefully.

Ankaris and Mabona both looked back at me, then at each other.

"Not here," she said.

"Why not?" he demanded. "Or are there more lies you want to try and cover up?"

"There are truths that should not be spoken where others can hear," she told him. "A Court on the edge of being shuttered and a room full of bodies aren't the place for this conversation."

"Again, I'm feeling lost here," I noted. "And I can't help but feel I should be part of this."

"He needs to leave here with me," Ankaris told my Queen, as if I wasn't even speaking.

"He is my Vassal," she hissed. "He is mine and he stays where he wills. Do not challenge me, Ankaris."

"Perhaps," he conceded. "But he deserves to know the truth about how you've *lied* to him."

For the first time since she'd arrived, Mabona's Power suddenly filled the entire empty space of the massive Court. Shadows and fluttering wings echoed across my vision and hearing alike as the Queen of the Fae reached the end of her patience.

"*I have never lied to him,*" she hissed, each word hitting the air like falling tombstones as her Power bound the attention of everyone around here. "*And I will NOT permit you to.*"

Out of the corner of my eye I saw Eric and Inga both crumple to their knees. The remaining Hunters followed, our Queen's Power sweeping over the Court as she unleashed her will.

Even Ankaris seemed cowed, but he faced her anyway.

"Mabona...he is my cousin," he finally said, something in the Power in the room carrying his words only to me and her. "If you have never lied to him, then tell him the truth now. Let him understand why he is the Hunt's."

"I. Will. Not. Lose. Him."

The words were ground out, each one a body blow to the entire room.

"Then tell him everything," Ankaris told her.

Shadows swirled in upon us and the Court was suddenly gone. Mabona's Power swept us through Between faster than I could ever move, and then the three of us were suddenly outside. A wind swept over us, and I didn't recognize the hill for a moment.

Then I saw the lights of downtown Calgary to the south of us and realized she'd transported us to Nose Hill Park, the closest thing Calgary had to a moor. Her Power still surrounded us, shielding us from outside view as I stood between the two members of the High Court.

It took me a moment to even realize I was standing. In the same moment she'd teleported us several dozen kilometers, Mabona had healed my spine and arm. I still wore my weapons and the new suit she'd fitted on me.

She was suddenly clad in a long, flowing black dress, very different from the pantsuit she'd arrived in. Ankaris had shifted too. Now he was clad in emerald-green armor and antlers framed his head, the Horned King challenging his mistress for honor and truth.

"We will not be heard or seen here. This truth will bring the Masks upon us," Mabona said quietly. "Upon you, Jason."

"They'll work it out," Ankaris replied. "They'll realize once they know a *changeling* killed Andrell."

She sighed.

"You asked me once who your father was, Jason," she reminded me. "Would you know now?"

"I get the feeling I need to know now," I said. "Andrell said he knew who I was. That he'd killed my father."

"If he was at the Battle of Tír na nÓg…then yes, he did," Mabona confirmed. "He was one of many, but his hands would have killed your father."

"You're stalling," the Horned King said. "*Tell him.*"

Mabona sighed.

"Your name…is incomplete," she told me. "Mellie knew the whole thing. She would never have told you it. It was part of what we did to protect you." Mabona shook her head. "I *hated* your mother, Jason, but I owed your father everything.

"Your name is Jason Alexander Odysseus Kilkenny Calebrantson," she said flatly, the extra names ringing like the tones of a massive bell and feeling *right* in a way I could never describe.

"Your father was Calebrant, Lord of the Wild Hunt, bound by oath and Covenant never to sire a child with a mortal or changeling," she continued. "The blood that flows in your veins is that of a Power, of a Horned King."

"Of my uncle," Ankaris told me, and I understood why he looked so familiar. The features that looked familiar on the master of the Wild

Hunt were the same features that looked back at me from the mirror every morning.

"Covenants say that the Powers of the High Court shall have no children," he continued. "That allows the extra Gifts they possess to be willed to their successors. The edge that would have made me a Power like your father runs in *your* veins."

That was impossible. I was just a changeling...and yet somehow, I knew they spoke the truth.

"I loved your father," Mabona admitted. "More than life itself...but when he became Lord of the Wild Hunt, he told me we could never be together. I...tried to impose on his Vassalhood. He defied me...and then spent a century avoiding me."

"That's why the Hunt wasn't there when the Masked Lords starting murdering members of the High Court," Ankaris told me. "We learned too late, only when his half-forgotten Vassal connection to Mabona warned us she was injured."

"He saved my life—by taking the blow meant for me," my Queen told me. "It killed him. He killed them as well, but they broke the will and the life of a Power.

"And he told me that he'd made a mistake while he was dying. That Melissa Kilkenny was pregnant with his child. And he demanded that I swear to protect both her and the babe, that I shield them from his enemies and mine."

"So, you told no one," Ankaris concluded. "You should have told *me*."

"Honestly? For the first decade or so, I thought you knew," she admitted. "If Calebrant would have told anyone, it would have been you."

"I didn't know," he told her. "Obviously. Or I would have seen him guarded his entire life, Hunters and Valkyries at every corner."

"I think he's better off for that."

"Do I get a say in this?" I asked snidely. They kept talking past me like I didn't exist.

"Plenty," Mabona snapped. "You are my Vassal...but I have other Vassals among the Hunt. More, I owe you a boon. I swore I would release you from service to honor—and you have served beyond any reasonable demand tonight."

"And the Wild Hunt needs you," Ankaris told me. "You are the son of my uncle—you are my cousin, and the blood of the Horned King runs in your veins. To the Seelie and Unseelie, rules and blood define everything.

"Among the Courts, you are and will only ever be a changeling, but that is not your birthright. That is not your place. By blood, by gift, by right, by Covenant—you are a Noble of the Wild Hunt and your place is by my side!"

36

I STOOD between two gods on a windswept moor, and I had no idea how to process what they'd just told me.

My father was a Power, the Horned King. That made me…what? Still a changeling…but also apparently a Noble of the Wild Hunt.

One of the gods standing around me had been my father's lover. The other was my cousin. And it seemed that I was being asked to choose.

"What…" I swallowed. "What happens now?"

"That's up to you," Mabona told me. "If you would serve me still, you can remain here. You can also serve me in the Wild Hunt. I will not deny you, wherever you go…but if you would be released from my service, I owe you that."

"It…is up to you," Ankaris agreed. "Your place is by my side, but I will not demand anything. You must know what you are…and know that what you are makes you a target."

"A target?" I asked carefully.

"The Masked Lords were defeated by Calebrant," the Lord of the Wild Hunt told me. "He did…*something* I don't understand. He broke the spell they used to strike him down."

"It's a complex ritual that uses an old power focus, one there's no way they can duplicate," Mabona explained. "He blood-bound it. He was a *Power.*"

"Blood-bound?" I asked. I could guess...I realized what they meant.

"They have *Esras,*" Mabona continued. "The Spear of Lugh, the first Horned King, before there even was a High Court. Forged in the fire and blood of another time, the hands of a dozen Powers have wielded it. Such things become greater than any hands could ever make.

"And they forged their ritual around it. With *Esras* and their ritual and twenty-one Lords and Nobles, they can strike down the Powers. But Calebrant stole *Esras* from them. They may hold it, they may conceal it..."

"But without a warrior of Calebrant's blood, they can't wield it," Ankaris finished for her. "While I was the only one left, we weren't overly worried. They'd need *Esras* to defeat me. But you..."

"Wouldn't they need me to wield it for them?" I asked. "I can't see that happening."

"The spell can also be broken with blood," my Queen admitted. "They don't even need to take you alive, Jason. If they have enough Lords to repeat the ritual to use the spear, they have enough Lords to complete a ritual to use your blood to unlock it."

"So, once they realize I exist..."

"They will hunt you to the ends of the Earth. Nowhere you go will be safe. Anyone who stands with you joins a war that we'd hoped was over."

"But your very existence gives them the possibility of unleashing that stolen weapon," Mabona told me. "You are the key to their revolution ever succeeding."

"So, if I stay here, continue as I am, they'll come for me?" I asked.

"Yes," she admitted. "Your protection was keeping you secret, but they'll work it out when they realized a Hunter's changeling fought and killed a Fae Lord."

I couldn't leave. I had friends, almost family, here. I couldn't leave Mary behind.

"But if we're going to end this, we have to fight them," I said levelly. "We need to let them come to us. So long as they hide, they can try and find something else to use for their spell. They can seek me, seek Ankaris…or they can seek another focus.

"We need them to come for me," I realized aloud. "We need to use me as bait…and if I'm going to be bait, it will be here."

I gestured at the city around me.

"Here I have friends, allies, tools," I told them. "A Wizard who owes me a boon. A woman who loves me.

"You want to make me a Noble of the Hunt? To stay a Vassal of the Queen? Then I say you need to come *here*," I told them. "We let them know I'm here. We let them come.

"And I will face them. As a Noble, as a Vassal, as my father's son… but I'll do it with my friends and my love at my side."

Ankaris laughed and gestured. A silver-hilted sword materialized in his hand and he offered it to me.

"So be it, then. Take the sword, Jason Kilkenny. You are a Rider of the Hunt, a Noble of the Wilds. If you would fight our enemies here, then we will fight them here."

I took the sword. I had no damn idea how to use it—I was more comfortable with the whip handle MacDonald had given me—but I understood what it was.

A symbol. Of who I was. Of who I had always been.

"My Queen?" I asked quietly.

"You are mine, Jason Alexander Odysseus Kilkenny Calebrantson," she told me. "Whether you are my Vassal or not, you are the child of the only man I ever loved. The Masked Lords *must* be defeated…and I swore an oath to protect you."

"Then let the bastards come," I told them. "We will fight them— with fae, with shifters, with a Wizard and the Powers of the High Court. If they want to burn the High Court down, then let them come."

ABOUT THE AUTHOR

Glynn Stewart is the author of *Starship's Mage*, a bestselling science fiction and fantasy series where faster-than-light travel is possible–but only because of magic. His other works include science fiction series *Duchy of Terra, Castle Federation* and *Vigilante*, as well as the urban fantasy series *ONSET* and *Changeling Blood*.

Writing managed to liberate Glynn from a bleak future as an accountant. With his personality and hope for a high-tech future intact, he lives in Kitchener, Ontario with his wife, their cats, and an unstoppable writing habit.

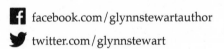

    facebook.com/glynnstewartauthor

    twitter.com/glynnstewart

OTHER BOOKS BY GLYNN STEWART

For release announcements join the mailing list or visit GlynnStewart.com

Changeling Blood

Changeling's Fealty

Hunter's Oath

Noble's Honor (upcoming)

ONSET

ONSET: To Serve and Protect

ONSET: My Enemy's Enemy

ONSET: Blood of the Innocent

ONSET: Stay of Execution

Starship's Mage

Starship's Mage

Hand of Mars

Voice of Mars

Alien Arcana

Judgment of Mars

Starship's Mage: UnArcana Rebellions

UnArcana Stars (upcoming)

Starship's Mage: Red Falcon

Interstellar Mage

Mage-Provocateur

Agents of Mars (upcoming)

Castle Federation

Space Carrier Avalon

Stellar Fox

Battle Group Avalon

Q-Ship Chameleon

Rimward Stars

Operation Medusa

Duchy of Terra

The Terran Privateer

Duchess of Terra

Terra and Imperium

Vigilante (With Terry Mixon)

Heart of Vengeance

Oath of Vengeance

Bound by Stars

Bound by Law

Bound by Honor (upcoming)

Exile

Ashen Stars

Exile (upcoming)

Fantasy Stand Alone Novels

Children of Prophecy

City in the Sky

CPSIA information can be obtained
at www.ICGtesting.com
Printed in the USA
FSHW02n0904050718
50150FS